WITHDRA

NO
DIVING

Sky Blue Water

The Mid-Continent Oceanographic Institute

 THE MID-CONTINENT OCEANOGRAPHIC INSTITUTE (MOI) helps young people navigate the latitude and longitude of reading, writing, and learning. Based in Saint Paul, it is the Twin Cities' premier portal for creative writing—giving muse and amusement to kids as they captain the stories of life.

MOI offers a range of programs, all free of charge, for students, classes, and schools throughout the Twin Cities metropolitan area. With a focus on project-based learning, MOI aims to enhance the educational experience of young people through cross-curriculum creativity. Our programs include after-school tutoring, writing workshops, in-school support, student publishing projects, and high-energy bookmaking field trips.

MOI is an approved community partner of both Saint Paul Public Schools and Minneapolis Public Schools.

MOI is working to become a chapter of 826 National, a nationwide network of writing and tutoring centers, each with a unique storefront designed to raise funds, inspire creativity in students, and serve as a gateway to the community. Founded in 2002 by award-winning author Dave Eggers and award-winning educator Nínive Calegari, 826 National's chapters offer a variety of inventive free programming.

MOI is a 501(c)3 nonprofit organization registered with the state of Minnesota. The authors and editors of this book have donated all royalties from the sales of *Sky Blue Water* to support MOI's free writing programs.

To learn more about MOI, visit http://www.moi-msp.org.

SKY BLUE WATER

Great Stories
for Young Readers

Jay D. Peterson and
Collette A. Morgan
Editors

Foreword by Kevin Kling

University of Minnesota Press
Minneapolis ≈ London

The University of Minnesota Press gratefully acknowledges assistance provided for the publication of this book by the John K. and Elsie Lampert Fesler Fund.

Published by the University of Minnesota Press
111 Third Avenue South, Suite 290
Minneapolis, MN 55401-2520
http://www.upress.umn.edu

ISBN 978-0-8166-9876-9
A Cataloging-in-Publication record is available for this book from the Library of Congress.

Design and production by Mighty Media, Inc.
Interior and text design by Chris Long

Printed in the United States of America on acid-free paper

The University of Minnesota is an equal-opportunity educator and employer.

22 21 20 19 18 17 16   10 9 8 7 6 5 4 3 2 1

Contents

Foreword

Kevin Kling

THERE ARE PLACES IN THIS WORLD, natural environments, that give us peace. Whether it's an ocean, a mountain, or a desert, there is a landscape that speaks to somewhere deep within each of us.

The shoreline of a Minnesota lake is that place for me. My blood pressure drops; regrets for the past and anxieties for the future melt into insignificance. I become aware of the sounds— the lapping water, a bee flying past, the wind rustling the trees, a chainsaw buzzing across the lake—and the feel of the sun on my face.

"Minnesota" in the Dakota language translates to "sky-tinted waters," which is where the title of this collection comes from. The bright blue sky is reflected in the water and the water is reflected in the sky so you can't tell where one ends and the other begins. The shore of a lake is a place of reflection.

How our lakes were formed is open to debate. Scientists think they were created thousands of years ago as a great sheet of ice receded north, gouging the surface of the earth and filling the holes with melting glacier. Some folks, mostly chamber of commerce members, believe our lakes are the footprints of Babe the Blue Ox, companion of the great lumberjack Paul Bunyan.

However they were formed, our state license plates say we are the "Land of 10,000 Lakes." In reality there are closer to fifteen thousand lakes in Minnesota. I often tell people, "If you start walking in any direction and are soaking wet within three miles, you're probably in Minnesota." We have more shoreline and more boats registered than any other state in the union.

We also have Lake Superior, known by the Anishinabe as Gich-igami. Lake Superior, the greatest of the Great Lakes, contains one-tenth of the world's entire fresh water supply. We did not learn its depth until fifteen years after we had walked on the moon.

I grew up near a small lake. We fished for bullheads in the hot summer, swam off the end of the dock, played King of the Mountain on the raft farther out. Every winter the lake would freeze before the first snow. When the ice was thick enough to hold a kid named Patrick Gilligan, we knew it was safe to play hockey.

When I grew older, we moved farther from the lakes. In the summers my dad loaded up the station wagon with supplies and took me and my siblings north into the Boundary Waters Canoe Area. My dad, my brother, and I would sit in our canoe and paddle all day. If we were thirsty, we would simply dip our cups in the lake. Dad would say, "I wonder how they got all these big rocks up here?" And then I would wonder, too.

The Boundary Waters are home to frogs, turtles, birds, muskrats, mink, raccoons, great blue herons, and wolves that howl all night. One morning we saw a moose and her two calves in our campsite. Every night we would see at least one shooting star. Sometimes we would see the northern lights. In the north, the heavens are open, and you can feel the spirits of the past, the first people, the voyageurs, the French trappers.

My dad was never more at peace than on those lakes. One time we were fishing, and his bobber was going under. I wondered why he didn't set the hook—you know, reel in the fish. Then I noticed that a yellow butterfly perched at the end of his fishing pole. Dad would rather lose the fish than disturb that butterfly.

I live near a lake now, in Minneapolis. At sunset, it looks like glass, reflecting reds and yellows. A loon, the state bird of Minnesota, calls, and I am transported to a place deep within myself.

The lake is where I bring my big questions. I'm reminded of my friends, my family, my childhood. In the solemnity of the moment I'm reminded of our short time on this planet and that these lakes we call "our lakes" had names long before we were here.

I find big questions in stories, like the ones in this anthology. Where did we come from before life, where do we go after life, what's funny, what's sacred, how do I fit in this world? Reading, like fishing, is not always about catching something. Whether I am sitting in a library, an ice-fishing house, or along the bank of a river, my thoughts dive down through the layers.

Down past the dam the beaver built
Past algae muck and silt
Down past dreams and wishes
Past tadpole, turtle, and fishes
Down where grows
The language every creature knows
Mammal, fish, and bird
More water than language more music than word
Down where everything is understood.
All is peaceful.
All is good.
Then back to the surface where sky meets water.
If the lake is visible and the wind is unseen,
With our stories we ride on the waves.

Introduction

Jay D. Peterson and Collette A. Morgan

As booksellers, we have a unique window on those special moments when readers and writers come together, moments that typically occur in private wherever readers read and writers write. Over the years, we have witnessed countless writers establish themselves as published authors, then perfect their craft from one book to the next, collecting more and more readers along the way. At the same time, we have often been privy to the magical moment when a young person first connects with the fictional character who will help make them a *reader*—for life.

Two years ago, we sat down and began hatching plans to publish a collection of stories by some of our favorite middle-grade and young adult writers from Minnesota, the state where we have built a community around our shared love of books. The purpose of the anthology, we determined, would be to celebrate the vibrant culture of youth storytelling here in Minnesota and to help connect readers from places both near and far with Minnesota's writers.

While our state may be known for its long, cold winters, there's a richness to each of our seasons that helps bring forth the stories we tell one another. True, those winters make us appreciate warm blankets, hot chocolate, and storytelling around the fire. But who could forget the joy that the first warm day of spring brings? The beauty of a maple tree in the fall? Or how much time there is to explore and hike and swim and play when summer days seem to last forever?

The best stories capture the changing of the seasons, the textures of the land, and the people around us. When you pair the ethnic diversity of our large urban areas with the beautiful and varied geological diversity of our state, it's no wonder we have such a breadth of talented storytellers in our midst. The bluffs and caves of the south help stoke our curiosity and imagination. The dense woodlands of the north give our stories an air of mystery and intrigue. Our larger cities deliver excitement and energy. And in between are thousands of lakes and miles of prairies, which is where we come together to listen to the tales be told. Minnesota is a great place to be a reader because it's such a great place to be a writer.

For the Dakota people and other native inhabitants of these lands, storytelling has been an essential way to share the culture and values of our region with children and grandchildren. The writers featured in *Sky Blue Water*, who come from as far north as Rainy Lake and as far south as Mankato, carry on that tradition when they write about our state. Some of these writers were born here and have lived here their entire lives; others moved to Minnesota from places as far away as Colombia and Vietnam. Regardless of how they got here, Minnesota is now the place they call home.

In the pages that follow, you'll encounter a neighborhood ghost (in William Alexander's "The War between the Water and the Road"), an invisible pet (in Kelly Barnhill's "Ozymandias"), an octogenarian pickpocket (in Julie Schumacher's "Strange Island"), and an elf-like creature with sensitive ears (in Lynne Jonell's "The Creature under the Bush"). Anika Fajardo will take you fishing with a pair of brothers, both named Eddie. Mary Casanova will take you back in time to the 1920s. And Pete Hautman will introduce you to a most mysterious food. As Dr. Seuss said, "Oh, the places you'll go."

Sky Blue Water: Great Stories for Young Readers encompasses stories and poems for both the intermediate and young adult reader. We organized them roughly based on the age range of the character and the difficulty of the text: stories for younger readers are toward the front; stories for older readers are toward the back.

We hope that you enjoy reading this collection and that it gives you a new appreciation for Minnesota—the Land of 10,000 Stories. Happy reading!

The War between the Water and the Road

William Alexander

OLIVER'S FATHER TOLD HIM that the park across the street used to be a lake. Most of what was now park, including the baseball field and the sledding hills, had been underwater—everything except for the two sets of swings at the top of the hill. He said that highway construction had cut into secret, underground places and wounded the lake. The water drained out, leaving just a small pond with hills on all sides.

"Why did they do that?" Oliver asked his father, who was cooking.

"Why did who do what?" his father asked, because he had already forgotten the topic of the conversation. He got very focused on his cooking. He kept the TV on in the kitchen, but he never watched, never really listened to what it said. He also never worked in a restaurant, at least not for very long. He didn't like to be rushed.

Oliver tried again. "Why did they drain the lake?"

"Oh, I don't know," Oliver's father said. He closed the oven door and stood up. "I don't think they meant to. But people who make highways don't care very much about lakes."

"They should," Oliver said.

The park across the street was one of Oliver's favorite places. He thought about what it must have looked like, all filled up with lake. He thought about the fish that must have died, surprised when it drained away. Oliver liked fish. He had goldfish named Donkey and Hodey. They were serial goldfish. The fish changed, but the names remained. Right now Donkey was silver and Hodey was orange.

Oliver decided to find those responsible for draining the lake and visit justice upon them.

He tried to think of suitably watery punishments. His cousins were known for filling pillowcases with ice cubes, or putting the hands of their enemies in small buckets of warm water while they slept, which would make them wet the bed. Their enemies were mostly younger cousins, all of them except for Oliver. Nobody played pranks on Oliver.

"Who built the highway?" he asked his father. He tried to ask like it didn't really matter, but at that moment it was the only thing that did.

"Don't know," his father said. "It was something like eighty years ago. More, maybe. Anyone who worked on that thing would be a hundred by now."

Oliver knew only one person who looked like they might be a hundred. Old Louisa spent most of her time sitting on a bench in the park, right next to the pond. Maybe she remembered the days of highway construction.

He got down from his kitchen chair and went to his room. He took a pirate coloring book from inside his pillowcase. The pillowcase had fish on it. So did the sheets. He flipped to the very back of the book, which was an old birthday present. None of the pirate pictures were colored in. None of the pages were marked at all, except for the last. He kept his list on the last page.

Oliver wrote "the lake" at the bottom of the list with a crayon. Then he returned the book to his pillowcase and went to find his coat and boots.

"Going to the park!" he shouted from the front door.

"Don't harass the ghost," his father called from the kitchen, like he always did.

The afternoon was cold and clear. There wasn't any snow. Halloween had just happened, and already it felt too cold for snow. Most kids in Oliver's neighborhood had dressed up as pirates for Halloween. Oliver had worn a miniature navy uniform. He didn't like pirates. They were thieves and oath breakers.

The park had two swing sets on the playground at street level, before the slope plummeted down to the pond. One was smaller and set up for younger kids. The smaller swings looked like armored underwear, impossible to fall out of. A more advanced swing set jutted up near the smaller one like a pirate ship bearing down on a weaker vessel. Three older girls were on the swings. Two older boys boarded the younger playground. They loomed over its only occupant, who held on to a ball as big as he was. The older boys looked like pirates. Oliver didn't know their names, but he recognized them. They had not dressed up for Halloween, but they had still gone door-to-door expecting candy.

One of the pirates kicked the kid's ball, hard. It sailed over the edge of the slope and hung there for a moment, held up by the wind—it was a windy day—or else by the air remembering where the surface of the lake used to be. Then the ball dropped down and out of sight.

"Stop it," Oliver said.

The pirates looked at him. Either one was twice Oliver's height, so the two of them together had the collective mass of four Olivers. They might even have been teenagers, technically. But he had said "stop it" in a way that wasn't a threat, a whine, or any other kind of complaint. He said it with the conviction that they actually would stop, and Oliver's was a contagious belief. The older boys caught it. They glared down at the intense eight-year-old who had given them the order, and then they moved aside.

"Come on," Oliver said to the smaller kid, taking his mittened hand. The two of them walked to the hill and down the switchbacking trail. This was Oliver's favorite sledding hill, whenever it actually snowed. The retreating lake had created excellent sledding hills on all sides. But Oliver refused to let accidentally positive consequences influence his conviction that the wounded lake required justice.

The ball had rolled out over the surface of the pond. The little boy started crying when he saw how far out of reach it was, but he cried quietly. Oliver approved.

Thin ice covered the pond. Ducks swam in one unfrozen corner. Crows stepped lightly on the ice and looked around. One walked up to the ball, pecked at it, and walked away.

Oliver couldn't find a stick long enough to reach the ball, so the two of them went around to the other side and threw rocks to knock it back onto shore. The rocks made holes in the ice. The little boy got tired of missing all the time, so he started to throw rocks at the ghost instead.

The ghost stood where it always stood, knee-deep in pond water. Its overcoat moved around it, even when there wasn't any wind, and it held out both arms as though holding an imaginary beach ball. One thrown pebble passed through the ghost's head and scattered the shape of it like candle smoke. The ghost's head came back together, sputtering and confused.

"I've seen it cold!" the ghost shouted, but not loudly. Even its shouts were quiet. "So cold that fires went walking to find someplace warm!"

"Don't harass the ghost," Oliver said, and the little boy stopped.

Oliver picked up a stone that felt good in his hand. He took aim and threw. The stone knocked the ball across the ice. It rolled within reach of the far shore.

"There," Oliver said. "Go get your ball."

The little boy ran around the pond for the ball and then took the long, switchbacked sidewalk to street level. Oliver lost interest in the kid as soon as he had his ball back. A wrong had been redressed. Oliver's work was done.

He looked around. He had been to the park hundreds and hundreds of times but without knowing that it had once been underwater. He looked up and pictured leaves floating high above him, where the surface used to be. He looked at the ghost and realized why its overcoat moved.

"That's where he sank down to," said old Louisa. She sat behind Oliver on her usual park bench. She looked like a permanent part of the bench. "He drowned when the lake was large. When this was the bottom of it. He sank this far. Once the water drained down to small we could finally come and visit him."

"Did you help build the highway?" Oliver asked. This was what he'd come here to know.

"Women didn't work road crews in my day," Louisa said. "But I knew some of the boys who built things, back then. One of the things might have been a highway."

"You don't remember?" said Oliver.

"Not especially," said Louisa, but she said it with a smile. "How can you not remember?" Oliver asked, not smiling. He had a very good memory, and he took things seriously.

"I remember more than he does." Louisa nodded at the ghost. "And maybe I remember the highway. The boys always shouted, 'Hurry up! It's going to explode!' when they put down concrete. It wouldn't really, but they all rushed around and smoothed it out like it might, because if it wasn't ready by the time it all set, then the concrete might as well have just blown up. All of it went on right outside my door."

"Didn't they know what it would do to the lake, when they built it?"

"Do to the lake?" Louisa leaned forward. She poured a little more of her voice into the words "do" and "lake." "Do to the lake? More like what the lake did to them, boy. They cut into some kind of river, down underground. I saw it happen. I was tending to things outside when the water lashed out at them, down in that trench, and it carried some of them away."

The ghost spoke up. "I've seen it so cold the sun came out at night, just to keep the moon warm." The ghost faced away from them, toward the middle of the pond. It always did. Oliver had never seen its face. "Moon couldn't make it across the sky otherwise. It was that cold. That cold."

Most people in the neighborhood said the ghost had fallen in by drunken accident, so Oliver had not written "the ghost" in the back of his coloring book. He didn't write down accidents.

"Do you know what his name was?" Oliver asked.

"Of course I do," Louisa said, "but he doesn't remember it, and if he can't remember, then I won't say. But he was one of those who worked on the highway crew, before this happened to him. I'll tell you that much. Now get going."

Oliver frowned. He had justice on his mind, but he didn't know where it should fall. The highway hurt the lake, and the lake hurt the highway. He wasn't sure whose fault this was.

He would have to investigate further.

"Bye," he said. Louisa waved good-bye. The ghost went on saying the sorts of things it usually said.

Oliver walked home. He walked steady and slow, pushing the air in front of him like it was lake water.

~~~~~~~~~~~~~~~~

Dinner wasn't ready yet. Oliver's father kept tasting and adding things. "Just a pinch," he said to himself. He didn't notice that Oliver was back. "Just a simmer. Almost there."

The news was on, but both Oliver and his father continued to ignore it. Oliver went over to the kitchen table and boxed with Bats the cat. He tried to touch the cat's torso without getting swatted. It took a lot of duck-and-weave to accomplish this. Bats seemed to like the game, and she never drew blood when she parried, but that wasn't self-control on her part; she had no claws.

Oliver's father said that a declawed cat was like a human with no fingers, or at least someone who went through life without ever taking their mittens off. Oliver had worn his own mittens for three days after his father said that, to express solidarity. Then he wrote "Bats" in the back of his coloring book and set out to find those who had declawed her so that he might visit justice upon them.

He hung flyers with pictures of Bats all over the neighborhood. Was this your cat? She had walked into Oliver's apartment one day, already a well-fed adult, and never left. Someone must have fed her before. Someone must have taken her claws.

Oliver found the former owner eventually. He was white, and tall, and he looked a little sleepy when he opened the door on a Saturday afternoon.

"Hello?" the man said.

"This used to be your cat," said Oliver, and he held up a picture.

"Yeah," said the man. "Looks like."

"Did you declaw her?" Oliver asked.

"Had to," said the man. "She ruined the couch."

Oliver fixed the man with a look, one that could take an apple off someone's head from a hundred paces. "You have to wear these for the rest of your life," he said. Then he handed over a pair of mittens and walked away. It didn't even occur to him that the man would question the rightness of this order and refuse to obey.

Bats wasn't allowed on the table, but this rule was never actually enforced. Oliver tried to touch the orange spot on her side. She swatted him away on the first two jabs, but then he faked left and tapped her with his right.

"Perfect!" Oliver's father announced, loud enough to scare the cat down off the table. Oliver and his father finally sat down to eat. The food was good.

"Dad," he said, "tell me more about the lake."

"Okay," his father said. "The water in your fishbowl overlaps with the water in the lake. It's all the same. It's how your gold-fish swim away when it's time to change color."

"You're making that up," Oliver said.

"I am not."

"How can Donkey and Hodey swim out of a fishbowl? It's a bowl. It's glass all around, and air all around the glass. It doesn't connect to anything."

"It does," his father said. "It's just that some of the water in the bowl is the same water as some of the stuff in the pond. And the ocean. And everywhere else."

"Is that why one corner of the pond takes so much longer to freeze over? Because it's really part of a lake that's also some-where else, somewhere warmer than here?"

"That's right."

"What about freshwater and salt water?" Oliver asked. "Some fish live in salt water. Wouldn't it mix if it's all the same water?"

"Hydrodynamics are tricky, I know."

Oliver did not want to talk about hydrodynamics. He wanted to talk about the lake that was not a lake anymore. He wanted to be sure which side to blame. "Tell me about—"

Oliver stopped, because his father had stopped paying attention. They both watched the TV on the kitchen counter. A reporter said that a highway bridge had collapsed earlier today. The TV showed it happening. The bridge had collapsed quickly, so the news kept showing the same video clip, over and over.

Oliver watched it collapse twice more before the news changed the subject and then cut to commercials.

He hated that bridge, so he wasn't actually sad to see it go. And he did not write accidents in the back of his coloring book. He did not write down the names of those who were simply unlucky, only those deliberately wronged. He had "Toyota" written down because somebody broke the windows of his aunt Bess's car in the middle of the night, and that was the name of the car. He had "Bats" in his book, because of her claws. He had "the lake," even though he was no longer sure that the lake was the wronged party. But he had not written his cousin Marcus in the back of his coloring book because a patch of ice on a very tall bridge was an accident. It was just unlucky. Everybody said so. But everyone in Oliver's whole wide family still avoided crossing that bridge, so Oliver wasn't sorry to see it collapse.

People on the TV talked about ice getting into seams and cracks, expanding. "Ice," Oliver said. "Again." He watched the bridge hit the river below in the same repeated clip.

Maybe the river took down the bridge as vengeance for what the highway did to the lake.

"Is all water really the same? On the same side?"

His father looked at him sideways. "Why talk about sides?" he asked, suspicious.

"Because the water hates the road," Oliver said. "And the road hates the water."

His father got up and stacked dishes. "If there's an old feud going between them, it's no business of ours."

"What's a feud?" Oliver asked.

"A feud is a war on a slow simmer. It's two sides looking for the wrong kind of justice." His father's tone meant that he did not want to discuss this topic any further, not at all. That tone never actually worked, not with Oliver. He saw the bridge hit the river, again, right before his father turned the TV off.

"That's not a slow simmer," Oliver said. "It took down the whole bridge. And it is our business because Marcus slipped off that bridge. Was it the road's fault, or the water's fault? We have to know."

Oliver's father turned away from the sink and gave him a long look. Oliver expected him to say some infuriating, dismissive thing, like he always did whenever Oliver took his leg-pulling too seriously—which was often.

"There is no right or wrong in a feud," he said instead. "That's why we're not in it. That's why we don't choose sides. Don't you go choosing sides."

This was intolerable. Oliver needed to know who to blame. He said so, several times, but his father washed dishes and refused to answer.

Oliver stormed into his room, took his coloring book out from inside his pillowcase, and stood poised with a crayon hovering over the back page.

He didn't know what to do. It didn't feel right to put the highway or the bridge on the same page as the lake. It didn't feel right to cross out the lake. He wasn't sure whether or not to add Marcus, whether or not he could blame that death on water.

He put the book away without writing anything.

Oliver did not sleep well that night. He could feel the edges of his coloring book through the pillowcase.

~~~~~~~~~

The next day Oliver still had justice on his mind. He went down to the park, down the switchbacking sidewalk path, which was made out of concrete and was therefore a kind of road. He circled the pond at the bottom and stared at it. Was it wronged, or had it done wrong?

He picked up trash as he went by. Littering was wrong, but he could fix it by gathering it up and throwing it away. He could almost fix it. Picking up trash helped keep the park clean, but it did not bring justice to litterers, so it wasn't satisfying.

"I've seen the wind blow so hard it blew a cookpot inside out," the ghost said when Oliver came near. Louisa waved hello from her favorite bench.

Oliver marched up and demanded to know about the war between the water and the road. She gave him a long look. One did not demand anything of old Louisa.

"Did your father tell you this?" she asked.

"Yeah," said Oliver. "Sort of."

"Your father is a legendary liar. Pay him no attention."

The ghost spoke up. "Seen the wind blow so hard it blew a crooked road straight and a straight road crooked."

Oliver would not be deterred, but Louisa would not speak of it further. A clash of wills built up between them—and then rain broke it apart.

Louisa turned her glare on the sky. "It wasn't supposed to rain today," she complained, "and here I am without my hat. This breaks the rules. They're breaking all the rules."

"Cold!" said the ghost in a muted shout. "Cold as witch tits! Cold as iron!" The ghost railed against the sky. Rain scattered the substance of its limbs as it waved both arms around.

A mist came down with the rain and froze on impact wherever it touched. Louisa tried to stand up, slipped on the newly icy sidewalk, and landed back on her bench.

"No good," she said. "Not hardly any good. I'll break both my hips, trying to get home."

"I'll help," Oliver told her, his ire forgotten. Something needed doing, and he was there to see it done.

"Might work," said Louisa. "Come here, let me lean on you. We'll keep to the grass, away from the sidewalk. Away from the road. That's where they'll fight hardest."

She leaned on him as they trudged up the steep, grassy slope. Frozen grass blades crackled underfoot. Oliver stuffed a handful of gathered trash in his coat pocket—a pink plastic lighter, a candy wrapper, and a greasy napkin that smelled like french fries.

"Supposed to be a truce," Louisa muttered. "Supposed to be a cease-fire these days, but first the bridge goes down and now we get bombarded. This will put potholes in the road like impact craters. This is full-on ugly. There was supposed to be a truce."

"Who called the truce?" Oliver asked. A truce wasn't justice. It was not satisfying. But if it ended a feud, then maybe it was something close.

Louisa didn't answer for a good long while. Oliver was about to ask again, and again, however many times it took, when she finally spoke.

"Your father," she said, "after that sad business with your cousin. Handsome boy, that one. Your father stepped out, straight from the funeral, and he brokered a truce. A liar can be a decent diplomat. He'd be furious at me if he ever found out I told you, so hush just as best as you know how."

Her apartment building stood on the opposite side of the park from Oliver's home. They made it to the top of the hill, where they stood and looked across a long stretch of street. Cars parked by the side of the road were already frosted over, every inch of them encased.

Old Louisa looked down at the slick road surface. She ran one hand through her hair, breaking up a layer of accumulated ice. "Nothing for it but to try," she said.

Oliver remembered some of the rules of war. He had a very good memory for rules. A medic could walk through battlefields unscathed. A medic could tend to the wounded. Both sides were supposed to honor that.

"Medic!" he yelled at the road.

Louisa jumped, startled. "Don't you have a pair of lungs," she said.

They inched across the road while ice fell from the sky and built up in layers underfoot. Oliver escorted Louisa onto the sidewalk, up to her steps, and safely underneath the awning at her own front door.

"Thank you," she said. "Very much. You'd best come in and drink something warm before you try to brave it back home." Oliver shook his head and gave her a crisp salute. He had practiced his salute for Halloween. Then he turned and made his way back across the road.

"You come back here!" Louisa called after him. "It isn't safe!" But he didn't come back, and she went muttering inside.

He should have gone in with her. He should have circled around the park rather than cutting straight through. But he didn't. The ice stood thick on every surface. The hillside all around the park made excellent sledding hills. Oliver slipped, and slid all the way down. He was moving in a world without friction. The pond moved toward him like someone had thrown it. Then he caught hold of Louisa's favorite bench before his momentum threw him out over the paper-thin ice. He got to his feet. He fell again, a hard fall, a hammer blow against the ground. His ankle twisted.

He lay there awhile with his eyes closed. He heard blood going about its own business inside him. He also heard the strain, the struggle, and the screaming as crystalline water pried bits of gravel apart. He had his ear to the ground over ice-covered sidewalk, where the fighting was thick. He lay there and listened to the war. It surrounded him. The cold violence of it would claim his fingers, his ears, and the tip of his nose if he stayed there—whether or not he chose sides.

~~~~~~~~~~

He had once watched his father break up a hallway fight between Bats and another apartment cat.

"Who started it?" Oliver had asked at the time.

"Doesn't matter," his father had said. He held spitting Bats over his head and kept the other cat back with one foot. He wasn't wearing shoes. The other cat wrestled with the foot and stuck claws through the sock. Oliver's father winced, but he kept at it.

"Who started it?" Oliver asked again. It mattered. It was the only thing that mattered.

"They're both in it," his father said. "They're both in, and we want them both out of it. First thing is to separate them, give them a chance to catch their breath." He sucked in his own breath when teeth found his toe. "This was a stupid way to do it, though," he admitted. "Run and fetch me a blanket."

Oliver ran for a blanket. His father dropped Bats. The two cats lunged for each other. Then Oliver's dad tossed the blanket over both. They yowled, surprised, and fought with the blanket rather than each other. The two cats fought their way out. The blanket lay still, defeated. Bats smacked the inert fabric once more, for good measure, and then both cats marched off to their respective apartment doors.

Oliver glared at the neighboring cat, certain that it had started the uneven fight—it had claws, and Bats didn't. He wanted to prove it. He wanted to punish it. He wanted to bring justice down upon it.

His father saw and recognized the look on his face. "Doesn't matter. Let it go. They were in it. Now they're out."

But it still mattered. Oliver didn't know how to let it go. But he also had no evidence, no real knowledge of which cat started the fight, so he was forced to leave the incident out of his coloring book.

<center>~~~~~~~~</center>

Oliver wondered about the ghost. He should have been able to hear it shouting from where he lay on the ground, on the ice, at the bottom of a lake that wasn't there anymore. He felt the heaviness of the water that used to be there pressing down on him. He wondered what would happen if it suddenly came back, all of it pouring down over the sides of the park in a surrounding waterfall. He wondered if he could swim to the top in time, or if he'd be stuck right where he was, looking up at the sky through four fathoms of lake water and trying to remember how fish are supposed to breathe.

He tried to open his eyes, but the eyelashes had frozen together. He pinched his lashes between fingertips to melt the ice, and then looked for the ghost. It stood frozen, the smoke of it roiling and agitated under a vaguely person-shaped coating of ice.

"You worked on the road and drowned in the water," Oliver said to the ghost. "Tell me which one is wrong. Tell me which one is wronged."

The ghost remained stuck in the cold that was all it ever talked about. So cold. Oliver wanted to do something for it, something warm, something hot and blazing. He wanted to set fire to the pond, to burn away the ice around the ghost, to make it stop wailing about the cold. In that moment he didn't care who had hurt the ghost, or why it died, or whether or not it was an accident. In that moment it no longer mattered. The ghost was cold. It needed to get warm.

Oliver found a rock, got to his knees, and tried to get to his feet before stumbling back to his knees. Then he threw it, hard. The ice broke around the ghost. The smoke of it rolled, sputtered, and raged.

"Cold!" it yelled out once it could yell, but the yelling still sounded like a whisper.

Oliver found a stick. He dug the trash out of his pocket and wrapped the greasy napkin around the end of the stick. Then he used the pink plastic lighter to light up the napkin. It took a while. There wasn't much fluid left, but there was a bit. The little torch blazed. It smelled like french fries.

He threw the little torch at the ghost, who was so cold and who spoke of nothing but the cold. Its billowing overcoat caught fire and burned quickly, hungrily, eager to soak up all the heat that flame could offer. The ghost burned blue like the flame of a gas stove. It smiled before it burned itself out.

Ashes swirled through the air as though the air were water at the bottom of a lake. Then the ghost ash seemed to notice that the air was air, and no longer water. It drifted down, settling on the pond ice, and melted the ice where it fell.

The rain stopped, just as surprised as Oliver to learn that ghosts were flammable.

Oliver took advantage of the pause in hostilities and put his hand to the sidewalk pavement. "Everybody just take a step back," he said. "I call a truce." He said it like he meant it, like he knew the water and the road would listen and do as he said.

He got up and stumbled across the crunching, frozen grass. He made it around the pond, across the park, and as far as the foot of the opposite slope. He sat back and stared at the hill, his favorite sledding hill. In his calm estimation he knew it would be impossible to climb, so he started screaming. "Medic!"

He kept shouting. His father finally came.

"Your dinner's getting cold," Oliver's dad called down from the top of the hill.

Oliver laughed. He rarely laughed, but now he couldn't stop laughing. "Cold as iron!" he tried to say, since the ghost wasn't there to say it.

"Just hold on," his father told him. He went away and came back with a sled tied to a length of clothesline. Oliver's father believed in clothesline, and not the clothes dryer, even in weather like this when he had to string wet wash across the hallway and the living room. The dryer agreed with this belief, because it was broken. They never got rid of it, though. Bats loved to sleep inside the broken dryer.

Oliver climbed aboard and went sledding, slow and in reverse. His father hauled him up, picked him up, and carried him home. Oliver held the line, and the empty sled followed behind them. Ice shattered under his father's feet where Oliver would only slide over the surface. The ice respected his father, or else it was afraid of him, or else it respected his office as a medic and a diplomat.

"They agreed to another truce," Oliver said.

"Good," his father said. "Just remember what I said about choosing sides. If you go looking for one side to blame, then you've joined the fighting, and you can't stand back and call a truce once you're in it."

At home he put Oliver in the bath, and then in bed. He tied a towel filled with ice cubes around Oliver's swollen ankle. Oliver kept his leg fully extended, kept his eye on the towel, and reminded the ice cubes about the truce.

On the last page of his pirate coloring book he wrote "road" beside "lake" and drew a square around both, cutting them off from the rest of the list and each other. It wasn't justice. It was something else, but it would have to do for now.

He still felt the edges of the coloring book through his pillowcase, but this time it helped him sleep to feel it there.

Dee Dee

Kurtis Scaletta

I KNEW MY GRANDMA wasn't like most grandmas. Other kids talked about homemade cookies and surprise gifts, about pancakes for dinner and ice cream for breakfast, about hugs and cuddles and five-dollar bills hidden in their jacket pockets to discover on the ride home. Well, my grandma never baked cookies, not even for Christmas. Since she was raising me, there were no rides home from her place, and she would be as likely to slip a rattlesnake in my coat pocket as a five-dollar bill. She sure didn't coddle me. She barely looked at me when I came home muddy and crying with skinned knees and elbows.

She didn't act like a grandma, and she didn't look like one. She was taller than most men, wide at the shoulders and lean as a post. She didn't need glasses or wear a hearing aid. She was strong, too—I'd seen her haul two fifty-pound bags of manure for the garden, one under each arm, like it was nothing.

She says our family has been in Wormel since the state was a territory and that we're descended from outlaws and cardsharps, treasure hunters and con artists. "And that's just the women," she says. Maybe that's why she is the way she is.

The reason my grandma was raising me is that my mother left me all alone when I was a baby. We were living in an apartment in Minneapolis. The neighbors called 911 when they heard me crying all night and realized nobody else was home. The police came and broke the lock on the door. They found me in my crib, my pajamas soaked because the diaper couldn't take any more. A judge said my mother was unfit to be a parent, and I went to live with my grandmother in Wormel.

For years I had nightmares where I was back in that apartment, lying in my crib and staring at a water-stained ceiling, hungry and alone and afraid. I shouldn't have remembered any of it, but I could remember every detail: the splashes of light on the high wall as headlights passed the window, the warm wet on my bottom and legs. I could barely remember my mother's own face, but I could recall the pebble print of the wallpaper and the baby blue crib sheet. I would wake up breathless and afraid, sneak into my grandmother's room, and crawl into her bed.

"Go on back to your bed," she'd grumble. "I can't sleep with you kicking me all night." She'd nudge me out, and I would creep back across the hall to my own bed, the sheets clammy from sweat, and lie there trembling until dawn.

But my memories of lying in the crib had no context. I only know the full story because I once found a business-sized envelope inexplicably shoved into a kitchen drawer where Grandma kept batteries, twist ties, packets of seeds, and other clutter. The envelope was printed in Grandma's hand: MANNY PAPERS. Inside I found two mimeographed pages, waxy to the touch and shot through with smudges. The document was organized under headings like THE FACTS and THE REASONS and FINDINGS AND ANALYSIS. The story of my infancy was all there, reduced to a few sentence fragments. I had believed legal documents were long and complicated, but when it came to babies and unfit mothers they were short and to the point.

One of the headings read SUPPORT & VISITATION, and the paragraph beneath it declared that my mother would pay $38 a week for my care and that "due to the lack of stability of the defendant, it is not possible to establish any visiting time with the child." I don't know if my mother made good on the support, but she made good on the lack of visitation.

In fourth grade a teacher told Grandma I was falling asleep at my desk, slinking away during recess to be alone. I was sulky and uncooperative. I wasn't meeting expectations, academically or socially.

"Has he been tested?" she wanted to know.

"Tested for what?" Grandma asked.

The teacher shrugged. "He might need help."

"I reckon he does," my grandmother said, and her tone suggested it wasn't the kind of help my teacher had in mind.

That Saturday Grandma hauled boxes down from the attic.

"Sick of all the clutter up there," she said. But she didn't seem to be throwing any of it away. She was looking for something. She searched one box after another, and set most of the boxes aside to be hauled back up to the attic. Only one box was spared, originally for store-brand diapers but now containing who knows what, and that one she moved into my room. She put it on the top shelf in the closet, which was already crammed full of things that weren't mine.

"Stay out of there," she told me.

"What's in there?" I asked.

"None of your nevermind," she said.

She returned the rest of the boxes to the attic and settled down with a book of crosswords and a pot of coffee.

I looked at the mysterious box and decided it was some of my nevermind.

I climbed on a chair and got a finger on the box and worked it to the ledge, tipped it, and caught it as it fell. I set it on my bed and opened it. The first thing I found was a white Bible with a gold clasp. I opened it and saw my mother's name scrawled in a childish hand. A wave of wonder passed through me. These were my mother's things, not my grandma's. My mother was a mystery to me.

There were photographs: one of a small girl holding a doll; one with the same girl, slightly older, standing with other girls in front of a sad-looking pony; one with the girl and my grandmother, younger but still recognizable. Everything looked terribly old-fashioned. The girls wore white blouses with big collars and black vests, bangs hanging over their foreheads. A series of class photos in grainy black and white; I had trouble finding my mother among the dark-eyed girls.

Under the pictures was the doll from the first photograph. It was smashed flat but it only took a moment to fluff it back to life. The doll had red yarn hair tied with yellow ribbons, a white dress printed with purple flowers, round black eyes, and a carefully stitched U-shaped smile. The doll was peach-colored except for her cheeks, which were painted pink circles. I liked her immediately.

I hid the doll in the messy blankets on my unmade bed and put everything else back where I found it, jumping to get the box back on the shelf and painstakingly nudging it back in place. Moments after I pulled the chair back to where it belonged, Grandma barged in and told me to take out the garbage.

That night I slept with the doll in my arms; her linen face was cool against my cheek. When I awoke the next morning sunlight poured through the windows. I had not had a bad dream all night. She seemed to smile at me. She always smiled, but this smile seemed to be made for the moment and for me. I bunched up the blankets and hid the doll in the folds.

"Stay here," I whispered.

That would do if Grandma didn't make the bed. Sometimes she did, and sometimes she didn't. I was lucky. After she washed the egg pan and plates, she looked outside and decided it was warm enough to garden.

"Might as well start prepping for the transplants," she said. She already had egg cartons full of dirt in all the windows, their cups sprouting green shoots. Grandma was serious about her garden. "You can play in the yard."

I usually jumped at the chance to be outside, but not with secret toys in the bedroom.

"I want to play inside," I said.

"Well, fine." She put up less of a fight than I expected. "Just stay out of trouble." As soon as she was outside I retrieved the doll. I played with it all morning, untying the ribbons and combing the hair with my fingers, retying the ribbons with nicer bows. I named her Dee Dee. Dee for doll times two for no reason. As soon as I heard the door creak open, I pushed her back under the covers, took up a cowboy comic, and pretended to be reading it when Grandma poked her head in and told me to wash my hands for lunch.

Later that day I found a shoebox and some old newspaper, laid the doll in a bed of paper, and shut it. I put the box in the closet, near some other boxes, and hoped that Grandma wouldn't remember that box used to be in the capsizing stack of boxes near the basement steps. I closed the closet door, opened it, and checked on the doll. She was still there. Her smile now seemed unsure; a smile plastered over worry. Grandma called me to dinner.

~~~~~~~~~~~

On Monday morning I woke up early and stowed the doll in her box-bed in the closet. I knew I couldn't risk bringing the doll to school. It wasn't because other kids would tease me, because they did that anyway. It was because of Todd Baker, a third-grader who rode the same bus to school. He was a year behind me in school, but at least the same height, maybe a bit bigger.

He'd been bothering me all year. One time he took my gloves and dunked them in cold muddy water. Another time he grabbed my hood and tried to pull my parka off over my head. He'd dumped my backpack into snowbanks more than once. I'd told Grandma, but she said I had to fight my own battles. There was no way I would let Dee Dee get discovered by Todd Baker. He'd rip out her hair and undo her stitches and rub her pink-cheeked face in the mud and stomp on her. I couldn't bear the thought of her being ruined. So I left her in her cardboard coffin and closed the door and went to school, feeling like I was leaving my own heart and lungs behind.

I dawdled over breakfast, thinking about Dee Dee and how I would barely get through the day without her. I thought again of taking her, even though I knew it was impossible. Then I had an idea.

I finished my oatmeal in a hurry and ran into my room. I shut the door, dragged a chair to the closet, leaped up, and dragged the box down. I made a racket, but Grandma was running water in the kitchen and didn't hear.

I opened the box and found the photograph—my mother as a child, playing with a doll. Playing with *my* doll. I slid the photo into my backpack, in the pages of a textbook, and put the box back where it belonged.

Grandma shouted from the kitchen. "If you miss that bus and I have to drive you, you *will* be sorry."

"I know! I know." I dragged the chair back and threw the door open. Grandma was standing there, filling the doorframe.

"You sure are making a big enough racket."

"Sorry." I didn't try to come up with a lie. Grandma never asked me what I was doing. I don't think she cared.

"All right. Well, get going."

~~~~~~~

The kids in Wormel went to a school in a nearby town. We caught the bus at one corner of the gravel parking lot of the Holiday store right off the highway. On good days I got there right when the bus did so Todd didn't have a chance to harass me. Unfortunately, the bus was late a lot, and it was that morning.

All the kids were there. Todd had his pick of kids to torment. There was fat Kimberly and pale Scotty who had asthma and frequently had to stop and suck on a plastic inhaler. There was Mel, short for Melody or Melanie, curling her lips back and baring her teeth. She always did that for some reason. She was in special ed. There was Theresa, the only black kid in Wormel. Todd never bothered any of those kids. He only bothered me.

"Manny, Manny, Manny," he said. He reached out and poked me in the shoulder. I swatted his hand away but said nothing. There's no comeback to your own name being used like a bad word. His sister Leah snickered. She was a fifth-grader and mostly ignored his attacks on me, but sometimes she encouraged him. Todd grinned and looked me up and down, trying to find something to mock—mismatched socks or frayed hems on my jeans. He caught a glimpse of my shirt collar and tugged on my coat zipper to get a better look.

"Woohoo," he said. "Fancy duds."

I was wearing a button-up shirt instead of a T-shirt. It was purple and kind of shimmered. I'd picked it off the rack at the Goodwill. Grandma told me I looked like a hustler. I didn't even know what that meant, but she bought me the shirt because it only cost forty cents and it fit me pretty well. I should have known better than to wear it to school.

"Your mother is doing a better job dressing you," said Todd.

"You mean his grandmother," his sister added, her voice with a nasty edge. "He doesn't have a mother."

"Oh, yeah." Todd faked a sad look.

By now everybody was watching. Kimberly blinked at me. Mel did that thing with her lips. Scotty withdrew his inhaler from his pocket—not sucking it, but keeping it handy just in case. They probably wanted to see if I would cry. Making me cry was easy, and kids made a game of it.

The bus appeared on the exit ramp. It would be here in a minute. Once it was, I could sit by a window and look outside so nobody could see my watering eyes. If I got a seat to myself, I could even sneak a peek at the photograph and see Dee Dee's reassuring stitched-on smile. The thought soothed me. The bus curved through the lot, and for a moment it sat with the door open while all the kids still looked at me.

"He's not going to!" Kimberly announced and bounded onto the bus.

I sat next to Mel. Other kids nudged each other. Nobody was supposed to sit with Mel unless they had to. I didn't care. Mel didn't talk. She was the perfect companion. I opened my text-book, pretended I was looking up answers to my homework assignment, flipping past the photo and getting a glimpse of my mother and the doll. Dee Dee looked proud of me.

I stole glances at the picture all day—when I needed to solve a math problem on the board, I pretended to look in my desk for a pencil. When we had quiet reading time, I tucked it into the pages of *Adventures in Reading* and turned to it several times during the story, which was about kids having a contest to see whose frog could jump the highest. I got the math problem right and answered all the questions about the story in the quiz at the end. At recess I left the picture behind and joined in a game of kickball with some other kids. I almost never did that, and they almost didn't let me play, but David W. said, "Aw, let him play. We need another player." David W. had a way of bending other kids to his will. I played on David's team and kicked the ball hard in my only plate appearance, hard enough that it bounced off Chad's hands and rolled to the fence.

The whole week went like that. In the evenings I would steal a little time to play with Dee Dee, and at night I would have deep and restful sleep. During the day I stowed her in the shoebox in the closet. I avoided Todd and did well in class and played kickball every day. I even had lunch with David W. and his pals. At the end of the day on Friday, the teacher patted me on the shoulder and told me I'd had a good week. I guess I'd met all of her expectations, academically and socially.

Of course it all fell apart that afternoon. On the bus ride home I thought about Dee Dee and how I could play with her that weekend if I wanted to, and since the bus was emptying and nobody was paying attention to me I reached down to get my bag and sneak a look at the photograph, but my bag was tipped over and unzipped, the contents spilling under the seat. I panicked, reached down to scoop it up before anybody saw, and realized it wasn't an accident. Todd was on the floor behind the next seat. I caught a glimpse of his corn-yellow hair before he disappeared.

He popped up jubilantly, waving the photo. "Manny has a picture of an ugly little girl!" he said. "Is this your girlfriend, Manny? She looks like a pilgrim."

"It's my mom."

"Your mom is a pilgrim?"

"Yes. Give me the picture."

He stared at it a moment, then ripped the picture in half and half again. He shredded it, sending the pieces out the window.

"Oops," he said. He looked around to see if anyone was laughing, but we didn't have an audience. Kids were scattered around the bus, looking out the window or talking. Even his sister was reading a paperback book three seats back.

Something inside of me smoldered. Todd could see his mother whenever he wanted. She wore tank-top shirts so the whole world could see her armpit hair, but she was a *fit* mother and probably never left him or Leah all alone as a baby. He knew who his father was. He was a carpenter or a repairman or something, drove a pickup truck with a banged-up fender, and wore a greasy Oakland A's cap for some reason. I didn't think he was from Oakland.

I almost forgot that I didn't even care about the photo because my mother was in it. It was because of Dee Dee, and I should have been glad that Todd didn't notice the doll or have the imagination to think the doll had anything to do with me carrying the photo.

"Are you going to cry?" he asked, leering and hopeful.

"No," I said. "I'm going to beat you up the second we get off this bus."

"Big words."

"Sorry, I don't know any shorter ones," I said. My voice was even. I never felt further away from tears. I was cool as dew on spring grass.

The bus was taking the exit to Wormel now, turning into the big gravel lot. Todd tried to scoot off early but was held up by Scotty and Mel in front of him. I was right behind him, hoisting my bag and planning my attack.

I didn't mean it only as a threat. I really was going to beat this kid up the second our shoes hit the dirt. He leaped off the bottom step and tried to run, but I leaped after him and swung my bag at his head. He staggered and turned around to face me, his fists held up like he was in some boxing movie. I swung the bag a second time, catching his fist.

On the third swing he caught the strap and pulled the bag away from me, but the moment his hands were full of it, I bulldozed him and knocked him flat in the mud.

I hammered on his face with the heel of my palms while he bucked helplessly. "Uncle!" he cried.

"What?" I didn't get what Todd was yelling about. Was his uncle within earshot? Was he expecting him to come help?

"He means you win," Leah said. "He quits."

"You quit?"

"Yes! You win!" Todd hollered.

I felt like I should extract something from him—a promise, or an apology. But a promise from Todd Baker wasn't worth the dirt from a dog, and an apology was worth even less. The kid would never be sorry about anything. I spat in his eye and pinched his nose and stood up. He scampered away, broke for home.

The bus driver had driven away, either not noticing our fight or not caring enough to stop it. Maybe once we were off the bus what we did was none of his business.

I hoisted up my bag and found Leah still watching me.

"You're older than him," Leah reminded me. "You beat up a younger kid."

"You watched," I said. "You're his big sister, and all you did was watch."

~~~~~~~~~

I went on home and found Dee Dee propped up on my pillow. Grandma must have been through the room. Since she was still there, I guessed it was okay to keep her. I picked her up, dumb with wonder.

"You wash your hands before you play with that," Grandma said. "You're filthy."

"Yes, Ma'am." She was right. My hands were covered with dirt and snot and spit. No blood. I hadn't beaten Todd badly enough to make him bleed. I put the doll down and started for the bathroom.

"The Baker woman called. She says you fought with her boy."

"I had to," I said.

"Glad you finally took care of it," said Grandma. Like I said, she wasn't like other grandmas.

I washed my hands and went to play with my doll.

Kings and Queens

John Coy

SNOW FELL IN WET, FAT FLAKES as Grandpa picked me up after school.

"Your mom's running late," he said. "How was your day?"

"Like usual. Boring. School's always boring."

"Boring? You don't know boring, Noah. School is much more interesting now than it used to be."

"No way." I set my heavy backpack down and buckled my seatbelt.

"When I was in fifth grade, we didn't have computers, Smart Boards, or the Internet," Grandpa said. "We didn't do interesting projects and make the kinds of things you do in art. You can't believe how boring school used to be."

The windshield wipers slapped aside wet snow as we drove out of the parking lot. I thought about all the math and science homework I had to do for tomorrow. "I bet you didn't have as much homework as we do."

"We had homework," Grandpa said. "Maybe not as much as you have now, but we had plenty of boring homework. Day after day, we did worksheets and passed them to the person behind us to correct while we corrected the ones from the person in front of us. Now that was boring."

Grandpa stopped at a red light and pointed at me. "I've got you beat on boring school by a mile. I'd love to be in fifth grade now. You know so much more than I did at your age. You get to see and do so many more things. When I was your age, we didn't have nearly the opportunities that you have now."

I stared out the window at the falling snow. Adults loved talking about how hard things used to be.

"There was one thing about my school that was better," Grandpa said.

"What?"

"We got recess three times a day."

"That's no fair."

"Yup, morning, lunch, and afternoon, but the reason we did was because school was so boring. That's my whole point. We had to have recess after being there for only an hour because we were already bored out of our minds."

I took my gloves off and wiggled my fingers. I couldn't wait to get home to play Minecraft. Homework could wait. After sitting in school all day, what I really needed was to lose myself in a different world.

"Today would be just right for one of my favorite games," Grandpa said.

"What game?"

"King of the Mountain."

I looked over at Grandpa and realized he wasn't talking about a video game.

"We used to get more snow when I was a kid, and when they cleared the playground, they piled snow into a big hill. At recess, we'd race out to the pile and try to get to the top. Everybody else had the same goal, so there was lots of pushing and grabbing. I loved that game."

Poor Grandpa. Kids back in the olden days got excited about being outside in the cold with a pile of snow. I was glad I lived now when I could stay inside and play all kinds of amazing video games.

~~~~~~~~~

The snow was falling heavier as Grandpa pulled in front of my apartment.

"Aren't you coming in?" I asked.

"No, I need to get home and clear some of this snow. Your mom will be back in half an hour. She said traffic was slow because of the weather."

"Do you think they'll call off school tomorrow? We need a snow day."

"Snow day? We never had those when I was a kid. The idea of

not going to school because of snow hadn't even been invented. You guys have it easy now."

"Thanks for the ride, Grandpa." I rushed in to play Minecraft.

～～～～～

The next morning, mounds of sparkling snow covered everything as light flakes continued to fall.

"Snow day?" I asked Mom, who was listening to the radio.

"Yes, six inches already," she said. "But I still have to work. I'll drop you off at your grandparents'."

"I'm old enough to be by myself," I pleaded. "I'll stay inside the whole day."

"What would you do?" Mom poured herself more coffee.

"Play Minecraft. I promise to stay right here."

"Your grandparents are happy for you to come over," Mom said.

"I'd rather stay here. Grandpa doesn't like video games, and he'll try to make me go outside."

"That's not the worst thing in the world."

"It will be boring." I trudged back to my room.

～～～～～

When Mom dropped me off, I hurried into the house and took off my hat, coat, and boots.

"What do you want to do with your snow day?" Grandma asked.

"I don't know." I sat down in front of the old-fashioned TV. It only got a few channels, and none of them were any good.

"I've got a five-hundred-piece jigsaw puzzle of the Tower of London and a one-thousand-piece one of the Taj Mahal," Grandma said.

"You can help me shovel," Grandpa said. "That's what I did all winter when I was your age."

"I'll stay inside." I wasn't into puzzles, but it sounded a lot better than shoveling all that snow.

Grandpa shook his head and muttered something I couldn't hear. Grandma got out the Taj Mahal puzzle and dumped the pieces onto the dining room table. They were tiny, and it looked like we could spend a year working on it and never finish. Making a puzzle or shoveling snow, those were two terrible choices. I wish Mom had let me stay home by myself and do what I wanted.

"Let's start with the edges," Grandma said. "That's the easiest way to begin."

I picked out edge pieces and we set them around the table. Grandma was really good at figuring out which pieces went where, but I wasn't.

I handed her two light blue pieces that she snapped into place on different sides of the puzzle.

"How did you know which one went where?"

"Look," she said, pointing to the box. "The colors are slightly different. You can see which one goes on each side."

I couldn't see much difference. Maybe Grandma had done so many puzzles in her life that it was now simple for her.

"What was school like when you were a girl, Grandma?"

"Oh, I loved school." Grandma fit three more pieces in. "I had a wonderful third-grade teacher named Mrs. Bryce. She knew how much I enjoyed reading and telling stories, so she encouraged me to write them down and bring them to school. She'd let me read my stories to the class, and I was surprised how much the other kids liked them. They kept telling me to keep writing because they wanted to know what happened next. That made me work harder on them, and through stories I made some great friends. I owe a huge thank-you to Mrs. Bryce."

"So your school wasn't boring?"

"Heavens, no. I loved being in school."

"Grandpa said his school was super boring."

"You know Grandpa. He sometimes exaggerates." She shrugged her shoulders and held out her palms. "But I don't think he ever had a teacher as good as Mrs. Bryce. He always liked to run around and be active, so I think school really was more boring for him."

I kept sorting through the pieces on the table, looking for the straight sides of the edge pieces. Just then, Grandpa came in and took off his jacket and pulled off his sweater.

"I'm too hot." He tossed it on a chair. "Once you get working, it feels good." He put his coat back on. "Change your mind, Noah? Ready to come out?"

"Nah." I shook my head.

"Talk about boring." He zipped up his coat.

"It's fine if Noah wants to stay inside and work on a puzzle," Grandma said. "I'm going to make some chocolate-chip cookies in a little bit. He can help me with that."

"I'd rather eat them than make them."

"Why don't you call a couple of friends and see if they'll come over to help shovel?" Grandpa said. "Tell them they can eat as many cookies as they want afterward."

"I don't think so." Grandpa didn't know that most fifth-graders don't do things for cookies. Maybe they did in the olden days, but not anymore.

"Sheesh." Grandpa went back out.

Grandma and I worked on the puzzle as the edges came together. She grouped pieces into colors and put sections together while I twisted one piece around trying to get it to fit into a spot that it wouldn't go.

Later, when Grandma went to the bathroom, I got out my phone and called my best friend, Rafe. He said his older sister was bugging him and when I asked if he wanted to come over and shovel for cookies, I couldn't believe it when he said yes. He told me to call Shawn, and Shawn surprised me by saying yes, too. I guess they were as bored as I was. Grandma was going to have to make a lot of cookies for the three of us.

When Shawn and Rafe arrived, they told me that Grandpa had already asked them if they were here to help shovel and how happy he was when they said yes. I introduced them to Grandma and got my coat and boots and hat on.

Outside, Grandpa gave me a smile and handed us each dented metal shovels. "Let's go to work, boys," he said.

The snow was heavier than I expected. We had to scoop it up and carry it over to the side of the driveway. With all the snow, I was afraid we might be stuck shoveling all day.

"This is nothing," Grandpa said. "When I was your age we could get a foot of snow. And we never got school called off either."

Rafe and Shawn were both good shovelers who worked hard, and I struggled to keep up with them. They acted like they enjoyed it, and Shawn even asked Grandpa questions about the olden days. I knew that was a guaranteed way to hear some long stories, but Shawn and Rafe didn't seem to mind.

After we'd gotten half of the driveway done, Grandpa's neighbor drove up in his pickup with a plow on the front. He rolled down his window, and he and Grandpa talked.

"Move to the side, boys." Grandpa waved us over in front of the house. "Ramon's going to plow us out."

"All right," Shawn cheered.

"We still get cookies," Rafe said.

Ramon had come just in time. My back and arms were killing me.

Ramon rattled the plow along the driveway and pushed the snow into a pile. Grandpa kept directing him to add more and the pile grew bigger and bigger.

~~~~~~~~~~

When Ramon finished, Grandma called out from the front door and handed Grandpa a container of cookies for Ramon and his family. He honked the horn and waved thanks as he drove away.

Shawn walked over to the pile for a closer look, and we followed. It was twice as tall as us, and chunks of snow stuck out at odd angles to form a mountain of different levels. We walked around it, looking at it from all sides. Shawn started climbing, but he slipped and slid to the bottom. I started up, but Rafe pulled me by the back of my coat. I broke out of his grip, but Shawn grabbed me from behind, and we both went tumbling down.

I zipped my coat tighter and saw Leah and Maya, twins from our class who lived next door.

"Your grandpa said we could play," Maya said.

"Play what?" Rafe questioned.

Suddenly, I knew the answer.

"King of the Mountain," I said.

"Queen," Leah corrected. "I'm going to be Queen of the Mountain."

Everybody rushed the hill. Leah grabbed one of Shawn's boots and Maya grabbed the other. Rafe and I rolled around like polar bears and ended up sprawled in the snow at the bottom.

Later, DeJuan and Armando, who lived across the street, joined in and so did Jasmine and Trina, friends of Maya and Leah's.

Shawn, Rafe, Armando, DeJuan, and I faced off in a multilevel all-star wrestling match. Maya seized the opportunity to scramble to the top, but her glory time was short because Trina pushed her aside. Armando crawled up and sent her tumbling. I saw an opening when everybody was focused on pulling him down.

I raced behind the hill and climbed quickly. When Armando slid down, I scrambled up.

"Look," Rafe shouted.

"Get Noah!" Shawn yelled.

But it was too late. I was alone at the top, and I loved the view. I could see all the way down the street. I waved to Grandpa who was cleaning the edges of the driveway. He gave me a big thumbs-up. I was King of the Mountain.

~~~~~~~~~

Afterward, Grandma invited everybody inside. She'd made tons of cookies and had set out mugs of hot apple cider in the kitchen. Jasmine talked about how great it was to be Queen, and we all discussed our favorite parts of the game.

"I really like how we all had to work together to get Armando down," Shawn said.

"Yeah, but then you turned on me," Rafe said. "You double-crossed me."

"That was the only way I could be King."

"Leah and I decided to be Queens together," Maya said. "We were co-Queens."

"But then we got both of you down," Trina said.

"And then I got you," Jasmine said.

"Yeah," Rafe added. "The great thing is sometimes you have to work together, but sometimes you get your own chance to race to the top."

"But it doesn't last long," Armando said.

"That's right." Dejuan laughed. "You've got to enjoy it while you can because you know someone's coming to get you."

"And when you think you know who, somebody else surprises you from behind," Jasmine said.

Everybody was right. There were so many things to pay attention to in this game, and it moved quickly. I kept remembering what it felt like to be on top. Grandpa was right. King of the Mountain was a great game.

~~~~~~~~~~

After we'd all had as many cookies as we wanted, Jasmine and Trina spotted the puzzle. Rafe had been to the Taj Mahal with his parents so he was eager to see what it looked like put together, and Maya and Leah were puzzle experts. Their hands flew around the table grabbing pieces and locking them in. DeJuan and Armando were good, too, since their grandma liked to do puzzles; they worked together on their side. In no time the whole Taj Mahal was constructed, all one thousand pieces.

We all stood back and admired what we'd done.

"What are we going to do now?" Shawn asked.

"I know," I said. "Let's go back outside. I want to be King of the Mountain again."

Max Swings for the Fences

Anne Ursu

IT WASN'T AS IF MAXIMILIAN FUNK didn't know that things were going to go badly. After all, there's no good that can come out of being a new kid in school, especially when you've just moved halfway across the country, *especially* in the middle of the year. Nothing says *Give me a wedgie and hang me from the flagpole* like waltzing into a new middle school in February at a time when there are no other new kids to hide behind.

He knew things were going to go badly. If he knew just how badly they were actually going to go, though, he would have faked some illness that would keep him out of school for the rest of the year. Like bubonic plague.

So Max slowly got ready for his first day at Willard Middle School, spending more time than anybody ever had trying to decide whether it would be better to wear a sweater and T-shirt or sweater and button-down shirt. He just wanted to get it right. Max had spent his middle school life thus far working hard to be the sort of kid no one ever noticed, except perhaps to say, "Oh, I didn't see you there." Because there were only two ways to get noticed in middle school, and Max was never going to be the kid who got noticed in a Good Way, as if he were a basketball stud or did something amazing like winning an ice cream-eating contest or solving one of Mrs. Bjork's extra-credit word problems. So that left the Bad Way. Better not to be noticed at all.

When he got downstairs, his mom presented him with a Minnesota Twins cap, flashing him a huge I-know-I-ruined-your-life-but-I-bought-you-this-fabulous-hat-so-it's-all-better-now smile. "Now you'll look like a native," she proclaimed.

Max frowned. He did not wear baseball caps. Baseball caps only served to emphasize his ears. Which were already doing a fine job of emphasizing themselves.

"Mom," he said, not trying to keep the exasperation from his voice, "baseball hats are for jocks. I can't stride in there pretending I'm a jock." Middle school kids could smell posers like a T. rex could smell a lame triceratops. It was a biological fact.

"You *are* a jock!"

"I play *tennis,* Mom."

"That's a sport!"

"Trust me. It's not the same thing."

"Come on, honey. Don't be nervous. Everyone's going to love you."

"It's February, Mom. Nobody cares."

"Of course they care!" she said. "You have so much to offer them!"

Max tried to keep from rolling his eyes. Every mother thought her kid was extraordinary. By definition, at least 75 percent of them had to be kidding themselves.

"Anyway," she added, putting the cap on his head, "this town's nuts about baseball. Just tell everyone at school you're from Beau Fletcher's hometown. They'll think you're a celebrity!"

Max sighed. Beau Fletcher was the veteran all-star third baseman for the Minnesota Twins, a two-time MVP, future Hall of Famer, and the greatest thing to come out of New Hartford, New York, ever. People in New Hartford said Beau Fletcher's name with this dazed reverence, like he'd invented soup or something. It didn't matter whether he was a nice guy or anything. All that mattered was that he hit a jillion home runs. After Beau donated some money to help rebuild Roosevelt High's athletic fields, there was a movement to rename the school after him. After all, what had Franklin Delano Roosevelt done for them lately? In New Hartford, Beau Fletcher mattered so much that the universe needed to make people who didn't matter at all just to keep everything in balance.

People like Max.

And then it was time to go. Max's dread followed him to the car. It huddled its overgrown body into the backseat and kicked Max's seat the whole way to school. It lurked behind him as he went up the steps to the school and through the doors and down the hallway following the signs to the main office. And then, right before Max went in, it wrapped him up in an icy, immobilizing embrace—and then disappeared suddenly, leaving him all alone.

And that's when everything changed.

Because in the main office stood a woman, and next to her was a girl. And she was the most beautiful girl Max had ever seen. The girl had long, thick, wavy hair like a mermaid might have. And it was a rich, dark red, the kind of color that should only exist in a Crayola box or maybe a very special kind of slushie. And her eyes, her eyes were green like emeralds. Or kryptonite.

Max's ears flushed.

"This is your official new student buddy," the woman, who had apparently been talking for some time, said. "Molly Kinsman. She's in sixth grade too."

"Hi, Max," Molly said, smiling a smile that would need no orthodontia. "I'm going to show you your classes and stuff, okay?"

Max opened his mouth but couldn't come up with a response. This was the sort of girl who would never pay attention to him unless she was assigned to. Her eyes were so green. Who did they remind him of?

"Ready?"

"Catwoman!" he thought. Except he said it out loud. His mouth hung open.

The girl blinked. "What?"

"I mean, yes," Max said. "I'm ready. Thanks. Thank you. Ready, Freddie!"

He closed his mouth. Molly gave him a curious look, then led him around the school. She chatted as she showed him his locker, the gym, the library, the cafeteria. And Max just followed, nodding and grunting like an ape desperately trying to hide the fact that it had just been body-switched with a sixth-grade boy. But, he reflected, at least nodding and grunting was better than babbling. If he started talking, who knows what ridiculous thing would come out of his mouth next?

Molly dropped him off at his homeroom. "So, come find me in the cafeteria at lunch, okay?" she said brightly. "You can sit with us."

And then she turned and left, her invitation hanging in the air.

Max stared. Did she really want to hang out with him? Or was it just part of her job description?

Max sat through his first three periods wishing he were a different sort of person, the kind who might impress a girl like Molly, the kind who had anything interesting about him at all. If Molly thought he was cool, then surely the other kids would too. And then they wouldn't string him up on the flagpole by his underwear. There was a lot at stake.

Plus, then he'd get to hang out with her.

At lunchtime, he surveyed the cafeteria, and his eyes instantly found Molly's red head as if drawn there. His stomach flipped. *Don't blow it,* he told himself as he walked over. *This is your chance. Ready, Freddie.*

Molly was sitting at a table with a blond girl and a tall, dark-haired boy. Max gulped. The boy looked like the wedgie-giving sort.

"Hi!" Molly said, smiling up at him. "Max, this is Jenny, and this is Logan. Guys, this is Max. He just moved here."

Max sat down and attempted to look interesting.

"Oh, do you like the Twins?" Jenny asked, nodding to his hat.

"Oh, well, you know," Max said, "my mom gave this to me . . ." He cast a look at Molly. Should he play it like someone who loved baseball or someone who didn't really care that much? Was Jenny looking at his ears?

"Dude," said Logan, leaning in suddenly. "What position do you play?"

"Uh," Max looked around. Molly and Jenny were staring at him expectantly. "What do you mean?"

"What do I mean?" He nodded to Max's hat. "Baseball. Practice starts today!"

Of course. Logan was clearly a crazed jock who naturally assumed everyone around him was always thinking about baseball just because he was. Max looked at the girls but couldn't read them.

"Baseball?" he said. "It's February! There's snow on the ground!" There. That was a good, noncommittal answer.

"So?" Logan asked, looking at him as if he'd said fish sticks were best when made out of people.

"The all-city sixth-grade tournament is coming up," explained Jenny. "We lost it last year. We're starting early."

Logan straightened. "*We* didn't lose anything. Last year's sixth-graders did. But we're going to get it back this year. We have the best pitcher in the city."

"That's you, I assume?" Max said, half to himself. He knew this boy's type.

There was that look again. "Naw, dude. I'm shortstop. What about you?" He looked Max up and down in a way that reminded him of the way his mom picked out tomatoes in the grocery store. "We really could use a left fielder."

"Well, um, I don't really play baseball."

No one seemed to know what to say to that. Everyone suddenly looked down at their trays.

"I mean, I like baseball and everything," Max said quickly. "But I'm not very good at it. You know." He looked at Molly and laughed in what he hoped was a charmingly self-deprecating manner. "Everyone says I throw like a girl!"

The two girls turned their heads toward him slowly. Logan let out a long whistle.

Max grimaced. He just made himself sound like a total loser. "I mean," he said quickly, "I play tennis."

Logan blinked. "What?"

"Tennis. You know." He mimed a forehand for their benefit. Max actually had a very good forehand. But this is the sort of thing that's hard to show in mime.

Logan scrunched up his face. "My *mom* plays tennis."

Max did not know what to say. Many people's mothers played tennis. It did not mean there was something fundamentally wrong with the sport itself.

"Anyway," Logan said, "I gotta run to the library. See you later, Molly, Jenny. And—" he turned to Max, "you too, Venus!"

Max blinked. Oh. "More like Serena," he muttered defiantly.

Logan looked at him, and then a smile spread across his face, and it was the most delighted evil smile Max had ever seen—sort of like how Lex Luthor might look if he unwrapped a present Christmas morning and found the keys to global thermonuclear destruction.

"Right!" Logan said, laughing. "See you, Serena."

He left. Max looked at the two girls, who were distinctly not looking at him.

"Serena's better," Max explained.

And then silence, great and terrible, and Max felt himself fading into the wall, and along with it, all his prospects for a happy middle school life. Jenny shifted, then said she'd better go to the library too and got up and left, giving her friend a look that told Max that Molly was definitely hanging out with him because she was assigned to. He stuck his fork in his mac and cheese and attempted to jiggle it.

"So," Molly said after a pause, "where'd you move from?" Her voice sounded flat. Max didn't understand. Was the tennis thing that dumb?

"Um, upstate New York. A little town called New Hartford. You've probably—"

Molly's eyes grew large. "That's where Beau Fletcher's from!"

Oh. Right. "Yeah, I know."

And then Molly looked up at him again. "Did you . . . know him?"

And there was that spark in her eyes again—Max might even go so far as to call it a glow. And it would be a terrible, terrible thing to extinguish that glow again; why, Max didn't think he could live with himself.

"Know him? I mean." Max shifted. "Oh, well, I don't like to—"

As he talked, he was aware that his sentence was a runaway train picking up speed—but it didn't matter, for Jenny appeared again behind them just then to derail it. "Hey, Molly," she said, "do you want a ride to practice after school?"

"Practice?" Max said, still choo-chooing on. "For what?"

Molly's eyes narrowed. "Um, baseball."

There are times in a boy's life when it is wise not to speak the words in his mind. But Molly's hair was the color of a cherry slushie, and Max was not wise.

"You go to watch baseball practice?"

Jenny exhaled. And the glow in Molly's eyes turned into something else entirely.

"I'm the pitcher," Molly said, each word an ice cube slipped down the back of Max's pants.

Jenny rolled her eyes. "The best one in the city," she added, and then sighed epically and stalked away. Molly glared at Max for another two beats and then tossed her hair and got up and turned to go. Max's heart leaped out of his throat, followed by some words he didn't even know were there.

"He's my dad!" Max said.

Max froze. The words floated in the air. He blinked at Molly. Maybe she hadn't heard.

"Who's your dad?" she said, taking a step closer.

She'd heard.

Now, if you were sitting on the outside of this situation, you would recognize this as the point where things could have been saved. But if you were inside it, you would see nothing at all to do except open your mouth and say, "Beau Fletcher. Beau Fletcher's my dad."

Molly stared. And Max, Max stared too. Max's dad was not in any way, shape, or form Beau Fletcher. Max's dad lived in Poughkeepsie and franchised tanning salons.

Molly tilted her head and considered Max for one moment. Two. Max did not move. Inside, he could feel his intestines begin to unravel.

"You expect me to believe that?" she asked. But her voice didn't sound hostile. Just curious.

"I know," said Max. "It's really weird."

"But—" Molly's brow contorted, "Beau Fletcher's not married. He never has been. He's married to the game!"

Max nodded solemnly. "I know."

Molly's eyes widened, and then she too nodded, because she was a girl of the world. She sat down next to him. Max exhaled.

"So, why don't you have the same last name?" she whispered, leaning in to him so close Max could touch her hair. She smelled like cupcakes.

"Oh," said Max. "Well, you know, my mom raised me. He wasn't really around till I was a little older."

She gasped. "Does the school know?"

"Oh, you know." Max could not decide whether to nod or shake his head, so he jerked his head in a direction that could best be called diagonal.

"Wow," breathed Molly.

"So," Max said, blinking spasmodically. "Don't tell anyone, okay? It's really important." He cleared his throat. "It would be weird, you know?"

"Right," said Molly. "You don't want people to like you just because you're Beau Fletcher's son!"

"Right," said Max. *Just you*, he thought.

Molly stared at him as if expecting him to say more, and when he didn't, she just nodded as if she understood. His intestines curled back in place. Molly would never betray him. And her Catwoman eyes were fixed on him as if he himself had invented soup. Maybe the gods of middle school were finally smiling at him.

It was a little lie, that's all.

~~~~~~~~~~~

That night, Max went straight up to his room. He had work to do. He was no longer a boy-ape body-switch victim. He was a liar now, and that changed everything. Liars had information. They stuck as closely to the facts as possible. Liars kept control of their words. And they did not *ever* babble.

This was going to be a challenge.

He spent the evening reading up on Beau Fletcher. Nobody could talk about him without gushing over his stats: one jillion home runs, and a bazillion hits, and some crazy-high OPS, whatever the heck that was. It was like Beau was so amazing they had to make up a statistic for it. Most of the biographical stuff Max knew, of course—in New Hartford they taught Beau

Fletcher history sometime between the alphabet and scissors. But buried in interviews were some interesting bits of information, things that brought out the picture of Beau Fletcher the man, the sort of thing you might know if he were your dad. Like he was scared of spiders. And he ate a pastrami sandwich before every game. And he was allergic to strawberries. And his favorite movie was *Wall-E*. In Minnesota, he was a spokesperson for milk and even had his own ice cream flavor, which might be the coolest thing that could happen to a person ever. He could probably get it for free whenever he wanted, too, because they can't possibly charge you for your own ice cream flavor.

In short, Beau Fletcher was the sort of guy who, if you were going to have a famous guy for a dad, would be a great dad to have. Max was pleased.

He strode into school the next morning armed with everything there was to know about the life and times of Beau Fletcher, in case Molly decided to quiz him on the finer points of his dad's food allergies. But it wasn't Molly who accosted him as he walked to first period. The hand that grabbed his arm was Jenny's, her blond ponytail bobbing determinedly behind her.

"Molly told me," she whispered, her voice electric.

Max froze. "She did?" He turned slowly to look at her.

"I can't *believe* it!" Jenny said.

"You can't?"

Her blue eyes were sparkling. "No, I mean, it's *amazing!* But you know—" she tilted her head, "you look like him a little. Especially in the ears."

"Oh," said Max. "Look, Jenny . . ."

"I know, I know. I can't tell anyone. You don't want kids to like you just because you're Beau Fletcher's son, right?"

"You promise?"

"Swear!" Jenny said, holding her hands up.

As she disappeared into the stream of students, Max tried to slow down his heart. Jenny believed him. And, more important, Molly believed him. That's what mattered.

He finally saw Molly at third-period English. She was waiting outside the classroom. For him.

"Hey," he said, because that is the sort of thing sons of baseball players say.

"Hi," Molly said. She looked around and then whispered, "I got a present for your dad."

"What?" His ribs abruptly cinched together.

"Yeah!" She reached into her bag and pulled out a little Wall-E pin. "I thought it could be, like, a good-luck charm, you know?"

"His favorite movie! How did you know?"

"I know everything about him! He's my favorite player of all time. Maybe he could wear it in the dugout someday so I could see? You could ask him that, right?"

"Right," Max said. "Sure!"

"Amazing," Molly said. "Oh, hey—" a look of regret crossed her face, "did Jenny talk to you?"

"Um." Max shifted. "Yes."

She tilted her head. "I'm sorry I told her. It just came up, you know? She's my best friend. I don't want to *lie* to her!" Her nose wrinkled up at the very thought.

"No, of course not!" Max said, wrinkling up his nose even more. "Just, um, don't tell anyone else, okay?"

"Oh, you don't have to worry about me," she said.

Max smiled. Of course she wouldn't tell. And if Molly told Jenny, Jenny was trustworthy too. And anyway, Molly wanted to hang out with him now. And that was worth anything.

~~~~~~~~~~

Something changed in Max that day. For the first time in his life he was someone who was Someone, the sort of kid people noticed. In a Good Way. After all, if a girl like Molly believed he was the sort of kid who might have a baseball player for a dad, well, maybe that's who he was.

It would be the best thing ever to have a major league baseball player for a dad. And not just any major league baseball player. Beau Fletcher, one of the best. When Max was little, the Twins' mascot would've come to all his birthday parties, and all the kids would think that T.C. Bear was his best friend. Beau would have taken Max to the ballpark all the time. Max would run around on the field, take grounders from the other players, drink Gatorade in the dugout, and tell all the kids in school about it the next day. Sometimes Max would bring his friends, too—but only sometimes. And his dad would go to his tennis matches whenever he could and cheer louder than all the other dads combined. And everyone would point and say, "That's Beau Fletcher! Cheering for his son! Tennis is a real sport!" But they'd still play baseball sometimes. Beau would pick Max up from school, and they'd go to the fields in the back of the school and play catch as dusk slowly fell—father and son, night after night, just like it was supposed to be.

As Max walked through the hallways that day, he could feel himself standing taller, walking assuredly, like Logan and all the other kids who mattered. And the funny thing was, it worked. By the end of the day, he could feel the crackle in the air as the kids around him noticed him, sense them make way as he walked past, hear the staccato whispers, and see the fingers pointing—

Uh-oh.

"Hey!" A boy from his English class grabbed him on the shoulder. "Do you think your dad could come to school sometime to autograph? I have baseballs like you wouldn't believe!"

"Um—" said Max.

"Man!" A girl with a unicorn on her shirt sidled alongside Max. "Your dad is, like, my favorite player of all time. I named all my gerbils after him. Do you think I could meet him sometime? I won't be weird!"

"Uh—" said Max.

"Serena!" Logan was standing in front him, grinning. "You were kidding when you said you couldn't play, right? You gotta come to practice. Hey, think your dad might come? Give us some tips?"

And that's what it was like as Max made his way through the throngs of adoring Beau Fletcher fans to his locker. He grabbed his jacket, then looked inside his locker as if it might be a very nice place to stay for a while.

"Hey!" Molly appeared behind him, looking very happy.

He stared at her, pale and shaking. "Everybody *knows!*" he whispered.

Molly let out an exasperated sigh. "Oh, Jenny! Gosh, she always does this! You can't tell that girl anything!"

Max blinked at Molly. Everything inside him was blank, a pocket of nothingness floating in endless space.

"Don't worry about it. Listen." She leaned her head toward him, voice thick with excitement. "I want to meet him."

"You do?"

"Please?" She put her small, pale hand on his arm. Max almost gasped. "He could help me with my changeup! We could just meet. You can do that, right?"

Max's stomach was a pit of boiling tar, and all his innards were slowly descending into it. "Molly, he wants it to be a secret—"

"I know, but it's just me. Tell him I'm the only female baseball pitcher in the sixth-grade tournament. Won't he think that's cool? Anyway, he must want to meet your friends. Doesn't he?"

"Molly, um, he's so busy, and—"

She looked at him, her eyes not exactly losing their glow but shifting a bit. "You mean you can't set up a dinner with your own dad?" She blinked. "Why not?"

Max froze.

"Molly!" The word exploded out of his mouth. One breath. Two. Oh, God. "I lied," he said finally.

She drew up. "What? What do you mean?"

This was it. This was his chance to come clean, to end this. And then he'd just be normal Max again, the kind of kid guys like Logan step on in the cafeteria, that girls like Molly never even think about. And this look she was giving him now—a little confused, a little hesitant, a little hurt, all because of something he'd done—no one would ever look at him this way again. He could write a poem about this look, if only he knew how to write a poem.

"I mean," he said, "I let you think something that wasn't true. Beau . . . my dad . . . he doesn't know about me. That's why we don't have the same last name."

Molly gaped. "Wow," she finally breathed.

"I know," he said, shaking his head with as much sincerity as he could muster. His lungs felt like they were about to crack into bits and puncture various vital organs. "They dated one summer. My mom was a lifeguard at the pool in college, you see. I guess they'd broken up by the time she found out she was pregnant. And by then he'd been drafted into the minors, and . . . my mom never told him. She raised me on her own." His breath slowed a little. This was good. This sounded plausible. Max was pretty sure he'd seen something like it on CBS once.

"I'm sorry I lied to you," he said, making his face as sincere as possible.

"It's okay," she said. "What matters is that you're telling the truth now."

Max could do nothing but nod.

"Does *anyone* know?" she whispered.

"No," he said. "Mom told everyone my dad was some guy in Poughkeepsie. I believed it most of my life."

"I can't believe it!" Molly bit her lip. "Don't you think he'd want . . . to know? I mean, if I had a son—"

Max just shrugged, as if this was the stuff of grown-ups and he could only wonder at it.

"I bet," Molly said, her face so close her hair brushed against his arm, "if Beau Fletcher met you, he'd just know. He'd look in your eyes and see something. He'd *know.*"

There was something buzzing in Max's ears now, and Molly sounded very faint. "Yeah. Maybe," he said. That would be something, wouldn't it? To look into your long-lost dad's eyes and see recognition there.

"Oh, Max," Molly said. She stared up at him. "Your story is incredible." And with that, she slipped into his arms and gave him a squeeze, as quick and magical as a fairy blink. And then she was gone. But Max did not move, not for a long time.

~~~~~~~~~~

Max went home and planned on spending the weekend in quiet contemplation. There was a chance that it was over—that Molly, out of the goodness of her heart, would tell everyone to stop talking about it so Max would not have to feel bad about the dad he never knew. It was the sort of thing she would do. Eventually, it would all die down—and if not, he'd just stay under his bed until college.

He was allowed to entertain this delusion for about twelve hours.

The next morning, he awoke to his mother knocking on his door. "Max," she called. "Wake up. You have a visitor!"

A few minutes later, Max went downstairs to find Molly sitting in his living room, wearing a baseball cap and looking impatient.

"Come on," she said. "You're going to be late for practice!"

Max shook his head. "Molly, I told you, I don't—"

Her eyes got big. She seemed to be trying to tell him something, and Max wished desperately he spoke girl. "Yes," she said, voice full of portent. "You do."

He nodded. Like he could ever say no to Molly.

Max's mom smiled. "Honey, are you playing *baseball*?"

"That's right!" Molly said. "He tried to get out of it, but we thought he might have natural gifts."

Max stopped. Had Molly hit those last words a little too hard? His mom seemed to be looking at her a little strangely, but then just turned and gave Max a smile. A few minutes later he was wearing sweats and sitting in the backseat of the Kinsman family's SUV, Molly next to him.

"Molly, what—"

"Shhhh," she whispered, pointing to her father, who was driving. "We're not going to practice. Look!"

She held out a flyer. Max looked at it. And everything inside of him turned to goo. There were a lot of words, but only three stood out to him:

MEET BEAU FLETCHER

Max gagged.

"Can you believe it?" Molly whispered. "It's a charity thing. My dad got tickets as an early birthday present. You get his autograph and everything!" She produced a baseball from her bag and held it out like an apple.

"Uh-huh," Max said, very, very faintly.

"I think you should just tell him! Walk up to him and tell him who you are!" She looked at him expectantly. "You can do that, right?"

"Molly, I-I don't know."

Her eyes narrowed. "Max, come on. He's a world-famous baseball player! He must have a kazillion dollars. He should be taking care of you and your mom! I mean, if he's your dad . . ."

"Molly," he said, though his throat was closing in, "I-I can't do that."

"Why not?"

Max opened his mouth and closed it like a goldfish.

"Yes, you can, Max. I know you don't like to make trouble. But if not for you, then for your mom! Anyway, don't you think he'd want to know about you? His son? Isn't that fair to him? Give him a chance to *do the right thing.*"

Mouth opened. Mouth closed. And again.

"And if you don't want to tell him," she said, "I will . . . unless you can give me a good reason not to."

Silence settled in the car then, thick like eternity.

"No," said Max, voice like a strangled squirrel's. Molly raised her eyebrows. Open. Close. Open. Close. "I'll do it," he said finally.

There was no way out of this. She would hate him if she knew the truth. He would be a laughingstock. He would spend the rest of the year hanging by his underwear from the flagpole. Max had made his bed; now he had to strangle himself with the sheets. He turned and looked out of the window.

At best, Fletcher would just think Max was crazy. He would sign his baseball, wonder at this boy's obvious brain damage. And move on.

And at worst, at worst, well—

Max closed his eyes for the rest of the car ride.

Molly's father dropped them off at a hotel, and they walked in slowly. Molly was practically buzzing. Max felt like toxic sludge. His intestines kept looping in on themselves. She led him through the lobby into a big ballroom and to their place in line.

"You want to do this, right?" she asked as they got in line.

Max nodded weakly. The line might have taken six minutes or six days, Max wasn't sure. Whatever it was, it wasn't long enough, and soon Max and Molly were next in line to see the white-toothed, curly-haired, iron-jawed, big-eared pride of New Hartford, New York. Max had seen Beau Fletcher many times on TV and on billboards and in the eyes of kids around him who thought maybe they could be great someday, too. And he'd always seemed like he only existed in two dimensions. But here Beau Fletcher was a person. A very large person, but a person nonetheless.

"You go first," he said to Molly.

Molly nodded. "Second thoughts?" she whispered.

"No," he said. "No. Definitely not." After all, he told himself, she had a point. If Beau Fletcher had in fact been his dad, telling him would be the right thing to do. Definitely.

And then the usher urged her forward. And as soon as she was in front of Beau, her eyes lit up and a shy smile appeared on her face. "Hi," Molly breathed to Beau. "You're, like, my hero."

And judging by the expression on her face, Max knew it was true. He was lucky his dad wasn't some utility infielder.

Fletcher gave her a smile. "I'm flattered. You are . . . ?"

"Molly," she said, handing him a baseball. "To Molly."

It must be something, Max thought, seeing the excitement flash in Molly's eyes, to make people feel like this. Like they mattered.

"Any message?" Fletcher asked.

"Um, Strike 'em out?"

"You play softball, huh?"

Molly straightened. "No. Baseball."

"Baseball!" Fletcher laughed, and flashed Molly a smile full of charm. "Do you throw like a girl?"

Molly blinked and took the baseball back. She stood there for a moment, staring at Fletcher. Something passed over her face. Then she turned to Max. "Batter up," she said, her expression inert.

And that was it. There was no waiting anymore. Max stepped forward.

"Hello." Beau Fletcher looked up at him with an automatic smile. He really was a large man. He could probably crush Max with one arm. But he wouldn't. Beau was a good guy; Max could see that now. Just because he was the greatest baseball player in the world didn't automatically make him a jerk. "Um," Fletcher said, and Max realized he was staring dumbly again. "Do you want me to sign something?"

Max thrust the baseball in his general direction. Beau Fletcher poised his pen, and in two blinks, the ball was signed in thick black ink. Molly poked Max in the ribs. "Do it," she hissed.

"Um, Mr. Fletcher," gasped Max. Beau glanced up at him. "I, um . . . I'm your son."

Behind him, Molly exhaled. Beau Fletcher sat slowly back in his chair.

"Excuse me?"

"I'm your son. Um. You don't know about me, but—my mom—um . . ."

Fletcher drew back and eyed Max for a moment. His eyes narrowed. "Look, kid," he said, leaning in, "I'm pretty sure that's not true." He articulated each word carefully.

Max tried to speak the truth with his eyes. *I know. I know. But play along, okay? Please?* Beau Fletcher was a good man, the kind of man who inspired people, who made them feel like they mattered. This sort of thing happened with kids and professional baseball players all the time. They had a connection. The baseball player looked the kid in the eye and saw the wish in his heart—hit a home run for me, come visit me in the hospital, pretend to be my dad . . .

Beau Fletcher did look Max in the eye. And he leaned in. And Max leaned in, too, because he could do nothing else.

Beau said something to Max in a low voice, and it took Max a minute to process the words, because Beau was not playing along. Beau said something baseball players are never, ever supposed to say to kids.

Max stared. Tears burned his eyes. And then Molly pushed next to him. "What did you just say to him?" she spat.

"Are you in on this, too?" Fletcher said.

"I used to look up to you," Molly said. "You were my hero."

Fletcher stood up a little. "I don't know who put you kids up to this." Behind them, people began to murmur. And Max could not move at all.

"What's wrong with you?" Molly continued. "You're on commercials for *milk*! And you're nothing but a jerk!" She pounded on the table.

"Hey—" Fletcher looked around. "Keep it down."

Yeah, Max thought. *Keep it—*

"This is your *son*!" she proclaimed.

Silence, all around. And stares, from every direction. The usher stood dumbly, as if none of his usher training had prepared him for this.

Molly straightened and looked around. "That's right," she said to the crowd loudly. "This is his son, Maximilian Funk from New Hartford, New York. His mom raised him all by herself. And Beau Fletcher won't even acknowledge him."

Two security guards appeared next to them and grabbed both their arms. And then they were being hauled out of the room. Max caught one last glance at Beau Fletcher, who was watching them go.

Then they were outside the hotel. The security guards yelled at them for a while. Molly's big green eyes looked so confused, and Max wanted to help her, protect her, but he could not because this was all his fault.

When they were alone, silence settled around them like dust. And tears rolled down Max's cheeks. And he turned to Molly and began to speak.

"Molly, Molly, look. I'm sorry. I can't take it anymore. I lied. I lied about the whole thing. I just wanted to impress you. I wanted you to like me. It got out of hand. I'm so sorry. You're so tough and brave and amazing and—"

He couldn't go on. Molly was staring at him coolly. Her Catwoman eyes looked suddenly as if they might be capable of terrible things.

"I'm so sorry," he said again.

And then one corner of Molly's mouth drew up. "Oh, Max," she said, her voice suddenly feline. "I knew you were lying the whole time."

"Wha—?"

"It's the stupidest story I've ever heard."

"Then what . . . ?"

"Because you expected me to believe it. I wanted to see how far you'd go. How stupid you thought I really was. Turns out pretty stupid. Why, because I'm a girl? Or because I'm good at baseball? Or both?"

"No, I—"

She tossed her red hair, and it looked like fire. "You're just like everyone else. All you care about is being cool. Nobody cares what a person is really like."

"No, no, that's not—"

"And besides—" Molly took a step closer. She stared him down.

Max could not move.

"Now you'll never, ever say you throw like a girl again." Her eyes narrowed. She leaned in and hissed, "You *wish* you threw like a girl."

Max stared. His mouth hung open. Molly suddenly seemed six feet tall, and her eyes took your secrets from you. Max felt what it was like to step into the batter's box and see her staring at you, to look into those eyes as she probed you for your weaknesses. And he knew without a doubt that he, like every sixth-grader in the city who would face her that season, had just struck out.

The Creature under the Bush

Lynne Jonell

JANE PRESTON WAS QUIETLY DITCHING her gluten-free sandwich under the bushes next to the chain-link fence that surrounded the schoolyard when she saw the leaves move and the flash of an intelligent eye. She thought it might be a squirrel or maybe something even more interesting, like a very small fox.

"Enjoy the sandwich," she said, doubtful but hoping for the best. Her mother was going through a gluten-free phase lately, and Jane was suffering in patient silence until it was over. She had to get rid of the sandwich before school, because if the lunch ladies saw her throwing food away, they'd report it. You were not supposed to waste food at the Rosemary Perkins Day School because it wasn't respectful to Mother Earth. Or something.

Jane saw the thing—whatever it was—again during Supervised Recess, which basically meant gym class but outdoors. Tanner, on the other team, had kicked the ball into the bushes and Jane had to run to get it. She reached down for the ball and thought she heard a small, shrill voice say, "Got any more?"

She turned, startled, but then Peter and Abby and Michael all screamed at her to throw the ball already. Tanner was running for third, and Jane had to hurry away.

After school, Jane dawdled in the cloakroom until Lindy went on without her. Jane and Lindy were supposed to walk together to school and back—it made their mothers feel safer—but Lindy was one of those spectacularly boring people who never had anything to say. Except sometimes she talked about other people, a little meanly, and laughed. Jane did not want to investigate what was in the bushes near the chain-link fence when Lindy was with her.

So Jane was quite alone with no one watching when she knelt down by the bushes, pretended to tie her shoe, and looked straight into the eyes of a—something.

It was bigger than a squirrel, but smaller than a fox. It had oversize, pointed ears that looked excessively hairy. Its eyes were too big for its face, its chin too small, and its nose was long and knobby, like a sweet potato. It looked like a very small, very ugly person who had baked too long in the sun and gotten as dried out as a piece of old leather. It was wearing something that looked like a mitten with raveled edges, tied around the waist with a shoelace.

"Well?" it demanded. "Got any more?"

Jane breathed through her mouth. The power to speak seemed to have abandoned her.

The creature's nose curled down in disapproval. "What are you, a frog? Are you planning to catch flies with your tongue?"

Jane closed her mouth with a snap. She shook her head mutely.

"And I keep *asking* you." It raised its voice to a piercing whine and articulated each word. "Got—any—more—food?"

"At home," Jane whispered.

The creature sprang to grip the neck of Jane's cardigan sweater. It dug its long fingers into the knitted wool and peered up into her face. "Is your home in a forest?" it asked hoarsely. "Do you have caves?"

Jane moved her head back a fraction. "We have trees in our yard," she managed to say, her voice a little breathless. "And sometimes I make a cave with a blanket over the picnic table."

The creature's face was so near that Jane could count the black pores on its forehead and smell its sour-pickle breath. She turned her head slightly aside and wondered if it would be rude to plug her nose.

"But do you have . . ." the creature's throat bump bobbed up and down, and it trembled. *"Bells?"*

"What kind of bells?" Jane breathed shallowly from one corner of her mouth.

"Loud bells! Long bells! Bells that ring and ring and then

hordes of children race in or out, screaming like harpies on a wild night! That building right there—" he pointed to the school with a trembling finger, "has a bell." The creature dug its clawlike hands deeper into Jane's sweater. "The noise! The pandemonium!"

"If you hate bells so much," Jane said, "why do you live in a schoolyard?"

"It didn't used to be a schoolyard. It used to be all forest! But they put up houses on one side, and then the other, and they built that infernal bell house they call a school, and now they've dug up the last patch of woods to put up that!" The creature waved a wan, despairing hand at the apartment complex under construction across the street. "There was no place left for me to go but these bushes, and ever since then you don't know how I've suffered . . ."

He gulped back a sob. "Just look at those horrible machines! They RUMBLE. They BEEP. They HONK. I ask you—with refined and delicate instruments like this, how can I be expected to tolerate the noise?"

"Instruments?" Jane asked.

The creature swiveled his head until Jane was looking into one very large and hairy ear. "Instruments of hearing! My eardrums are *highly* sensitive. I simply cannot be expected to tolerate the noise of the modern world."

"Oh." Jane twisted a bit of her hair around her forefinger. "But where did you come from in the first place? And what are you, anyway?"

The creature cleared his throat. "I came from across the sea, a couple hundred years ago, give or take. A lot of us came then. And I'm a—" The creature slid its eyes away from Jane's and muttered something that sounded like "bold."

"What did you say?" Jane asked.

"You can call me—er—Karl."

"But I still didn't hear—"

"TAKE ME HOME WITH YOU!" Karl howled. "PLEASE, PLEASE, PRETTY PLEASE WITH A GUGELHUPF ON TOP!" He scrambled inside Jane's sweater, stretching out the neck in the process, and popped his head out again through a space between the buttons.

Jane cleared her throat. She wasn't sure what a gugelhupf was, and she didn't think her mother would be happy if Jane brought home a strange creature without permission. On the other hand, Jane's cousin Bill might like it very much.

Bill was coming to visit for two weeks while his parents were away. Jane admired her cousin, but he was two grades ahead of her, and he was not easy to impress. He could run farther, climb higher, read thicker books, and he wasn't afraid of snakes. He played with Jane now and then, when he had nothing better to do, but mostly she got the feeling that she bored him.

Jane looked down thoughtfully at the shabby little creature. Karl was not exactly impressive, but he was certainly interesting. "Do you mind not digging your fingers into my sweater like that?" she said. "My mother will kill me if I snag it."

"Kill you?" Karl peered up into Jane's face again. "Is your mother so very violent? Is she a troll?"

"It's just a figure of speech," said Jane. "What I mean is, she'll get mad. And she'll go mental if she sees you, so you'd better stay hidden."

"She won't see me," Karl said with a snap of his long fingers. "Grown-up people never do."

~~~~~~~~~~~~~

This, as it turned out, was true. When Jane walked in the door, the creature leaped out from inside her sweater to the kitchen counter where he did a whirling dance around the toaster, apparently looking for crumbs.

Jane's mother only stared vaguely in his direction. She asked her daughter the usual questions about homework and how her day had gone and mentioned that Bill was riding his bike straight to their house from school.

"Though I don't know why his mother lets him," she added. "I don't think he's nearly old enough to ride that far on his own." She gazed in the direction of the counter and blinked. Karl was down on his hands and knees, reaching into the sink.

Jane said faintly that lots of kids rode their bikes to school.

Mrs. Preston blinked again, and a small worried line appeared on her forehead. "I seem to be having trouble with my eyes. I keep seeing this sort of brown flicker around the edges..."

Jane gave the creature a meaningful stare. Karl held up a bit of food he had found. It looked like a stray flake of cereal (gluten-free). He pointed to the flake of cereal, then to his mouth, and raised his eyebrows in a clear question.

Jane nodded. Of course he could have an old soggy flake of cereal! *Just—get—out!* she mouthed silently and jerked her chin slightly in the direction of the stairs.

Karl popped the flake in his mouth, somersaulted off the counter's edge to the floor, and scampered up the steps, chuckling to himself.

Bill arrived on his bike, looking superior. "No offense, but this could be a boring two weeks unless we think up something interesting to do. Got any new games?"

Jane ushered him into her bedroom, where the creature was bouncing up and down on her pillow.

Bill's knees gave way, and he sat down on the floor.

"Interesting enough for you?" Jane asked.

"Rah-ther," said Bill, who had been reading a lot of British books lately. He had also just had a unit on folklore at school, so he had an idea what the creature might be.

"A pixy? A goblin?" He dug in his satchel, pulled out a folder, and ran his finger down a list. "Let's see. Brownie, knocker, bogie... hey, does he look Swedish to you? He could be a tomte."

Jane shook her head. "He said he was something that sounded like 'bold.'"

Bill's finger stopped on a word. "Got it. He's a kobold!"

Karl turned red to the tips of his ears and dove under the pillow. "Don't believe everything you read about me," he said, his voice muffled.

"A household sprite," Bill read aloud, "originally from Germany."

"Are you from Germany?" Jane lifted the pillow and peered beneath.

"Deutschland," Karl mumbled.

"That's what the Germans call Germany," Bill said in an instructional tone. He frowned. "It says here that kobolds are bigger, though."

"I shrank," Karl said, his voice muffled. "Poor nutrition. Not enough gugelhupf."

"You'll get plenty to eat here," said Jane, suddenly cheerful. "If you hang around under the table at dinner, I can sneak you food off my plate. If you like gluten-free, I'll give you lots."

Bill read aloud, "A kobold likes to play tricks—"

"Not bad ones," said Karl, still under the pillow. "Funny ones! To make you laugh, ha ha!"

"—and sometimes a kobold will help with chores."

"I wish he would help with my chores," said Jane.

But as it turned out, Karl preferred to play tricks.

~~~~~~~~~

Jane had to admit that it was sort of amusing to watch Karl hide the car keys and then put them back in a place her mother had already searched three times.

And Bill could hardly keep from grinning when Mrs. Preston backed the car out and pressed the garage door remote to close it—and the kobold, inside the garage, kept pressing the button to make the door go back up.

But Jane felt a little bad about the tricks, too. So when she found out that the kobold could sew, she gave him needle and thread and told him to sew the missing button on her favorite shirt, to save her mother some work.

He sewed on the button. Then he made a few alterations to her old doll's bathrobe so he could wear something besides the mitten.

But he also sewed up the armholes of Jane's shirt so she couldn't put it on. And that night, after the table had been set for dinner, the kobold slipped in quietly and sewed the silverware to the placemats.

"Ha ha!" the kobold chortled when Father tried to lift his knife and the placemat lifted too, spilling his water glass.

Jane got the blame for that one.

Of course Bill was a guest, so no one actually accused him of letting the air out of Mr. Preston's tires while the car sat in the garage overnight. All the same, Bill could tell that his aunt and uncle were wondering about him, and he didn't like it much.

Bill and Jane searched the house and found the kobold in his favorite cave under Jane's bed (he liked the dust). They dragged him out and held on to his spindly arms.

"You've got to stop playing tricks," Jane said sternly. "Do you hear?"

"But they are funny, ha ha!" Karl twisted his hands together. "I heard you laugh!"

"We're not laughing anymore," Bill said, "because we're getting blamed for everything. Why don't you try to be helpful?"

Karl hung his head, scratched under one arm, and wiggled his long hairy toes. "What do you want me to do?"

Jane looked around her room. It was strewn with stray socks, books, games with pieces missing, an old dollhouse she didn't play with anymore but couldn't bear to get rid of, her softball glove, a rucksack from camping, school papers, a geode that she couldn't bring herself to smash open in case it was a disappointment, and a diorama from last year's Native American cultures unit.

"You could straighten up this place," she said.

The kobold looked puzzled. "What does that mean—straighten up?"

"Put things in order," said Bill.

Karl dug some wax out of his ear and looked at it fondly. "All right, then."

In the morning every shoe in the house was lined up in the hall, neatly arranged from smallest to largest.

Jane was roused out of bed by her annoyed father and told to put all the shoes back in their places. She and Bill had to polish them first, for a punishment. It took hours. "You were supposed to be helpful," she told the kobold, "not play more tricks."

"I was helpful!" The kobold opened his eyes wide. "I found every single shoe, from the basement to the attic, and put them all in order."

"You sure did," said Bill, grumpily buffing Mr. Preston's black wingtips.

The kobold was helpful in the kitchen, too. He turned up the burner on the stove so the soup would boil sooner. It did boil sooner—it boiled over—and it put out the flame. The house filled with a smell of gas and everyone had to go outside until the gas company came to see if there was a leak. Jane's mother was really very angry about that one. She told Bill and Jane that they were grounded for the next two days.

They talked it over at the top of the stairs where they could keep an eye on Karl, who was climbing the banister.

"I can't even really blame your mom," said Bill in tones of gloom. "Who else is she going to think did it? She can't even see the kobold."

"Or hear him," said Jane, as Karl slid down the banister with a particularly piercing *wheeeeeeee!*

The kobold slid off the banister and shot straight into a potted plant. There was a crash.

Jane looked resignedly down at the broken pot and the dirt strewn all over the floor, and went to get a dustpan and broom. "He's got to go," she whispered to Bill. "And the sooner, the better."

But when they broke the news to him, the kobold shook his head. "This is my house now. You offered me food when I first came, remember?"

"What?" Jane was having difficulty following his logic.

"If you give a kobold food when he first arrives at your home, it means you're inviting him to stay as long as he wants. And I want to stay for a long, long time," he added with a leer.

Jane frowned. "I didn't give you any food when you came to the house. I gave you a sandwich in the schoolyard."

Karl waggled his ears. "I found a cereal flake on the counter, and you nodded when I asked if I could have it. You offered. I accepted. That's been an unbreakable contract between humans and kobolds for a thousand years, and you can't get out of it. I'm yours for good, even if you don't appreciate me."

He stomped off to Jane's bedroom and kicked the door in

passing. From the hall, Jane saw him lift the bedskirt and crawl into the space beneath her bed. He sneezed twice, faintly, and then there was a sulky silence.

Jane pressed her hands to her forehead. "It's bad enough when he tries to help or make us laugh. But now that he's mad . . ." Her voice trailed off.

Bill put his hands in his pockets. "You're in deep trouble."

"Me? What about you?" cried Jane.

Bill shrugged. "I'm out of here when my parents come home."

"Coward," said Jane.

Bill grinned. "I'm not saying I won't help you. But we've got to do something fast, or you'll be grounded for the rest of your life."

Jane sniffled. "What can we do? He's going to stay here as long as he wants!"

Bill rubbed his ear. "Then we just have to make him want to leave."

"He won't," Jane said gloomily. "He told me this was the best place he'd ever lived in. He likes wearing doll clothes instead of old mittens. He likes the central heating. He even likes the gluten-free stuff."

"But what doesn't he like?"

Jane looked thoughtful. "Well, he does hate—"

The phone in the hall rang shrilly. Jane jumped.

"Bells! Bells! Bells!" came a thin angry voice from Jane's bedroom.

Jane and Bill both began to smile at the same moment.

~~~~~~~~~~

They mapped out their campaign like two generals planning a war. They wrote down their battle plan in a lined notebook and synchronized their watches. Then they collected their supplies for Project Evict Kobold.

A box in a basement closet yielded an old rattle from Jane's toddler days, a See 'n Say farm animals toy, and a baby doll that cried "Mama."

They found an Indian gong on a shelf in the guest room,

wind chimes in the garage, and a box fan under the stairs. They located two alarm clocks—one that buzzed and one that beeped. Bill unscrewed the bell from his bike and programmed his cell phone with a new ringtone. And then they got a large piece of cardboard and made a big sign. They quietly staked it in the front yard, near the street, just as it was getting dark.

At 9:43 p.m. precisely, just as a steady snoring came from under Jane's bed, Bill's cell phone (which had been conveniently left on the floor) rang with "Kick Me Baby One More Time" (volume at ten).

The kobold screamed.

Jane was terribly apologetic. She shut the cell phone off and tucked Karl back into his cave, wrapping him in an old, raveled towel for a blanket. Strangely, in the process, a loose thread got wound around the kobold's leg. The thread stretched along the floor for a couple of feet, where its other end was tied to Jane's old baby rattle.

By 10:22 p.m. the kobold had settled down enough to begin snoring again.

At 10:23 p.m. Jane got up to go to the bathroom. She stepped on something that squished beneath her foot.

"MAMA!" shrieked the baby doll.

This time the kobold said a word that Jane was not allowed to say. He stalked out from under the bed in a fury—and the rattle came dragging noisily behind.

It made a strange, ghostly sound in the dark bedroom. Karl tried to move away from the noise, but the noise moved with him. He ran, yelping, and the rattle bounced along behind, making a noise like dry bones.

Jane dropped to her knees, landing on the baby doll's stomach again (*MAMA!*) and snagged the rattle on the kobold's third time around the room. She quietly bit the thread in two, thinking (not for the first time) that she was grateful her parents' bedroom was on the other end of the house, and tucked Karl in once more.

Unfortunately for the kobold, just as he got to sleep the alarm went off with a loud *buzzzz buzz buzzzzzz*. As soon as he recovered enough to snore again, Jane decided she felt hot and turned on the box fan. The moving air stirred the wind chimes that she had hung from the overhead light fixture, and the light tinkling sound lulled her back to sleep. The kobold didn't like it, though. He leaped onto the bed and tried to wake Jane up, but she mumbled and rolled over. Somehow her hand was holding a mallet, which hit the Indian gong on her bedside table with a fine, resonant *BONG*.

"Aiiiiieeeee!" screeched the kobold, and he ran out of Jane's room for the refuge of Bill's.

Bill, who had had the foresight to tie a string between his big toe and the doorknob, woke up when the door swung open. He waited until the pattering feet of the kobold came near, and then promptly rang his bicycle bell some six or eight times.

"Oh, sorry!" said Bill. "I was giving the alarm—I thought you were a burglar! Did you come to play?" He switched on the light and turned the arrow on the See 'n Say farm animals toy to a picture of a black and white cow. A mournful *moooooooooo!* came from the speaker as he pulled the cord.

Karl shuddered and clapped his hands over his large and hairy ears.

"Don't like that one? Okay, how about this?"

Baaaaaaa!

"No? Let's try—"

Oink oink oink!

"And here's my favorite."

Cock-a-doodle dooooooooo!

Karl wailed aloud. He whirled, ran out the door, and promptly tumbled down the stairs. Jane and Bill followed the bumping sounds and found him hiding under the sofa cushions with his fingers wedged deep into his oversized ears.

"Poor thing," whispered Jane. "He's had enough for one night."

Bill folded his arms. "He brought it on himself. Don't forget we're starting again first thing in the morning."

Jane picked up the whimpering kobold and cuddled him in her arms. "Come on, back to your cave. I'll turn off the fan, and it will be nice and quiet—"

"For a while," muttered Bill.

Jane shut her door tightly and rolled the kobold under the bed.

At 6:00 a.m., the clock radio turned on with a harsh *beep beep beeeeeeep.*

"Turn it off! Turn it off! Turn it off!" Karl shrieked, pulling at Jane's hair.

Jane sleepily hit the snooze button and sat up in bed. The kobold didn't look good. His eyes were red and wild, with dark baggy shadows beneath them. His fingers twitched nervously, and his ears were pointing in two different directions. But his chin—what there was of it—was held high, and he was glaring like a tiger.

"I know what you're trying to do. Both of you!" he snarled, as Bill came in the room. "You're trying to drive me out."

"Who, us?" Bill arranged his face in a look of spotless innocence. "How?"

"With the bells! With the chimes! With the buzzing and the beeps! With the incessant never-ending godforsaken ringing NOISE!"

Bill plopped into a chair and swung one leg over the armrest. "That's how life is in the modern world. If you want to stay here, you'll just have to get used to it."

Karl puffed up his cheeks and made a derisive sound. "I won't go, I tell you. I like this place. It's warm! It's cozy! I'm getting lots of things to ea—"

Honk! Honk!

A car zipped past on the street, honking merrily. Jane and Bill waved from the window.

Honk! Honk! Honk!

Bill examined his fingernails. "See what I mean, Karl? Life in the city is just noisy. And you can't blame Jane and me for cars honking."

Honk! Honk! Honk! Honk! Honk honk honk honk HOOONNNNKK!!!

"Aauuuugh!" The kobold dived beneath Jane's pillow, screaming and kicking. "Has the whole world gone crazy? Make it stop! Make it stop!"

Jane lifted a corner of the pillow. "If we make it stop, will you go away?"

Karl sat up, wet-eyed and trembling. "But where can I go?"

"We'll find you someplace nice," said Jane. "Do you promise to stop playing tricks until we do?"

The kobold nodded sullenly.

"Is that an unbreakable contract?" Bill asked.

Karl sighed. Then he spit on his hands, smacked the spit on Jane's palm, and turned around three times. "Now it is."

Jane privately wiped her palm on her pajamas.

Bill strolled out of the room, whistling tunelessly. Jane wandered over to the window and watched out of the corner of her eye as Bill reappeared in the yard. He yanked up the sign that said "HONK! IT'S MY BIRTHDAY!" and stuffed it in the trash bin.

"What on earth possesses people to honk this early in the morning?" Mr. Preston's voice got loud and then soft as he passed Jane's door, grumping to himself.

"Coffee," mumbled Jane's mother as she, too, passed Jane's bedroom. "I need coffee. Badly."

Jane turned to the kobold. "We will find you a nice place to go," she repeated in a whisper, "but remember you have to stop playing tricks. And helping," she added hastily.

"You'd better find a nice place in a hurry," said Karl. "I don't know how long I can bottle myself up."

~~~~~~~~~~

They worked on the problem all morning.

Karl had a lot of requirements. Running water. Woods. People to play tricks on. A cow.

"A cow?" said Bill.

"Or at least milk," the kobold said firmly. "One of my best tricks is making the milk go sour. But I can't do it in this house. You keep it in that big cold box and it stays sweet *forever*. Oh, and I want fire in a real fireplace. Not like here."

"What's wrong with our fireplace?" Jane set down her pencil and flexed her hand. The list of Karl's needs kept getting longer, and her fingers were cramping.

The kobold sneered. "It's *gas*. You light it by flicking a switch on the wall."

"What's wrong with that?" Bill asked.

"There are no cinders!" Karl's voice rose with temper. "No ash! No smoke! Nothing to blow into people's eyes!"

Jane tapped her pencil thoughtfully. She was beginning to get an idea. She could feel it growing, right on the edge of her brain . . .

"Marshmallows," she murmured.

"Huh?" said Bill.

"Marshmallows!" Jane clapped her hands. "Look, Karl, marshmallows are sticky and sweet, and people toast them over the fire. The minute they get a nice golden brown, just when they're almost perfectly toasted, you could—"

"I could blow on the fire so it would burn one side black!" Karl leaped to his feet, his hairy ears wiggling with excitement.

"Or you could make them fall off into the ashes," said Bill, who had experienced this more than once.

The kobold erupted into giggles, rolling on the bed in delight. "Now, *that* would be a trick to make you laugh, ha ha!"

Bill put his head near Jane's ear. "What are you saying? You want to toast marshmallows over a campfire in the backyard? That won't help much—"

"Not in the backyard," Jane whispered.

Bill frowned. "Where?"

Jane leaned forward. "The kobold likes things the way they were in olden times, right? They didn't have refrigerators. They used fires for heat, and there were forests and huts and things. Not so many buildings. Not so much noise."

Bill nodded slowly. "Back to nature, sort of."

"Right, but back to nature with *people*, so he can play tricks. People who toast marshmallows and put up tents and go—"

"Camping!" Bill laughed out loud. "Brilliant!"

Jane blushed. Bill had never called her brilliant before. "Only I don't mean one of those city campgrounds. We need a state or county park, with forest around the campsites."

Bill nodded. "He could sour the milk and blow smoke in people's faces and make marshmallows fall off into the fire, and it wouldn't be any different from what always happens when you go camping."

Jane grinned. "He could put ants in the sugar—"

"And push swimsuits and towels off the clotheslines—"

"And dump over trash cans like raccoons do and make tents fall down in the wind and the rain, and it will be just the same as usual. We won't even need to feel guilty."

Bill snapped his fingers. "Got it. Waxacatchy County Park! It's not even that far, and it has caves, too!"

"Perfect," said Jane, feeling that one compliment deserved another. "I bet my parents will drive us there, if we ask."

~~~~~~~~~~

But they wouldn't.

"It's not warm enough for picnics yet," said Mr. Preston. "And I'm very busy this week."

"I am, too," said Mrs. Preston. "And besides, you two haven't behaved very well lately." She looked at Bill and Jane's dismal faces and relented. "Well, if you are good for the rest of Bill's visit, then perhaps I will take you on the last day before his parents come back."

Jane and Bill stretched their lips into smiles. They said thank you. Then they went to Bill's room to talk things over.

"Karl will never last that long," said Bill gloomily. "He'll have to play some sort of trick, or he'll bust."

"He did promise," said Jane, without much hope. She slumped into the curve of her chair.

Bill lifted his head. "Hey, maybe we could take him there on the bus! I bet there's one that goes out that way."

"How would we find out?" Jane was doubtful.

"I know how to read a bus schedule. You can get them at the library."

Jane picked at the armrest, frowning. "Well, even if there was a bus—which I doubt—my mother would never let me go. She still can't believe your mother lets you ride your bike to school. What happened, anyway? Your mother used to be worse than mine."

"Not worse," said Bill. "Just trendier. My mom does the latest trend first—like going gluten-free—then she tells your mom, and then you're stuck with it."

Jane was exasperated. "And we don't even need to eat gluten-free!"

"Hardly anybody does," said Bill with authority. "Most people just do it because it's the fad. My dad says my mom goes through fads like a kid through a bowl of M&Ms. She did the sugar detox and power yoga and crystal healing and the colloidal silver thing and—well, anyway, she's way past gluten-free. She's into free-range kids now. That's why I can ride my bike to school."

"Free-range kids?" Jane was doubtful. "That sounds like she wants you to ride a horse or something. You know, like 'Home on the Range.'"

"Nope. It just means that it's healthy or something to let kids roam free and explore. My mom got a book about it, and all of a sudden she was letting me ride all over the place. She even let me take the city bus. She says it builds confidence or something." He grinned. "It's the first trend she's ever been on that I actually like."

Jane stopped slouching and sat up straight. "Do you know where that book is? Could you get it?"

"Sure. It's on the coffee table at home. Hey!" Bill's eyes brightened.

"Great minds think alike," said Jane. "You get the book on your way home from school tomorrow. I'll ask my teacher if I can do an extra credit project on—um—bus trips. Between that and the book, I bet it takes us only two days."

~~~~~~~~~~

It took three. First they had to strategically place the book so that Jane's mother would notice it on her own—"We can't be too obvious," said Jane—and then Mrs. Preston had to actually read it. By the end of the second day, though, Jane's mother was halfway through the book and beginning to nod her head as she turned the pages. By the third day, she was reading whole paragraphs to Mr. Preston.

Jane's father looked pleased. "I've been saying everything that book says all along," he said. "Kids need to explore and learn things on their own. How else are they ever going to grow up?"

Jane judged the time was ripe to mention the extra credit project. For his part, Bill found the bus schedules and mapped out a plan. They would have to take two buses and transfer once, but he was right—a bus went right past the entrance to the county park.

Mrs. Preston would not let them transfer buses. In spite of what the book said, she wasn't willing to go that far. But she did drive them to the second bus stop and said she would meet them there on the return trip. She never noticed Karl, nestled in Jane's backpack, and no one on the bus noticed him either, except for a small child whose mother told him he had a wonderful imagination.

The kobold loved the wooded park. They took him past the lake, down the hiking paths, and around to the campsites and the showers and the trash bins. They watched from behind the bushes as he blew ashes into the face of a woman trying to light some coals, made a little girl's marshmallow drop off into the dirt, and tangled the guy ropes for the tent so that the man trying to put it together said, "Whoever put this tent away botched the job," and his wife answered, "I think *you* put it away, dear," and they almost got into an argument. Karl listened from under the picnic table, chuckling at the mischief he had caused.

But the kobold helped, too. He quietly coated the bottom of a cooking pot with soap, so that it would be easier to scrub after being on the fire. He threw himself in front of a baby boy who was toddling toward a sharp ax stuck in a log. And when a woman put out chocolate on graham crackers for s'mores, he took a square of chocolate and ate it peacefully with an expression of bliss on his knobby little face.

"He's not really bad," whispered Jane. "He just likes to make things happen."

Bill grunted. "Good thing he's not going to make things happen for us anymore."

They walked a little distance away, and Jane motioned for

Karl to follow them. "Do you like it here?" she asked the kobold anxiously.

Karl gazed off toward the lake. He could see canoes on a rack, and ducks swimming in a marshy area near the shore, and several interesting possibilities occurred to him for funny tricks, ha ha! "What about when it gets cold?" he asked. "And where are the caves?"

They showed him a trail map, with the locations of caves clearly marked. "And the park is open year-round," said Jane. "People come here to ski and slide, and if you get too cold in the cave, you can live in the visitor center. It has central heating," she added brightly.

"Pity the park rangers," Bill said under his breath.

The kobold turned around and around, surveying the park as a king might survey his kingdom. "Cows?"

"I saw some in the pasture across the road," said Bill.

"And listen!" Jane waved her hand at the woods and lake. "What do you hear?"

The kobold cocked his head. Above him, a bird trilled, and somewhere a squirrel chattered. The breeze brushed through the leaves with a swish like a soft broom, and in the distance small waves slapped merrily at the shore. His large, sensitive ears quivered slightly.

"No bells!" said Jane.

Karl clasped his hands together as reverently as if he were in church, and his breath came out of him in a sighing gust. "All right, I'll stay here. Good-bye." He turned to the woods and began to walk away.

"Wait!" cried Jane. Now that it came to it, she was strangely reluctant to let him go. "Will we ever see you again?"

Karl's mouth widened into a slow, delighted grin. His cheeks bunched up like apples until his eyes were mere slits of mirth. "Would you like a last trick?" he asked. "A trick to make you laugh, ha ha?"

"No," said Bill, "but—"

"Yes," Jane said, even louder.

The kobold spit on his leathery palms and waved them over

his head in a complicated sort of motion. Then he winked, one eye after the other, and trotted off toward the tall trees.

A brisk little breeze sprang up, blowing smuts and leaves and smoke from the campfire their way.

"That wasn't much of a trick," said Bill, coughing as he tried to dig a bit of ash out of his eye. "You should have known he was only looking for a chance to be mean. Come on, we have to get to the bus stop."

Jane said nothing. She was watching two small, rectangular bits of paper whirling and blowing toward them in the smoke. She reached up her hands and caught them.

"Look," she said.

Bill looked. He read the small print. "Bus passes!" he breathed. "Good for the whole summer!"

"We can come back," said Jane. "Anytime we want."

Bill looked at Jane with distinct approval. "Nice catch."

"Good old kobold," said Jane happily, and they ran for their bus.

The Blue between Us

Joyce Sidman

On the bluffs
over the blue lake with no rim
beside the great drop
into blue air
we squat, cull berries
from warm thickets
rub mist from blue skins
quarry veins of blue

As the blue-green
bramble scribes our skin
the lake-blue nuggets
pile in our palms
we dream of blue boiled down
between buttery crusts
lips stained with blue syrup
rendered essence
of blue

And when we rouse
like bears above the bracken
to greet each other
sunlight roars in our ears
bliss beats between us
and the dizzy sky
burns
    blue
        blue
           blue

Fishing

Anika Fajardo

EVERY SUMMER, WHEN EDDIE COMES to stay with us, Mama calls me Little Eddie. Most mothers give their children different names, but not ours. My half-brother was born in Mexico long before I came along, and Mama named him Eduardo. When I was born on a snowy day in Minnesota eleven years ago, Mama named me Edward. So we're both Eddie. Big Eddie and Little Eddie.

The only summer he didn't visit was when he was sixteen and his dad was sick. I was seven that year and the summer was long and quiet. Mama talked about going to Mexico to visit Guadalajara where she grew up and where Eddie was born, but then Eddie's dad died and we never went. And then my dad died last Christmas. Now we're the same, me and Eddie. We're half-brothers with no fathers and the same mother. And the same name.

The first Saturday Eddie is here, it's sunny and warm. When Mama catches us on the couch watching TV, she says, "Vete!"

Since I wasn't born in Mexico like Eddie, Mama and Eddie mostly speak English to me in an accent that chops off the *s* and *p* sounds. I didn't know Mama had a funny accent until I was in first grade. My friend Liam and his mama met us at the beach and Liam's mom had said, "I love the way you talk, Lidia." She smiled, her blue eyes hidden behind big black sunglasses. "It's charming."

On the way home I had asked Mama what "charming" meant.

"It means she thinks I sound dumb," Mama said. If you listened close enough, you could hear the *b* fall off the word dumb like a pirate walking the plank.

"Don't let Little Eddie sit around all day," Mama says, poking a finger at my belly, which is a round mound under my shirt. My face gets hot, and I know I'm blushing. I never see Eddie blush, and maybe that's because his skin is too dark to see it turn colors. His face is the color of coffee with a little cream, the way Mama likes it. My face is the color of the sand at the playground. He and Mama match like two brown molasses cookies.

"Take your brother fishing," Mama tells Eddie, even though she hates fishing. She says she hates the waiting, the little hooks that can send you to the emergency room, the tiny scales that fly around the kitchen and get stuck under baseboards, the eyes that look at nothing. But Mama can't hate fishing that much because she always cooks what we catch in hot oil that spatters on the stovetop.

"Vete," Mama says again, and even though I don't know very much Spanish, I know she's telling us to get out of the house. She wags her finger at Eddie, but she's smiling and happy. Mama is always happy when Big Eddie is here. It makes me wish he would stay with us always, not ever go back to Mexico.

I try not to think about Eddie going back. Every June, when the summer seems to stretch on forever, I always say, "We have three *whole* months!"

Mama watches us as we head toward the lake, me with the fishing tackle, Eddie with the big red cooler. She must not be thinking about Eddie going back either because when I turn around, I see her on the front step grinning like she can't wait to fry up the fish we're going to catch.

"Hey, Eddie," I say when we get to the corner. "We're going to catch a lot of fish, right?"

"We'll see."

"Hey, Eddie," I say. "I'm going into middle school this fall." I tell him in case he doesn't remember.

He nods but doesn't say anything. He just keeps walking.

"Are you thinking about staying this year?" I ask. Every year after Eddie leaves and it's just me and Mama again, I wish I had a full-time brother. After he graduated from high school, we thought he might stay in Minnesota, but last year he worked for his uncles in their factory. Eddie says it's hot all the time in

Guadalajara and that banana trees grow along the side of the road, but I'm not sure I believe that part. Maybe he doesn't want to stay. "I mean, maybe until Christmas at least?"

Eddie just looks at me and grunts. I think that might be a no, but since he didn't actually say no, I think it might also be a maybe.

"There's the lake, Eddie." I take a deep breath. I can smell the green lake weeds.

When we're at the shore, I check the dock. Eddie gets antsy when the fishing dock is crowded. "Only a few guys today," I tell him, even though he can see for himself.

"There's the dude with the radio," he whispers.

This man in a dirty blue baseball cap is here every summer. And every summer, country music—which both of us hate—warbles out of the radio. Actually, I don't really hate country music because sometimes it sounds nice and sad like the way I feel on Sunday nights before I have to go back to school. But Eddie hates it. He only likes hip-hop and Mexican music. Although, if you ask me, some of his Mexican music sounds a lot like the guy's country music only in Spanish.

"I'd like to see what would happen if I pushed that thing into the lake," Eddie says, pointing with his chin as we get closer. I laugh with Eddie.

"Pendejo," Eddie mutters. I know this is a bad word in Spanish. Eddie can be a little scary. He is tall. Taller than my dad. Taller than his dad. Eddie wears size twelve shoes, and Mama always jokes she could use one of his shoes as a canoe. He likes to wear shoes that make his feet look even bigger: high-topped sneakers or pointy-toed black dress shoes with little laces that go through eight holes. He's so tall, people ask him if he plays basketball, but Eddie hates basketball.

"Mornin'," says the radio guy as we pass him on the fishing dock.

My brother doesn't say anything, but he doesn't kick the radio overboard, either. So I think that's a good sign. Eddie just walks all cool like guys in movies. By the end of the summer, all the regulars will know Eddie just like they do every year.

And just like every year, Eddie takes me fishing almost every evening. On the walk to the lake, he tells me stories about the fish he catches when his *tíos* take him to Puerto Vallarta. He tells me about living with his grandma and sleeping in his dad's bedroom that still has all his old photo albums. I listen to his stories. I follow Eddie to the lake. I try to copy him—the way he walks, the way he ties the lure on his line, the way he holds his pole. The dock has little cutouts along the wooden railing where you can rest your pole, and we both stand with our lines in the water, waiting. Eddie leans his elbows on the wood, but even though I want to be like him, I never do that because once I got a splinter. Eddie broke it off when he tried to take it out with his grubby fingernails. When we got home, Mama used a pin to dig it out. First she lit a match and ran the pointy part of the pin through the flame, back and forth.

"Sanitizing," she said when she caught me watching bug-eyed. When the splinter was out, little bits of black ash were left in a trail on my arm.

Eddie catches lots of fish, but they're all small ones, most of them too small to keep. Every day that Eddie doesn't catch that big one reminds us that he's going back to Mexico in September. Eddie unhooks the little bass and sunnies and tosses them back. I can't help wonder what happens to those fish after they go back in the water.

Whenever I complain about not seeing any fish in the weeds, Eddie says, "Patience." And then he shushes me. Eddie doesn't talk, just watches the water turn pink and orange as the sun sets. "Just because you can't see them," he tells me every time, "doesn't mean they aren't there."

So we fish every day, and even though I like it, I realize Mama is right about one thing: fishing can be boring. I get bored. Liam comes along a couple times. While we wait for the fish to mistake one of our lures for a real minnow, Liam and I talk about middle school and which teachers we might have, but that just seems to annoy Eddie. Sometimes we try asking him about when he was our age, but he gives us that look that says Keep Out like one of those signs on a tree house.

By the end of the summer, Eddie's plane ticket is a rock that we keep stubbing our toes on. Mama scrubs and irons his clothes before folding them into stiff squares of blues and whites and greens. She buys me new notebooks and socks.

I complain, "We *only* had three months."

And before I know it, tomorrow is my first day of school. And the date on Eddie's plane ticket. But me and Eddie aren't thinking about tomorrow. Eddie's watching TV and I'm sitting on the couch with him, hoping he'll take me fishing one last time. He has his big feet propped up behind my head on the back of the couch. They smell like dead fish, so I'm secretly relieved when Mama warns him, "If you have time to watch TV, you have time to vacuum, mi'jo."

I don't know very much Spanish, but I know *mi'jo* means *my son*. Mama calls him *mi'jo*, even though we're both her sons.

When Eddie still doesn't move his big feet, I say, "Eddie, can we go fishing?" I know he's mad that he's been catching little throwaway fish all summer, so I say, "Maybe we'll catch a big one this time."

I can tell Eddie doesn't think so, but he gets up anyway. "You get the tackle. I'll get the cooler."

We meet in the front yard. I rest the fishing rods on my right shoulder. It's hard to carry two. They knock against each other and the lines keep getting tangled. But Eddie has the red cooler that's heavy with ice. "Just in case," he says like he does every time.

"There's the lake," I say the second I spot the sun sparkling off the water. Before we cross the street, we wait for a garbage truck to turn the corner. It smells as bad as Eddie's stinky feet. I plug my nose.

"I know that's the lake. We've only been here about a million times." He sounds mad, but his eyes are squinty in that good way when he's just joking with me.

When we get to the dock, Eddie says, "What's up?" to the radio guy who's in our usual spot. He doesn't say it mean or anything, but the man reels in his line and moves over without saying anything. He doesn't turn off his radio, though.

"Get your line in, Little Eddie," Eddie says to me. He really wants to catch a big one.

I look down and see the plants waving in the water. I don't

see any fish, but I know they're down there. I hook a bass lure on my line and the little pink rubber fish jiggles as I lift the rod and swing it over the dock and into the water.

"Watch out!" Eddie shouts. I almost clobbered him. He has that look on his face he gets when he doesn't want me to bug him. I try not to bug him. But it's hard sometimes.

"Oops," I say. I can feel my face turning red. I don't always understand the difference between being an annoying little brother and just being me.

"Move down if you're going to be wild like that," Eddie says. The guy with the radio gives me a look like he's glad he already moved. I watch my line trail through the water as I move down one slot and get farther away from my brother.

When I feel a pull on my line, I shout for Eddie. He comes over and helps me get the fish—about seven inches—off the hook.

"Good job, Little Eddie," he says, which I think is nice of him because he hasn't caught anything today.

I catch three more fish, each one a little bigger than the last. The last one I catch is almost as big as my arm from my wrist to my elbow.

"Might as well string these up, leave them in the water, Little Eddie," he says. "Keep them fresh for Mama." He doesn't look at me when he says this, and I feel bad he hasn't caught anything.

I loop the stringer through the mouths of the four bass I caught and dangle them in the water. They get excited when they hit the cool and murky lake, thinking they're home free. Then they thrash and fight until they realize they're caught for good.

Eddie leans over the railing and casts his line again. I think of my four fish in the water and hope he catches something soon. It's getting late, but the sun is still hot and he loosens his white button-down guayabera. I unbutton the top button of my polo shirt.

Suddenly Eddie wheels around.

"Did you see that?" Eddie makes a strange noise somewhere between a laugh and a cough like a hook got caught in his throat. "That thing just ate your fish!"

He's yelling and laughing and spinning, and I can't understand what happened.

"Your fish," he explains, rocking on his high-tops like he's ready to take a jump shot off the dock, "is bait!"

I lean over the railing and see that my smallest fish has been decapitated or whatever the opposite of that is. Its bloody head is still hanging from the line, but the body has been chewed right off.

"Get those fish in the cooler, bro."

He's laughing and muttering and I pull the three fish—and the fourth head—out of the water and dump them in the cooler where they look shocked by the cold ice cubes. I feel sorry for the fish. I imagine them, swimming around their green plants, minding their own business. Next thing they know, their whole world is different. Over, actually.

"Wait," says Eddie. "Toss me one of those."

I stare at him and then at the cooler. I don't know what he means. I wonder if this is what it's like in middle school—everyone constantly talking and you don't know what any of it means.

"The fish," he says. Even though he didn't say I'm dumb, I can feel the silent *b* hanging in the air.

"Here's what I'm going to do," Eddie says as soon as I've handed him one of the bass. He proceeds to loop his line and hook around one of the fish from the cooler. "Go after your own kind, hombre," he says, lowering the squirming fish into the water.

He's got an audience now. It's the last weekend of the summer, and the lake is busy. Two girls from my school have stopped on the dock, straddling their shiny bikes and watching my brother. I see Liam and his mom eating ice cream cones, and I wave, wishing I could hold up my string of fish for them to see. The other fishermen are watching out of the corners of their eyes. The radio guy has even shut off the country music.

"Never gonna happen," he says, turning his baseball cap around to get a better look.

Eddie doesn't turn around. He's leaning on the railing looking at nothing, humming a tune, one of those Mexican boleros.

And then there's a tug and a splash.

"Damn!" he says suddenly. Mama doesn't let him swear, but I won't tell her. "Get over here, Little Eddie," he says. I stop noticing the crowd. Eddie is pulling on his rod, leaning back just a bit.

I pull my line out of the water as fast as I can. I learned the hard way that if you let go, you might lose your rod. Earlier in the summer I scratched a mosquito bite and the whole fishing tackle fell in the lake. Eddie dove in and got it. Both he and the fishing rod were covered in green waterweeds.

"Little Eddie!" Eddie shouts. "Get over here now!"

I run across the boards of the dock, and as I run the water makes tinkling sounds lapping against the floats. I look down and see that one shoelace is untied. I hope, as I'm running toward him, that I don't trip.

"Take this," Eddie says, handing me the rod. I grab the handle and hold tight to its cork grip. I can see where Eddie usually holds it. It's blackened with sweat, grease, and fish guts.

While I have the handle, Eddie is pulling on the rod. The line is like a dot-to-dot: the dock is one and the surface of the lake is two. I imagine a fish down deep in the water: three.

Now we're both pulling on the rod and the fish—or whatever is down there—just hangs on tighter.

Last April a city work crew put in a new sidewalk in front of our house. After they were done, a square of yellow tape was supposed to keep me out. But I knelt down in the grass and felt the cement. It was cold and damp. Even though it was still wet, it was harder than I thought it would be. A twig had fallen into the cement. I tried to yank it out but it was stuck. The rod is just as stuck as that twig had been.

"Hey, man!" shouts Eddie.

The guy who turned off the country music points at his chest as if to say, me?

"Yeah, you," Eddie says. "We need some help. This little guy isn't strong enough."

I feel my face burn. I want to prove to Eddie that I'm strong enough so I pull harder. I might be little, but I'm sturdy—Mama always says so. Without letting go of the rod, I back up to get better traction. As I do, I realize one foot is stuck, and I look down to see that I'm standing on my shoelace and moving my other foot at the same time. I flail and drop backward to the wooden planks.

Luckily Eddie has hold of the rod. The other guy jumps like an alarm just went off. I watch as the two of them pull and swear. They swear and yank, and suddenly the line flies out of the water. Everything is a blur. Huge slimy thing. Thrashing tail. Broken line. Bent rod. Stomping shoes.

I look down at the fish flopping on the dock. I'm not sure, but I think it's a northern with its mean eyes. Whatever it is, it's bigger than three of Eddie's shoes put end to end.

"Little Eddie," he says, "get me the cooler."

I scramble up. I drag the red cooler by its handle. I can hear the melting ice sloshing inside. This is where Eddie's fish will go. And from the cooler it will go into the freezer, cut up into meal-sized pieces that Mama will fry in hot oil. And I think maybe this fish—this huge, gigantic, marvelous fish—will make Eddie want to stay.

Now the creature starts really struggling again, like it has one more chance to survive. Eddie kneels down next to the fish. It still has the hook, and I can see teeth lined up. He reaches for the fish's gaping mouth. It feels like I'm watching in slow motion as Eddie puts his hand inside the fish's mouth.

And then he starts shouting, almost screaming like a girl. I see blood, Eddie's blood. And now it feels like we're in fast forward. He's shouting but he's also laughing. His blood is mixing with the fish's blood, and I feel a little sick but also excited.

"It bit me!"

More swearing. More laughing. He's using words I've never heard before. Words in English. Words in Spanish.

He's wrapped his finger in the shirttail of his guayabera. A splotch as red as the cooler spreads across the shirt. Eddie stands up. He can only use one hand so he kicks the cooler closer to the monster. The ice sloshes.

"Help me get this thing in here, Eddie," my brother says to me.

My brother needs my help. He can't do this without me.

I wrap my arms around the smelly, slippery fish and heave it into the cooler on top of the little bass I caught. My polo shirt is wet and smells like that garbage truck. Eddie's fish is so big, we can't close the lid of the cooler all the way. Its tail flops out one side. Eddie rests both our rods on his shoulder, and we each take one handle of the cooler.

"Some fish," says the guy with the radio as we walk past him.

Eddie doesn't say anything, but I nod. It is some fish, I think.

As we march home in the dusky light, the fish like an emperor between us, I realize that Eddie finally caught the big one. And it took my little fish to do it. Eddie might not be there when I get home from school tomorrow, but also, I think, he might.

Strange Island

Julie Schumacher

IN HIS OLD AGE MY GRANDFATHER LEARNED how to steal. He got pretty good at it. It was my job to "keep an eye on him" from two thirty to five thirty every weekday during the summer, between the time my aunt left for work and my mother got home. Sometimes when we got back from our walk to the drugstore or the ice cream shop or the tennis courts or the lake, I would find him—how the heck did he do it?—with something new in his hands.

A pack of bubblegum cigarettes. A little girl's plastic barrette. A pen. A bottle of juice. A broken watch. And once, a credit card, which I think he lifted at the drugstore when I was over by the magazine rack and the cashier and the customer weren't paying attention. My mother nearly lost it when she found that card. "Adam. You can't let him do that," she said, as if it was my idea, as if I'd pulled my grandfather aside and taught him the ABCs of being a thief.

He didn't used to steal; at least, that's what my mother said. But he didn't used to live with us, either, so maybe she didn't know.

Every afternoon, before my grandfather and I finished our walk, I tried to find out if he'd picked up anything he hadn't had when we started out. Which was fairly awkward. He was my grandfather and a skinny old man—was I supposed to frisk him? Once, when he was sitting on his favorite bench in front of the lake, I stood up and took a deep breath and told him he had to empty his pockets.

He pasted an innocent look on his face, all surprise and white eyebrows.

"Come on," I said. "You know what I'm talking about. Let's see."

Like a slow-motion magician, he took a black plastic comb from his shirtfront pocket. It must have been 85 degrees outside, but he was wearing long pants, a long-sleeved shirt, and a tweed jacket.

"Keep going," I said. I talked fairly loud; he was hard of hearing. "You know that's not what I'm looking for. What else have you got?" I stood in front of him, blocking his way.

Someone shouted behind me, but I paid no attention; the lake and the strip of gravelly sand in front of it (the beach was a giant cat box, my mother said) were full of people. It was a weekday, but the sky was as blue as a balloon, and the walkways and the water and the sand were full of bikers and swimmers and strollers and ice cream vendors and volleyball players and people lying around getting cancer because of the sun. There were leftover streamers on the slide and on the swing set from the Fourth of July.

I felt a hand pinch my shoulder.

"Why are you bothering that old man? What are you doing, robbing him?"

I turned around and saw Iris Dunn: Iris who had sat in front of me for a whole year at school, Iris who consulted a Magic 8 Ball during class, Iris who stored pens and pencils and even a ruler in her hair, using the tangled multicolored clump on top of her head like a personal supply closet.

"Um, what?" I asked.

"Leave him alone," she said. "Or I'll call the lifeguards."

"What would the lifeguards do?" I asked. "There's nobody drowning."

"They'll call the police," Iris said.

My grandfather stood up and held out his hand.

Iris shook it. "Nice to meet you," she said.

I told my grandfather to sit back down.

Iris looked shocked. "Sir, do you want me to call someone?" she asked.

"Wait," I said. "Don't. Don't ask him a question." I tried to wedge myself between them because I knew what was coming.

"Don't you dare push me." Iris curled up her lips and showed me her teeth. "Sir, is Adam bothering you?" she asked. "Do you want to get away from him?"

"Iris, wait, he—"

My grandfather nodded.

"Okay, that's it," Iris said. She cupped her hands around her mouth and screamed for help.

~~~~~~~~~~

Lifeguards, park police, Minneapolis police, and a large group of interested bystanders were gathered around the wooden bench where my grandfather sat, looking cheerfully out at the lake, while Iris Dunn accused me of threatening a senior citizen. Luckily my mother picked up on the second ring, and I put my phone on speaker and passed it to one of the lifeguards, who held it so that the entire crowd of people—people who were probably hoping to see me arrested or at least put in handcuffs—were able to learn about my grandfather's "situation." Which was basically this: He'd had a stroke—which is like a heart attack, I guess, but in your brain. My aunt and my mother were making arrangements to move him into a "home." Because of the stroke he couldn't talk. He couldn't read or write, either. As if there were a trapdoor in his head, the whole English language had fallen out of his brain. He still listened if we talked loud enough, but we weren't sure what he understood. No matter what question anyone asked him, he nodded yes.

"Wow. 'Yes' as an answer to every question. That must be terrible," Iris said, after the police decided not to arrest me, and the mob dispersed. "I'd probably go crazy if I couldn't talk. I talk all the time."

"Yeah, I noticed that," I said. Iris and my grandfather and I, along with two park police officers, were waiting for my mother. She had left work early—she was a receptionist in a dentist's office—and I could already hear her beginning a dozen sentences with "Adam, I thought I told you . . ."

"I guess I should have known you wouldn't have robbed him in broad daylight," Iris said. "Not right here where people could see you."

I was about to ask if she thought I would rob him after dark, but she lowered her voice and leaned toward me, her damp, mint-flavored breath in my ear. "He's staring at the water. What is he looking at?" she asked.

"I don't know," I said. A little boy in a bathing suit was playing with a plastic T. rex in the sand near our feet. "He likes the water. We're here every day."

Iris cocked her head, the striped topknot of her hair tilting to the left like the Tower of Pisa. "He's looking at the island."

I shrugged. The lake had a tiny island in it, about a quarter mile from shore. The island was covered with tall, thin trees that swayed in the wind.

"Adam's grandpa? Sir? Is that what you're looking at? Are you looking at the island?" Iris asked.

My grandfather nodded.

"Cool," Iris said. "And are you thinking that—"

I cut her off. "You don't have to wait with us," I said, hoping she would go home.

But she didn't. "It's a strange little island," she said. "Sometimes you see lights on it at night. I have a theory about islands. Do you think your grandfather's upset about the police?"

"I don't know," I said. He didn't seem to be upset, but I didn't know him very well. Before his stroke, he had lived in Oregon, and we saw him every other year at the most. The few times we visited, he'd spent all his time chopping and stacking firewood out in the yard.

"Wait. Hang on a second," Iris said, grabbing both of my wrists with her hands. "Why were you trying to make him empty his pockets?"

My mother's car, spraying gravel, pulled into the lot. I shook Iris off. "Long story," I said.

~~~~~~~~~~

During the year, Iris and I went to a charter school; it was one of those "alternative learning academies" for kids who were weird enough to get bullied at all the regular places. I'd gone to three different public schools in Minneapolis, where the teachers loved to tell my mother about my lack of motivation and "un-realized potential"; this was a cue for her to send me to another new school. I don't know what Iris's deal was, but she obviously didn't care about fitting in.

Now that she had humiliated me in public, Iris seemed to assume we were friends. My grandfather and I saw her two days later, down at the lake. She was sitting on a flowered bed-sheet (the kind with elastic at the corners), a little girl's plastic thermos and a tote bag beside her. "I was hoping I'd find you here," she said, putting the book she'd been reading facedown in the sand. Several plastic straws and a large striped feather protruded from the oversized knot of her hair. "Hi, Adam's grandfather. I brought you something." She rooted around in her canvas bag. "Hey, Adam, have you finished the cultural exchange assignment?"

"The what?" I asked. My grandfather sat down on the bench behind me and stared out at the lake.

"From Ms. Langmuller's class. Remember when Ms. Lang-muller gave us those names and addresses from different countries—kind of like pen pals?"

"Maybe," I said. "But it's July. I'm not doing homework until September."

"But it's a summer assignment," Iris said. She wore round yellow sunglasses that were too big for her face. "Don't you remember Ms. Langmuller telling us to bring our culture jour-nals to school on the first day of fall?"

"Hm," I said. This sounded vaguely familiar. I remembered Ms. Langmuller handing out some sort of packet of instructions in June. Our school was so small we were going to have the same teacher for English and social studies two years in a row.

"Aha! Here they are. Look, I brought cards," Iris said. "But instead of ace, king, queen, they have pictures." She shuffled the cards, and I saw drawings of a paintbrush, an elephant, a camera, a drum. "Adam's grandpa? What do you think?"

It wasn't a yes-or-no question, but my grandfather nodded yes anyway.

Iris laid out the cards on the bench, but of course some of

them immediately slipped through the wooden slats and fell in the sand. She was chattering away, but I had stopped paying attention. That was what happened to me at school: things were announced and explained at the front of the room while I was buried in some kind of underground chamber of thoughts, and I usually resurfaced in time to hear someone say, "That's it. Are there any questions?"

The wind had picked up, and the surface of the lake was slicing back and forth like a thousand soft blades.

"See?" Iris jabbed me with a pointy elbow. "He can make sentences with these."

My grandfather glanced unenthusiastically at the cards, nudging some of them through the slats in the bench. The ones that were left: pictures of an ice cream cone, a drinking glass, a boat.

"He likes ice cream," I said. "I guess that's a sentence."

But Iris was peering at him over her yellow sunglasses. "A glass of water and a boat," she said. "He probably wants to say something about the water. And, hey, he's always staring out at the island."

"He's just looking at the lake, Iris," I said. But all three of us turned and looked at the island, with its columns of trees.

"Do you know what I—Dang!" Iris said. A few of her cards blew away in the wind. She chased them past the swings and under the monkey bars down the beach.

I noticed that my grandfather was wearing a silver Mickey Mouse keychain like a ring on his finger. "Where did that come from?" I asked.

My grandfather nodded.

There were no keys on the keychain, and it was tarnished and didn't look like real silver, so I dug a hole and buried it deep in the sand.

My grandfather had turned back toward the lake. "Are you really looking at the island?" I asked.

He nodded.

"Or are you just nodding because I asked you a question?"

He nodded again, then held out his hand to show me four bright blue golf tees.

"Wow," I said. "We didn't even go near the golf course today. Are those from last week?"

A heron, legs dragging behind it, lifted off from the reeds.

"I don't get how you're doing it," I said. "And I don't even know if you understand me or if you know who I am."

My grandfather nodded and pressed the golf tees into my hand.

Iris jogged back, out of breath, and plopped herself down on the wooden bench. The feather had fallen out of her hair. "You can borrow these," she said, holding out the cards, but I told her we didn't want them.

"Why not?"

"Because he's not going to spell out a sentence," I said. "And we have cards at home."

That night, on the floor by my grandfather's chair after dinner, I found a gold ID bracelet. I picked it up before my aunt or my mother could see it. There was a tiny monogram on a plaque in the center: *ID*, it read, and at first I wondered why the person who owned it didn't inscribe it with her initials, and then I realized that they *were* initials—for Iris Dunn.

~~~~~~~~~~

My grandfather was supposed to move into his "senior residence" in September. My aunt and my mother talked about how nice it was going to be, how friendly and cozy: there was a music room, there would be activities, my grandfather would meet people during social time and meals, and we would visit him, probably once a week. But whenever they talked about the move, I got a queasy feeling. I knew we couldn't leave him alone in the house all day once I went back to school, but I couldn't picture him making friends, and his "residence" wasn't very close to the lake. Wasn't there something else?

No, my mother said. His new home would be comfortable; he would be fine. (This was exactly what she told me whenever she sent me to a new school, dropping me off in a building that smelled like boiled food and antibacterial soap—the smell of the place where you ended up when no one knew where you should go.)

By early August, even though my grandfather didn't talk, he and I had developed our own method of communication. It went something like this:

Me: Are you ready to go out? It might rain today; do you want a jacket?

My grandfather: [stares at the floor]

Me: Okay, no jacket. Are you ready? I'm your grandson, remember? My name is Adam. You live here in Minneapolis with us.

My grandfather: [lifts his hands, palms upward, and raises one eyebrow]

Me: Yup, it might rain. But we'll take a chance. If it pours, we'll come home.

My grandfather: [picks up an empty bottle of pills on the counter]

Me: The drugstore? No. No way. Last time we were there you stole some toothpaste, and they almost called the police.

My grandfather: [opens the door to the closet]

Me: I know; we have plenty of toothpaste right here. So you do want your jacket?

~~~~~~~~~~

It sometimes took us almost an hour to get out of the house.

Iris was usually waiting on the wooden bench by the lake, her multicolored hair piled high on her head and her ID bracelet circling her arm. When I gave the bracelet back to her, I told her I'd discovered it lying on the sand, but she had sniffed out the truth. "It's totally understandable," she said. "At least, I understand it. He's trying to communicate with us." She didn't appear to be bothered by the fact that my grandfather had stolen her bracelet right off her wrist. "He's gathering things together. You said he's moving soon, didn't you?"

In the past few days, my grandfather had managed to steal a baby's pacifier, a mini-notepad, a half-eaten sandwich, and a bottle of nail polish—he nicked the nail polish from Iris's bag. I said I didn't think nail polish and pacifiers would be much use to him at the Cypress Senior Residential Home.

"That's because we don't know yet what he wants to do with them," Iris said. "They might be symbols."

I was tired of Iris and her weird theories. Several chopsticks protruded from the tangled funnel of her hair. "Hey, Grandpa," I said. "The things you're stealing—are they symbols?"

My grandfather nodded.

"Or is Iris full of crap?"

A pause, and he nodded again.

Iris hugged her knees to her chest and looked out at the lake. I was starting to wonder if I should apologize, but then she asked if I had started the pen pal assignment.

"No." Actually, I had poked around on my mother's laptop, in case Ms. Langmuller had left some instructions on the website at school, but I didn't find anything, and when my mother saw me at the computer she delivered a twenty-minute speech about Internet safety, convinced that I was arranging to meet a child trafficker at midnight or handing over her bank account numbers in a phishing scam.

"If you lost the name and address of the person you're supposed to write to, I could ask Ms. Langmuller to send them to you," Iris said. "She lives down the street from me, a block away."

I imagined Iris camped outside Ms. Langmuller's house in a flowered tent. "Why does it matter to you if I do the assignment?"

She shrugged. "Because it's interesting. You get to talk to someone on the other side of the planet. You get to know who they are." She went on to explain a wacky sci-fi idea about the earth as a drop of water and the people who lived on the drop of water as tiny organisms who needed to communicate and learn about each other's lives.

"That makes no sense at all," I said. "Plus, it's totally weird."

Iris said I was cynical, and I told her I didn't think she knew what "cynical" meant.

My grandfather was staring out at the lake.

"You know, if you come here at night and stand on the shore," Iris said, "sometimes—"

I cut her off and said some mean things to her, I don't know why, but it was already too late to take them back when I heard them, one after the other, coming out of my mouth. Iris was the only person my age I'd hung out with that summer, but I didn't want her telling me she knew what my grandfather was thinking, because no one could know, and he probably didn't understand us, and what did it matter anyway if we were all just going to get old and then die? What was the point, and why was Iris bothering to nag me about a stupid assignment, telling me to communicate with a stranger I would never meet, when I couldn't even talk to my own grandfather, who was sitting right on the bench at my side? I didn't say all of those things, but I told her my grandfather and I were tired of her, her hair was ridiculous, and she should leave us alone.

Iris stood up. She put on her yellow flip-flops, stuffed her things in her bag, then kissed my grandfather on the forehead. "I do know what 'cynical' means," she said. And she walked away.

When my grandfather and I got home an hour later, I saw Iris's yellow sunglasses poking out of the top of his jacket pocket. They were plastic and didn't look expensive, so I threw them out.

~~~~~~~~~~

About a week before he was supposed to move to the Cypress Senior Residential Home, my grandfather died. He went to bed at night, and in the morning he didn't wake up.

After the funeral, after the polished box was lowered into the ground, I went to the lake. It was windy and cloudy, and other than the lifeguards, almost no one was there. I hadn't seen Iris since the day I'd yelled at her on the beach, but I walked up and down in front of the playground and the paddleboat rental, in case she showed up. School was going to start in five days.

It began to rain, a few fat drops hitting the sand, and then water came streaming sideways out of the clouds.

By the time I got home, I was soaked. In the hall, my mother or my aunt had hung my grandfather's shirts and jackets on a hook by the door, probably getting ready—the clothes would never fit me—to give them away.

I gathered the jackets up in my arms and pushed my face into the scratchy fabric. And here is the part of my story that you may not believe. There was something in one of my grandfather's pockets—one of Iris's cards. It was a cartoon drawing of an island with a little cluster of trees, and clipped to the edge of the card was a piece of paper with an email address, crumpled and torn. Right away, without thinking, I knew what it was.

~~~~~~~~~~

My mother's laptop was on the table. I booted it up and smoothed out the crumpled fragment of paper. I opened my email and typed the address and then tried to think about what I should say. I pictured my grandfather staring out at the island. I remembered the shine on the lid of his coffin, the way it sank like buried treasure into the ground.

Hello, I wrote. *I should have written to you before, but I lost your address. I don't even know if this address is right. I found it in my grandfather's suit. He died.*

But there must have been a missing letter or number, because I got an error message back right away.

~~~~~~~~~~

Ms. Langmuller, I know I should have started this assignment in June. I should have worked on it when Iris reminded me that it existed—and now I won't see her anymore, because you told me she's moved to a different school. And I'm sorry about that, and I wonder—if you see her—if you would tell her I'm sorry. And I know you might not accept what I've written here, but there's no other way to tell this story except the way that I'm telling it.

I typed every possible missing letter and number into that email address, but each time I clicked *send* I got another error message.

Finally, after studying the address a bit longer (it's not the address that you gave me), I thought I had it figured out. I typed in what I was sure was the right version and clicked *send*.

And I know you might think I'm making this up or making an excuse for not doing the assignment, and you can dock me the points, I don't care. I just want you to know that I got a message but I don't know who sent it—the address doesn't make any sense, but I didn't get an error message. I got an actual message. Here's what it said:

Your grandfather says he will be happy here. He is reminded of home.

Ozymandias

Kelly Barnhill

LISTEN. MY NAME IS JACKSON MARKS and I have an invisible dog.

I know what you're thinking.

But it isn't like that, I swear.

I've had him now for four years. I don't know how old he was when he showed up, but he hasn't grown. The top of his head reaches my knee. He's got wiry fur and skinny legs and a tail that whips me in the face when he jumps in my bed and turns around and around until he finds a comfortable spot. I suppose his coat would be softer if I gave him a bath—and believe me, I've tried. But he's invisible. And he doesn't like baths. So.

Which means that I have a dog with too-long nails and probably fleas and mange growing on his skin and a mouth that has never seen the business end of a toothbrush.

And I love him, you know? He's my best friend. My only friend.

He's slower now than he was four years ago. He's missing teeth. His back left paw drags a bit when he walks. I can hear it. And he whines if I scratch his left hip. And, ugh. He reeks. Really bad. I'd take him to a vet, but my mom doesn't think he exists, and anyway, how much experience does the average veterinarian have in the care and management of invisible canines? Not much.

(And yes, I looked it up. Invisibility is not covered in vet school. It doesn't show up in their curriculum. And I checked the online Ask-a-Vet who told me to stop making stuff up. Whatever. Maybe he wasn't even a real vet.)

But it's worrisome, you know? Because I feel like he's getting worse. I know he's worse. He's sitting on my feet right now, and the stink of him is so powerful that I'm losing my appetite—

which is good, actually, since I give him half of my food. My mom hands me my burger. For every bite I take, I give one to the dog. I have tried buying dog food, but my mom freaks every time. I think she thinks I have some kind of eating disorder or mental illness, though I don't know that either would make a person start eating dog food. Instead, I have told her that what I want to eat is meat—red and bloody and lots of it. Which isn't true. I don't even like it much. But I give it to the dog. And he likes it plenty.

My parents don't notice.

My mom puts another burger on the electric fryer and sits down, serving herself a mound of salad.

"Sweetheart," she says, staring at me over the upper rims of her cheap glasses.

Great.

She never calls me sweetheart unless I'm in for it.

The dog shifts on my feet and whines. He knows where this is going too.

Lyla, my kid sister, gives me that look. "Mom," she says, "he's making dog sounds again." She acts like she doesn't notice the dog. But I have seen her feed him pieces of her dinner too. She's just jealous that he likes me best.

"Am not," I say—which is, I might point out, the truth.

"Jackson, we've talked about the dog sounds."

"Whatever."

"What's that smell?" Lyla says, giving me an evil look. I make a barfing face right back at her.

"Jackson, don't make barf faces at your sister. We need to talk about something, and it is important."

I make a show of checking the watch that I don't actually own. "Geez, it's already seven," I say. "I better—"

"You better nothing. I spoke with Mrs. Lewis-Keene."

That's not actually her name. Her last name is Lewis and her husband's last name is Keene and their son Dylan's is hyphenated, and my mother knows this because she goes over to her house for a monthly craft night with the other moms in the neighborhood. None of them actually craft anything as far as I can tell. They just use it as an excuse to drink wine and swear a lot.

"Look," I say. "I don't care what Dylan says. I didn't do it. Nobody saw me do it."

Lyla snorts into her hamburger. I want to smash it into her nose. The dog thumps his tail on the ground in an ardent, Lyla-loving tail wag. Traitor.

"Those two statements are nonsupportive, young man," my mom says. "Dylan's injuries speak for themselves."

"Dylan has bite marks, Mom. Like with canine teeth. And a narrow jaw." I show her my metal-encased incisors. Other kids at school have braces with slim rubber pads and barely there wire. I have what looks like a medieval torture device. Thanks, lousy dental insurance.

"I'm just saying." My mom purses her lips. She does this when she doesn't believe me, even though the evidence that I am guilty of something doesn't add up. It's easier just to pin the fault on Jackson. I don't blame her—not really. Everyone else does it too.

"How about backing me up for once? And anyway, if the bites were from me, they would have been flat. My front teeth are not capable of needle-sharp puncture wounds. Learn anatomy, Mom. Geez."

She rested her eyebrows on her fingertips and heaved a sigh. "Just. Honey? Apologize. Even if you didn't do it. He says you did. She says you did. I can't explain the bites either. Sometimes we apologize for the crazy things that people think." She gives me a pointed look. "Some of us have gotten good at it."

"Mom."

"Jackson. Dylan was your best friend. He has only ever tried to be nice to you! I don't know why you have to be so horrible to him all the time."

The dog sits up and growls. Mom doesn't notice.

I let my head fall to the table, resting my forehead on the salad that I have no intention of eating anyway. To call Dylan Lewis-Keene a jerk would be an insult to jerks everywhere. It's true that we were friends back in the days when eating sand in the sandbox and running through sprinklers while your moms gabbed for hours were all you needed to call a kid your friend.

But then we went to school.

And things have been pretty much universally terrible ever since.

Dylan Lewis-Keene is not my friend. And my mom—and I love her, I honestly do—is an idiot.

"Where's Dad," I ask, realizing that my jaw is clenched so tight my teeth are about to shatter.

I don't have to ask this. Dad isn't home yet. Of course he isn't. He probably won't be for a while. He's a janitor at Lyla's school. Though they don't say "janitor" anymore. They say "engineer." But that just confuses little kids because they wonder where his striped hat and train are. The district keeps cutting the janitorial positions as a way to save money. At the same time, they cram their buildings with more and more students, making them harder to clean and maintain. So my dad stays later and later, doing work that he doesn't get paid for. He calls it "doing my best to keep an eye on the public's purse," but I don't see anyone else having to stay late for no pay because fourteen kindergartners decided to pee themselves at once.

"Your father will say the same thing as I'm saying."

"Arf," says the invisible dog.

"Don't you take that tone with me, young man."

"It wasn't me!" I begin, but my mom puts her hands up defensively.

"Don't even," she says.

I get up, grab my burger, and leave the kitchen. The dog gets up too, following behind on his clicky little nails and his back-legged limp.

"Finish your dinner," my mom calls back at me.

"I have what I need," I say. "I'll eat it in my room."

My dog follows me in. When I close the door, I let him have it.

"Bad boy," I say, putting my hands on my hips and leaning aggressively over where I think he probably is. "Baaaaad boy!"

(How do I know he's a boy? Well, I know, all right?)

(Fine. He likes belly rubs. And he's invisible, so you can't exactly see where your hand is headed, and sometimes . . .)

(Look. Just forget it. My dog's invisible. He's a boy. His name's Ozymandias. And shut up.)

Anyway. As it turns out, he's next to the bed, but my aggressive leaning seems to be doing the trick. He's whining and thumping his tail on the ground.

"Bad boy," I say again for good measure, but apparently it was too much, because suddenly there is a small puddle of . . . gross.

"That's nasty, Oz," I say.

He yips in response. I throw an old T-shirt on the urine—it was from bible camp and I only wear it to bed or at the school helping Dad when he has to go in on weekends—and I sit down on the bed. Oz takes this as some sort of indication of forgiveness, so he jumps onto my bed next to me. This actually takes several tries. He's not as spry as he used to be.

And he's right. I do forgive him. For everything. When you only have one friend in the whole world, it's not a good idea to alienate him. Even if he's a dog. Or an invisible dog. Oz climbs onto my lap and pushes his weight into my belly. I scratch his ears. He sighs his doggy sigh, and it nearly kills me.

~~~~~~~~~

Oz showed up four years ago after a particularly terrible day in third grade. I won't go into it much, except to say that Dylan Lewis-Keene was more than involved and the teacher found me shoeless, pantsless, and shirtless in the schoolyard. (I did, however, manage to hang on to my underwear. A small victory.)

No amount of tears and explanations would make the teacher believe that this wasn't something I had done myself. I didn't even know where my clothes were. Dylan stashed them somewhere. The garbage, probably. I got suspended for one day for indecent exposure. Which was kind of nice, actually. It was like a vacation.

Anyway, both of my parents had to work, so I was left at home. Dad took the television with him in his car and Mom took the computers. They bought some cheap math workbooks that were so boring and easy, I nearly exploded. About halfway through the day, the doorbell rang. I wasn't supposed to answer the door, but I did anyway. No one was there. Just a basket with nothing in it except a blanket and a note. I reached in and touched . . . fur. Fur that I could not see. And a soft, damp tongue licked the back of my hand. I couldn't see that either.

"This is Ozymandias," the note said. "King of kings. Dog of dogs. Look upon his works, ye mighty . . . and so forth. If you love him, he will love you. If you take care of him, he will take care of you. That's a promise."

"Hello?" I called down the empty street.

"Arf," said Ozymandias. That's all it took.

I've loved him and taken care of him ever since. Despite everything. And while he has for sure loved me back, the taking care of me bit has been something of a lie. Oh, well. Nobody's perfect.

~~~~~~~~~~

The next day, I tell Ozymandias in no uncertain terms that he is not to follow me to school. It's too stressful. He's not as quick as he used to be, and he's not as good at dodging feet. I don't want him to get hurt. He's my only friend. And I'm sick of getting in trouble for tripping people in the hall when it wasn't me at all.

It's one thing to be the kid who everyone bullies. It's another thing to be the kid who everyone thinks is nuts. To be both of those things? Well.

Oz started coming to school with me in fourth grade and continued when I started middle school. Middle school is harder for an invisible dog than elementary school—the hallways are way more crowded, and you have to navigate them more often. Sixth grade wasn't so bad—Oz stayed mostly out of everyone's way. But this year has been . . .

I don't know.

It's like Oz has forgotten, you know? Can dogs go senile? Maybe it's senility or maybe it's confusion or maybe he's just tired of watching me take crap from everyone else.

Anyway, in sixth grade, Oz started nipping people who were mean to me. Which, you know, was everyone. Tripping them. Grabbing their bags. And since they can't see him and they can see me (and they already don't like me), who do you think they blame?

"Sorry, buddy," I say. "Rules are rules. No dogs at school." I can't see him, of course, but I can hear him moping. That pathetic whine. That exaggerated limp as he follows me downstairs.

My dad is at work and my mom is out jogging. Lyla's sitting on the couch. Even the way she sits is annoying. She has no reason to be up yet. Her school starts after mine, and Mom drives her. Younger siblings get all the breaks.

I knock back a couple protein drinks and force down as many boiled eggs as I can stand. Supposedly it'll help me build muscle mass. I'm still waiting. Lyla watches me from the couch, her mouth pressed into a self-satisfied smirk. She still won't admit it. I can see the depression the dog makes on her capris. I know he is sitting on her lap. I know she knows about the dog. But she won't say anything about it. And she won't back me up.

"Bye, dork," I say. "Bye, Oz." I don't actually make eye contact with my sister. There's not much point in it.

She addresses no one in particular. "Does anyone hear anything? It must be an invisible boy."

Ozymandias yips, and she produces a small bit of beef jerky from her shirt pocket. It vanishes from her fingers with a slurp.

No loyalty, that dog. I slam the door in disgust.

~~~~~~~~~~

At school, I instantly wish I had brought him with me.

"Psycho," say the cheerleader girls by the Smoking Door—which leads out to the courtyard where, rumor has it, Ancient Middle Schoolers of a Far-Off Age were once allowed to smoke. At school. Not anymore, of course, but you can still smell it when you go out there. It's like the ghosts of kids long dead from emphysema and throat cancer are haunting the place where their lives went horribly awry.

"Freak," say the B-squad wrestlers lingering in the PE hallway with towels around their waists, waiting for their turn in the showers and giving each other bare-skinned chest bumps and noogies and being hilariously un-self-aware of how ridiculous they look. At least I wear clothes to school, I think, but don't say.

Or at least they seem hilarious until two of them shove me against the cinderblock wall so hard my head knocks on the side and I see stars.

The hallway is no better. I am tripped, shoved, hip-checked, and spat on. Like any other Tuesday. But that isn't true. This is worse. Since Oz's attack on Dylan, things have been much, much worse.

I'm at my locker when I am suddenly not at my locker at all, but partially inside of it instead, with my skull cracked on the shelf and the door crushing me from behind. And a big, beefy someone pushing on the other side.

I don't even need to guess who.

"You're disgusting, man," Dylan hisses poisonously in my ear. "What kind of freak bites?"

"I dunno, Dylan," I say. "Maybe someone with sharper teeth than I have. And without braces." My lip scrapes against the silvery coat hook inside the locker, and the door catch pierces my shirt and strikes me on the skin of my torso. I would wince, but my face is smushed between the door and a metal shelf. I'm not afraid of getting stuck inside—or mostly not afraid. I mean, I'm small, but not that small. However, given the force on my shoulders from the door, and given the pressure on my skull, I am starting to wonder if I might be—while clearly too big— ultimately crushable.

And how would I live that one down?

"Everyone saw you," he croons. "Everyone thinks you're a freak."

"No one saw diddly, and neither did you. You know perfectly well what bit you, and you know it wasn't me. What the heck, Dylan? I already promised that I wouldn't tell anyone about—"

Dylan rears back and slams his body again against the door, nearly splitting the top of my skull right off. I should probably mention here that I am not entirely blameless in this whole scenario. I did say "Sic 'em, boy" to Oz. So.

"You shut your mouth, you sicko. No one would believe you, anyway."

Then he gives a vicious kick to my butt, and I worry for a second that my hip might snap.

And I think, it's true—no one would believe me.

And I think, I wish I were invisible like Oz.

The first bell rings. Dylan gives me one extra shove and heads off to class. Laughing. I extricate myself from the locker, pull myself together, and limp my way to geometry.

~~~~~~~

(It's true that I know Dylan's secret. I know about his dad and what he did. What he probably still does. I've known since third grade. And I never told anyone. Because I promised. If Dylan stopped beating me up for one second, I still wouldn't tell anyone. I keep secrets. But Dylan is too stupid to know this. Or maybe he just likes hitting. Maybe he gets that from his dad.)

~~~~~~~

I am marked tardy in geometry, which is my fifth this quarter, which means that I am officially absent even though I am there and doing my work because I am an excellent student. Not that it matters. It's kind of like being invisible.

In second period, I am pulled out to talk to the district psychologist. He lets me know that he thinks I am as crazy as they come. He doesn't say this, of course, but he basically implies it.

"Howdy, sport," he says, because his vast psychological training has led him to believe that I am the sort of person who might enjoy being called "sport." I roll my eyes. "How's the urge to bite today, buckaroo?"

"I . . . what?" I say.

"Like on a scale from one to ten."

I stare at him. "It's zero."

He writes something down. Chuckles. Writes another thing. "Well, that's a little hard to believe."

"Listen, um, whatever your name is."

"Reggie," he says.

"Okay, Reggie," I say.

"That's Dr. Reggie, to you, young man."

"Fine," I say. I want to bolt from the room. I want to be invisible. "The point is that I have no interest in biting anyone. Or anything. I barely like eating food. It's faster to slurp down a protein shake and does the same thing."

"Perhaps we should schedule some time with the nutritionist," he says, writing that down.

"It's not like that," I say. "It's just, I have a lot on my mind."

"Being in middle school is hard, eh, sport?" he says.

"You have no idea," I tell him.

I don't tell him about my dog. I don't tell him about what happens in the hallways, either. Neither would do me any good.

Dylan blocks my path on my way to earth science. He is flanked by four of his buddies from the football team, all of them almost as tall and dense as Dylan. Dylan's dad was kind of famous back in the day, and there are still posters of him from his local-boy-made-good days when he led the university to some championship and was offered a bunch of money to play for the NFL—where he lasted three weeks before he permanently wrecked his back. Now he coaches the high school team. And Dylan's back is—or at least was—covered in bruises. You do the math.

The football players crack their knuckles.

"You're invited to a party, freak," Dylan says. "After school. We're all . . ." He pauses and smiles. "Really looking forward to it." One boy opens and closes his hands, like he's itching to wring my neck.

"Well," I say. "Thanks for the heads-up." I stand my ground, trying to root my feet to the concrete floor. I know they're going to shove me as they go by, and I don't want to give them the satisfaction of seeing bite the dust. Not that they won't in a couple hours, but it's the small things that get me through the day.

As they pass and knock me this way and that in a muscled-shoulders gauntlet, I whisper something to Dylan as he walks by.

"Ozymandias says hello," I say. "And he can't wait to see you again."

Dylan turns pale. Oz has always freaked him out.

～～～～～～

A long time ago, after we were no longer friends (no one at school wants to be friends with the weird kid, after all), my parents decided to go out of town for their anniversary, leaving my sister and me in three-night sleepovers with friends. Lyla stayed with the girl who is still her best friend. I was sent to Dylan's house. It was as uncomfortable as you might think.

Oz came with me. That was also uncomfortable.

That was when I found out about the hitting. And saw it too. It was awful, but I promised not to tell, and I didn't. And Dylan found out about Oz. And he also promised not to tell, but he did. And his dad knocked him silly for being a nutso. Dylan never forgave me. Or Oz.

～～～～～～

Two of the football boys are in my gym class. Today, it's dodgeball. They spend the game conspiring to not get me "out" but instead to wail balls just next to me, thrown so hard they're practically traveling at the speed of light. My team thins and thins, and there are fewer places to hide. Finally, it's just me on the far side of the gym. They move up to the line. They hold their balls up high. And they let loose.

Wham.

Wham.

Wham.

"That's enough," the gym teacher says, laughing a little. "I think we can call him out."

Wham.

Wham.

Wham.

The balls hit my face, chest, legs, hips. I am slapped and pummeled silly.

"I said that's enough."

Wham.

"That's it. You two. My office. Now."

I'd like to think they got in trouble. They didn't. I saw through the window that they both were high-fiving the gym teacher.

~~~~~~~~~~

At lunch I fake a stomachache and say I'm going to the nurse, but really I go and sit outside. I figure, if I get caught, I'll just say that I had to barf, and the door was closer than the bathroom. I lean against the back wall and look up at the sun. I miss my dog. I miss him so much.

When Ozymandias first started coming to school with me, it was like I had gotten a brand new life. I didn't hate school anymore. I wasn't desperate to get home. I had Oz and Oz had me, and suddenly math class was a lot more fun. And language arts. And social studies. Who cares if the other kids snickered when I raised my hand with the right answer? Who cares if they glared at me when I scored 100 percent again or when some professor from the university came to give me extra enrichment or whatever? Who cares if the other kids accused me of smelling like wet dog? I had Oz sitting on my feet and licking my hand and resting his head on my knees. I had Oz pressing his belly against my leg. Oz was my friend, and I loved him.

I wish I hadn't made him stay home.

I wish he was here right now.

I wish I was invisible.

The football boys are going to beat me up. In about two hours. There is nothing I can do to stop it. There is no one who can take care of me. I am all alone.

"Oh, Oz," I say out loud. "I wish you were here." I wipe my nose with the back of my hand and dry my eyes with the knees of my jeans. "I need you, buddy."

No one hassles me on my way to tech ed. No one talks to me, either. It's like I'm invisible. It's nice, actually.

When the bell rings, I take my sweet time at my locker. Everyone ignores me. It's like they got the memo from the football boys and are keeping their distance.

Stay away from this one, says the sign on my back. He's ours.

My lip is cut. My butt is bruised. This is not enough for them. Nothing will ever be enough for them. I shoulder my bag and slink down the hall.

My school is at the edge of town. There is only one road to take me toward home. I could cut across the field, but there are signs all over saying that it has just been sprayed and will give you cancer or something if you set one foot on there. It's probably a lie. The farmer just doesn't want kids cutting through his field. Still. I'd rather not get cancer.

Everyone else has left. There are a couple kids in the drama club practicing their scene on the steps, but that's it. I don't see the football boys, but I know they are nearby. Taking a deep breath, I step out onto the road.

There is a tap-tap-tap sound on the sidewalk to my left.

"Oz?" I say. But there is no Oz-like yip coming from the empty sidewalk. And anyway, it doesn't sound like Ozymandias's scritchy little nails on the concrete. It's louder. A bigger dog. It doesn't slow down, and it doesn't go away. It keeps up with me, at the exact same pace.

Then I hear another dog walking on the other side. I can hear it panting, too. I don't see it though. And from behind, I hear a baying sound coming from the backside of the school and careening around. Also invisible.

I keep walking.

To my left: a whine.

To my right: a scrambling sound.

Behind me: a small growl.

Up ahead: the football boys.

"Nice to see you, freak," Dylan says. One boy is holding a small bat—like maybe it came from his kid sister's tee-ball team. He hits it against his hand again and again.

I feel the press of a dog on my left. And the press of a dog on my right. I can feel a dog sitting on my feet and from the smell of him, I know it is Ozymandias. I can hear the whisper of a thousand paws gathering near.

Don't do anything stupid, I breathe.

"Listen," I say. "I don't know why you feel like you need to do this." I look at Dylan. "I didn't do anything to you, Dylan. I never would. And I never have. I'm not like that, and you know it."

I am talking about more than Oz's attack. Dylan's face turns hard.

"You know what you did," he says.

"And you know who bit you. And you know it wasn't me."

"Crazy psycho," one of the football boys says. I never can remember their names. Chase or Chance or Chet or Chortle or something. They all sound the same.

"That's redundant," I say.

He turns red. "You're redundant." And I can tell he doesn't know what that means. I roll my eyes.

"I'm tired of waiting," another football boy says. He steps forward. I can hear one of the dogs move quick as lightning. "Ouch," he says, grabbing his leg. I haven't moved. He knows it wasn't me. Still, he looks at me accusingly.

"Whadja do that for?" he demands.

I shrug. "I don't know what you're talking about. I haven't moved."

He pulls his hand away from his leg. There is a bite mark.

The football boys take a step backward.

"Ouch," another boy says, pulling his hand to his chest. His palm is bleeding.

"Enough, Oz," I say.

Ozymandias thumps his tail against the ground. He whines.

"Call your dog off," Dylan says. He's freaked out now. He's standing behind his friends. His face is pale.

"My dog is sitting on my feet," I say. "But there are others. And I don't know if they will listen to me."

"Ouch," says one of the football boys. "Something won't let go of my foot!" His voice is thin and high and panicked. Like a little girl.

The air was suddenly filled with growling. I can't tell how many invisible dogs there are, but they seem to cover the street. I can see the grit on the pavement scattering this way and that. I can see the occasional puddle of pee.

"Seriously, man, this is crazy," Dylan says.

"The whole world is crazy," I say. "This is middle school, remember?"

"I'm outta here," Chase/Chance/Chet/Chortle says. And he takes off with the other three boys on his heels. Dylan can't move. His shorts and shoes and the back of his shirt are all held in place by invisible jaws. He stares at me, wide-eyed.

"It's not my fault," Dylan whimpers. "Everyone messed with you before. It's just . . . what people do."

"My dog is named Ozymandias," I say. "King of kings. Dog of dogs. Of course you know that already." The dogs swirl around me. They lick me and nip me and wag their tails. And suddenly, I can see them. All of them. There are hundreds, maybe thousands of dogs. They blanket the street. They are beautiful. And then they vanish. And then they come back. I am surrounded by invisible-visible-invisible dogs. My body sweats and shakes. I am hot and cold and happy and terrified. I look down. There is Ozymandias. I see him. His grizzled mouth. His rheumy eyes. His tilted expression, as though he is grinning at me. He's the most amazing thing I've ever seen. Then he is gone. And then he is back.

"Whoa." Dylan's eyes go a little bit wider. "You just, like, disappeared for a minute. And then you came back and you disappeared again. You're like a devil or something. Ouch!" A dog bit him.

Dylan is breathing hard. His face is pale with red blotches. He whimpers, then shakes his head. He saw the dogs for a second, I can tell. "My dad was right. You're a freak. And I'm freaking nuts."

"No," I say. "I'm not a freak, and you're not nuts. I'm just like you. We're the same. Messed up. Trying to make it through the day. Getting it wrong. Saying things we can't take back."

"You disappeared again."

"I gotta go take care of my dog. Stop being a jerk."

And then I disappear. Or I appear. I can't see Dylan. He can't see me. He is lost in a sea of dogs. And so am I.

~~~~~~~~~~

That was a week ago. I am still invisible. I have tried explaining this to my parents. They won't listen. Or maybe they don't hear me. I leave them notes. They throw them in the recycling, unread. Oz pees on the floor. They think the refrigerator is leaking. My sister hears me and Oz. She pays attention. She is not nearly as bad as I always thought she was. She has tried explaining things to my parents and to the cops who keep coming to interview the family about my disappearance.

Dylan tried explaining it too. His dad freaked out and checked him into the loony bin, saying that there wouldn't be any psychos in his family. Poor Dylan. His dad is a jerk.

The upside to all of this is Ozymandias. He is an old dog. I can't even tell how old. I've been able to give him a bath and brush his teeth. It's nice to be able to see him, even though I had to turn invisible in order to do it. I still don't know how. I guess Oz was taking care of me, just as I take care of him. I don't know how long it will last. Maybe forever.

I still sleep in my bed and eat from the kitchen, though my parents don't seem to notice. Lyla makes sure we get enough to eat. She also makes sure that Oz gets enough exercise. She keeps trying to explain to our parents, over and over, until she's blue in the face. She does this every day. She says she'll never stop.

Who knows? Maybe one day they'll listen.

Worry and Wonder

Marcie Rendon

AMY CROSSED HER RIGHT LEG under her left and leaned over her social studies book, pretending to pore over the pages. Instead, she used her black fine-point—always the fine-point—pen to doodle on her notebook cover. As Mr. Kreilkamp droned on about human responsibility and the environmental crisis, Amy wrote, graffiti-style, *Ick waa waa* with teardrops falling down after the last *waa* on the notebook.

Amy glanced up. Mr. Kreilkamp was on a roll. His arms were waving; occasionally he would use his right hand to push his black glasses farther up on his nose as he implored them to consider saving the world for their children by recycling plastic and putting their leftover lunches into the compost trash bin after school lunch. *Which is where most of it belongs as far as I am concerned,* Amy thought as she drew a metal trash can on the notebook cover with a school lunch tray flying toward it.

Mr. Kreilkamp went on about their future children and all the humans who would be born who would want to drink clean water and breathe fresh air. Amy wondered to herself how this lecture on future generations would tie into the physical education lecture on sexual abstinence the seventh grade had been given just the past Tuesday. One class was telling them to prevent future generations, and here was Mr. Kreilkamp, "Ben the Old Hen," as the students laughingly called him behind his back, telling them they needed to "prepare for future generations." She drew a tiny child curled in a fetal position inside one of the teardrops.

"Humans are a precious species, and we are on the brink of our own destruction," exhorted Mr. Kreilkamp. Amy sighed and put her head closer to her desk. She drew a heart around the teardrop with the small child inside.

Humans are precious all right, she thought, as a familiar dullness tightened around her chest and her stomach muscles tightened. She inked over *Ick waa waa* as she thought about the court hearing she had been at yesterday afternoon. She looked up and around at the other students in the classroom. Some were listening intently. A couple students were doodling on paper like she was. Jackson was daydreaming out the window.

Amy inked over *Ick waa waa* again and felt the burning of tears began to well behind her eyes. Furiously, she blacked out the crying baby in the teardrop. Yesterday in family court the ICWA attorneys, the ICWA child welfare workers, the ICWA guardian ad litems, ICWA ad nauseam, and the ICWA judge had ruled that, since no other relatives had been found, she needed to stay in foster care another three months. That no, even though her father had completed the mandatory psych evaluation, had found a job working on the new stadium, rented a two-bedroom apartment, and was living whatever the courts called a "sober lifestyle," he hadn't proved to the court's satisfaction that he was ready to assume full responsibility of her yet. By the way her dad hung his head, Amy had known he was frustrated. But when he looked up, he flashed her a grin and a wink. When he hugged her after leaving the courthouse, he had promised softly, "Soon, my girl, soon. Stay strong."

Soon wasn't soon enough. The bell rang, and all the seventh-graders hurriedly stuffed papers and folders and books into backpacks and rushed away from global responsibility. Amy was right with them.

~~~~~~~~~

That night, Amy sat in her room at the foster home doing her social studies homework, thinking about global warming, social responsibility, and humans as a precious species. Her mind drifted to the last time she had seen her mom, almost two years ago now. Her mom had kissed her good-bye and told her to behave herself and not stay up all night watching TV. She told Amy to keep the door locked and not to answer the door or the phone. Amy could still feel the spot on her forehead where her mom had planted a kiss before saying, "See you later, kiddo. You know your mom loves you." And with that, wearing her going-out clothes, her mom, her beautiful mom, had gone out and never returned.

There had been a few phone calls from states Amy had to look up online in order to know where they were. Her mom always assured her she loved her and would be back soon. As the month wore on the phone calls tapered off. And then her cell phone ran out of minutes. Not knowing what to do or how to do it, whatever "it" was, Amy continued to go to school as if nothing were different in her life. She cooked ramen noodles or mac and cheese for herself at night. She washed her hair and took regular baths. She rummaged through the couch, the dresser drawers, and under the bedroom rug to find quarters to wash her clothes in the apartment building laundry room. Rather than waste quarters on the dryer, she hung the clothes on hangers in the bathroom. When the food supply in the cupboards dwindled, she wasn't quite sure what she needed to do, so she began to stash school lunch sandwiches in her backpack and bring home stray apples and oranges that had been left on the lunchroom tables. It wasn't until the landlord, looking for rent, came knocking on the door on the fifteenth of the next month that Amy was busted. Up until then no one knew Amy was living on her own. Up until that time of her life, Amy didn't even know that rent was ever due. *Dang it*, she thought.

The very next morning, starting at 10:00 a.m. (English class time), Amy's life was filled with ICWA social workers, ICWA caseworkers, ICWA this, ICWA that. By then she had no idea where her mother was. And even less of an idea of where her father was. All she knew was that her dad was an ironworker. Before, whenever she would ask her mom about him, Amy's mom would say, "Ah, your dad, he's a good guy. He is. He's a really good guy. He's an ironworker. A hard worker. We just don't have the same idea of what a good time is."

Placed in an ICWA foster home, Amy spent her nights worried and wondering what kind of good time her mom was having without her. The foster home wasn't a bad foster home; the people were kind, and there was plenty of food. Amy could tell by the careful way they talked around her that they were trying to give her "space to adjust," a phrase she had heard her foster worker say.

One day, at the start of last summer's vacation time, her social worker had driven up in a county-issued black SUV. Amy was sitting in the backyard at the picnic table watching two squirrels run up and down a tree scolding each other when the social worker came out the back door and sat down on the picnic bench across from her.

"We heard from your mom," the social worker said carefully, setting her pen in a straight line vertical with the edge of the paper folder she had set down on the picnic table. Amy hated how the social worker and the foster parents, in fact, how all the adults in her life these days, would make statements while looking at her with careful, worried eyes. Amy knew they were worried she would dissolve into a tearful, puddled mess and/ or that she might turn into a raving maniac. Amy had decided a few months ago that a raving maniac was the way to go but hadn't found the right opportunity yet to have that fit. While Amy had felt a jolt in her stomach at the social worker's words, she only tilted her head slightly to acknowledge she had heard her.

"Your mom is in California." Amy knew where that was. "She isn't coming back." The knot tightened in Amy's stomach. Her eyes burned. The larger squirrel was chasing the smaller one down the tree, chattering wildly. A plane flew overhead, headed in the general direction of the airport. "We found your dad." Amy's heart flipped. The social worker paused. Amy looked at her sideways, her eyes telling the woman to continue.

"He's been working in the Bakken oil fields. Out in North Dakota." Pause. "Do you remember him at all?" the social worker asked. She picked up the pencil and tapped lightly on the picnic table. The squirrels glanced over at her briefly before continuing their game of chase.

Amy watched the squirrels. In her mind she saw a tall, brown-skinned man. His long black hair, pulled back into a ponytail, fell forward over his shoulder as he leaned down and handed her a snow cone. People milled around them, laughing, talking, while in the background she could hear the men singing at the drums and the jingle dress dancers dancing. The arena director at the powwow said into the mike, "Intertribal, everybody dance, everybody dance, hoka hoka, everybody dance." With the memory floating into the tree after the squirrels, Amy turned her brown eyes to the social worker and shook her head yes.

"He's on his way back here. He'll be here tomorrow. He'd like to meet you. Or meet you again, I should say."

Amy's eyes widened.

"I don't want you to get your hopes up. We don't know anything about what he's like."

"Am I going to live with him?" Amy asked in a small voice.

"Maybe. We'll see. We don't know. It will take a while. He will have to go through a home placement study. Find an apartment. Find a job here. Show the tribe and the courts he's stable and ready to be a full-time parent to you."

Amy's heart clenched. "My mom said he is a good man."

"We'll see," said the social worker. "Like I said, I don't want you to get your hopes up. I'll come pick you up tomorrow morning, and we'll go meet him. I'll take the two of you out to breakfast, someplace like Perkins or Bakers Square. That sound all right to you?"

Amy slowly nodded yes and turned her head back to where the squirrels were both sitting on a tree limb like best friends forever. She always marveled at how these new adults in her life always asked her permission as if they hadn't already decided how things were going to be. Perkins or Bakers Square? She didn't care. She was just glad he wasn't going to come to the foster home to see her. She didn't want to share meeting him, remeeting him, with her foster parents around.

She didn't remember sleeping at all that night. And the next morning she nervously sat outside on the front steps, waiting. She had changed clothes a zillion times, tossing shirts and pants and skirts back into the closet, onto the bed, onto the floor, finally seeking comfort in her oldest, well-worn, baggy sweats and a nondescript oversized T-shirt. The social worker had driven up, and Amy had climbed in.

She sat, buckled in the front seat. The black leather was hot from the summer sun. A year and a half ago, when she had first started this foster care journey, she wasn't allowed to sit in the front seat because she was too little. Back then the social worker had said, "If I get into an accident and the airbag goes off, you're so little you'll get crushed. You need to sit in back. It's the law."

Too little for an airbag but big enough to feed, clothe, and get myself to school for a month all by myself, Amy had thought to herself as she crawled into the backseat. So many nights she had lain awake in the foster home, wishing the landlord had never come to collect rent. But today she was going to meet her dad.

They went to Perkins. Too nervous, Amy couldn't eat the pancakes she ordered. Her dad looked exactly like the dad who had handed her a snow cone all those years ago at the pow-wow. He had a wide grin when he first saw her. While Amy could see the happiness in his eyes, she was too shy to say anything at all. When he asked her questions about school, she answered with yes or no. When he asked her what she liked to do, she shrugged her shoulders. He didn't look at her with worry. He didn't seem afraid that she was going to fall apart. Both he and the social worker ate and chatted about his work in North Dakota. He said he was happy to be back in the land of green—green grass, green trees, lots of water. "There was no damn water in all of North Dakota. Not like here," he said, pointing his fork out the window as if there were a lake right there. From where she was sitting, Amy could see the trees along the Mississippi River bank.

After he finished his eggs and steak, he ordered blueberry pie and cut it in half and put half in front of her. The half with the most ice cream. She ate it. He asked her about her mom and the night she left. He asked as if he really wanted to know, not as if he were shocked or mad at her mom or at her. Amy told him without the usual catch in her throat. When she was done telling her story, and how she had fed and gotten herself to school until the landlord showed up, and how mad she was at the landlord for turning her in to the social workers, her father looked at her quietly, then burst out laughing. "Well, dang," he said, "I'm glad she found you. If she hadn't come looking for her rent money, you might have been off to college without me ever getting a chance to lay eyes on you." When he was done laughing, he said, "Least I won't have to worry about feeding you once you move in." "Just kidding," he quickly said to the social worker. "I'm a mean cook. She won't be living on mac and cheese with me, that's for sure."

It was the first time Amy smiled that day.

<hr />

After that first meeting, the courts set up regular visits between Amy and her dad. They went to powwows that summer. Close ones that were within a day's drive because she wasn't allowed overnights with him yet. He took her to the White Earth Urban Picnic at Wabun Park to meet her relatives on his side of the family. He took her to Valleyfair and the state fair. Sometimes, in the evenings before sunset, he would come by the foster home and ask her if she wanted to go for a ride. By that time, her foster mom would say, "Yes, just have her home before dark."

She would sit in the front seat of his pickup truck, and he would drive her downtown and say, "See that girder way up there? The third one to the left of that orange crane? That's the one I worked on today." Other times they would drive up and down West River Road along the Minneapolis side of the Mississippi River while he told stories of buildings he helped build in Chicago or St. Louis or how the oil fields in North Dakota were destroying that state for human habitation. He would laugh and say, "Used to be only Indians lived in that state. That's how it's going to be once the white folks are done over there. Only the Indians will be left. Heck, we can live anywhere."

On one drive, after one of the hottest days that summer, they stopped and went for a dip in Lake Calhoun. As they sat in the pickup, Amy, wrapped in a beach towel, asked the question she had wanted to ask since that first day in Perkins. "How come you guys weren't together? You and mom."

Her dad turned the key in the ignition, pulled out of the parking spot, and drove slowly around the lake, all the way around the lake, the setting sun turning the sky purple and gold before he answered, saying only, "Your mom isn't a bad person. She just isn't exactly what one would call settling-down material. You know what I mean?"

Amy nodded yes.

"She loves you the best she can."

Amy nodded yes.

"Soon as this court stuff is over, things are going to be okay, girl, you got that?"

Amy nodded yes.

"We were two different people; our idea of how to be in life was too different to live together. She was a good mom to you while she was here, right?"

Amy nodded yes.

"And now I'm here. It's gonna be okay. Got that?"

Amy nodded yes.

~~~~~~~~~~

And that's where things were when they arrived in court yesterday. Waiting for the ICWA folks to grant her and her dad permission to get on with their lives. On one of their evening rides her dad had explained ICWA to her. He explained that ICWA stood for the Indian Child Welfare Act. He told her how in the 1950s and 1960s Indian children were taken from their families and placed with white families. How those children had grown up and fought to have federal legislation passed so that Indian kids, if they needed to be placed in foster care, would be placed with Indian families, like the home Amy was in, and how it was federal law, tribal law, that the courts and the tribes had to try and find immediate family for children to be reunited with, which is why the courts had found him and told him to come home to raise Amy. And if things had been right between Amy's mom and him, he would never have left in the first place. But he was here now, and that's what mattered, right?

Amy nodded her head yes.

There were nights when Amy still cried herself to sleep because she missed her mom so much. Her mom was beautiful. And funny. And fun. And gone. And she had told the courts she wasn't coming back for Amy. That hurt.

Yesterday, when the judge recommended she spend three more months in foster care, Amy hated ICWA. All the ICWA people seemed to be working to keep her from her dad, from a home with him, rather than working to keep them together. She stared at the cover of her social studies notebook where she had inked in *Ick waa waa* with teardrops falling down. Tears slid from her own eyes. She heard Mr. Kreilkamp say, "Human beings are a precious species." *If all humans were precious, why had her mom left her? If all humans were precious, why was she living with strangers?* Amy threw herself on the bed and cried herself to sleep.

Amy got up the next day and plodded through school. Two months went by in a heavy haze. One Saturday when her dad came to visit, they went to Dairy Queen. He said, "You know, part of what Indian foster homes are supposed to do is keep you involved in our culture. Our culture is more than just the pow-wows I've been taking you to. I talked with the social worker, and she said it's okay if my cousin Marie—you remember her from the Shakopee powwow? She's kinda chubby, has her nose pierced? She's going to come by and take you to a water cere-mony tomorrow morning."

"What's a water ceremony?" Amy asked.

"Not exactly sure," answered her dad, "'cause it's for women, 'cause women are the caretakers of the water. Marie will take you with her in the morning, down to the river. Guess they say prayers to the water, sing a bit. Smudge with sage; make a tobacco offering to the river. Here," he said, putting a small leather pouch on a long leather string around her neck. "There's tobacco in there. *Asema.* That's the Ojibwe word for tobacco. *Asema.* You just take a small pinch of it out of there for your tobacco offering."

As he talked, Amy remembered seeing him take tobacco out of a red pouch he kept on the dash of his truck and offering it out the window on some of their drives along the river or some-times by a tree at one of the lakes they visited. She closed her hand around the soft leather pouch.

When her dad dropped her back at the foster home, he said, "Oh, I almost forgot. Do you have a long skirt you can wear tomorrow when Marie comes to get you?"

Amy shook her head no.

"I'll call her and tell her to bring one for you to wear."

"Why?" asked Amy.

"I don't know," answered her dad. "Guess it's something like the Creator can't tell if you're a woman or a boy unless you wear a skirt." He was laughing and shaking his head as he drove off.

Amy was nervous and quiet as she rode in the car the next morning with her cousin Marie. Marie was a talker. She talked nonstop about the weather, her lazy kids, the woman at work who dyed blue streaks into her hair and painted her two-inch-long fingernails purple. Amy was grateful she wasn't required to respond.

When they got to the river, five other women were already there. Marie handed Amy a long strip of material and showed her how to wrap it around her waist to fashion it into an ankle-length skirt. Amy noticed all the other women already had skirts on. Once her skirt was on, Amy and Marie joined the women in a semicircle down at the river's edge.

One woman was apparently leading the ceremony. On the sand at their feet was a cloth. On it was a shell with sage in it, a copper bowl full of water, a drum, and a ceremonial rattle. After lighting the sage in the shell and smudging everyone with the smoke from it, the woman offered tobacco from a pouch to the women who hadn't brought their own. After each woman had said a short prayer, the leader then sang a song in Ojibwe. The only word Amy knew in the song was the word *asema*, the word her father had taught her the night before.

When the song was over, the woman instructed them to offer their tobacco and prayers to the river. Each woman walked down to the water's edge and brushed the tobacco off their hands into the water. When Amy looked up after offering her tobacco, a bald eagle flew the length of the river. The woman leading the ceremony whistled piercingly and said, "Miigwetch, Migizi."

Amy followed Marie back into the semicircle of women and watched as the leader picked up the copper bowl of water and said, "Now we'll sing the water song."

As the women lifted their voices in song, Amy felt chills run down her arms. The only word she caught in this song was *ni-bi*. She needed to remember that word so she could ask her dad what it meant. As the women sang, they passed the copper bowl around the circle. Some lifted the bowl to the sky; some held it to their heart. The last woman to receive the bowl of water walked with it to the water's edge. She lifted the bowl three times to the sky and the fourth time to the water itself before pouring the water into the river.

As Amy lay in bed that night, she thought about some of the words the woman leader had said at the ceremony that morning. The woman, whose name she couldn't remember, had said that women were the givers of life, that women were water. That every human started this life in water. That each human life was precious. *See, Mr. Kreilkamp, you aren't the only one who thinks so,* thought Amy. That the water was in danger and that the ceremony they were doing was offering prayers of healing to the water, so the water could continue to give life to humans. As Amy dozed off her last thought was, *But why did I have to wear a skirt?*

Amy dreamed. In her dream her mother danced, wearing a red dress, her dark brown hair flowing out around her. She smiled and waved before dancing off into a room with disco lights flashing. Out of another room came the ICWA judge. Instead of wearing a black robe, she was wearing a black velvet dress with floral beadwork across her shoulders. Intertwined with the flowers were beaded blueberries and strawberries. The judge sat at a table and picked up a knife and fork, one in each hand, and started banging them on the table, looking sternly at Amy. When she had Amy's full attention, she asked, "Do you know why Minnesota winters are so long?"

Scared, Amy said, "No."

"To teach us patience," the judge said in a gravelly voice. "We are thirsty for the berries after a long winter and are happy to have them." She then proceeded to eat from a bowl of blueberries and strawberries that appeared on the table before her. Out of the corner of her eye, Amy saw her dad standing in another doorway, ready to enter, grinning widely. Just as he took a step forward, the judge stood up. Before she walked away, she pointed at Amy's legs. Amy looked down. She was wearing a floor-length turquoise skirt. The judge said, "We wear that to learn self-discipline."

When Amy awoke in the morning, the heaviness in her heart was gone, the sun was shining, and her foster mother had blueberry pancakes ready for her to eat before she headed out the door to school.

Mourning Dove

Joyce Sidman

When I hear your call,
like a sip
of melancholy,
I want to fly up
and perch beside you:

two girls searching
the deep black
depths
of each other's eyes,
smoothing
the neat white
crescents
of our feathery skirts,
trying to make
the sound
of sadness
beautiful

My Icy Valentine

Kirstin Cronn-Mills

"You have to stop now! Like right now!" Chase sounds like he might flip out. "It's dark, this is a *frozen lake,* and I'm not going out there!"

My brother Brady hits the brake, not one to ignore such an insistent request but also not one to like it. "What's wrong with you?" The truck slides about ten feet.

"Chase, what's your deal?" I've never heard anyone screech like that.

"I can't do this!" He's heaved himself out the truck door and run back to the shore before I can say another word.

I look at Brady, and he's scowling big enough I can see it in the dim interior of the truck. "Sorry. Give me a second."

"This isn't worth the twenty bucks you promised me. And it's freaking freezing out here. Look." Brady points to the digital thermometer readout embedded in the truck's rearview mirror. Minus ten.

"But there's no wind. That's a plus." And I hop out to try and convince Chase to get back in the truck.

I find him standing on shore about ten feet from where the ice starts, looking nervous and shy but also slightly angry.

"I won't go out there. It's illogical. Physics won't let you drive a truck on ice." A fourteen-year-old guy in cowboy boots, a down parka, a face mask, and snowmobile gloves is invoking physics for why he's ruining my Valentine's Day surprise.

"Those boots can't be warm. I hope you have on SmartWool socks."

"These boots are plenty warm." Now he's indignant as well as angry.

"Whatever you say." I try again, making my voice as kind

and soothing as I can. "You have to come with us, okay? It's an adventure. You'll like it."

"No way. It's water." He looks very sure of himself, as if lakes are made of something else where he comes from.

"You're correct. It's water. But it's February in Minnesota and it's *frozen* water. Please get back in the truck, Chase. Please? It's cold out here."

Chase shakes his head. "Doesn't matter how frozen it is. You're crazy." He points at Brady's truck, idling behind me with Brady in it, waiting to take us out to the fish house. "If he's this close to shore, he can at least drive out if the ice gives. Not true if he goes any farther."

"If you don't get in the truck, you'll wreck everything!" I try to keep the tears out of my voice. He can't mess it up now. He just can't.

"Listen here, Lucy." He says that every day in study hall, when we talk about life and music and cows and air filters for semis—*listen here, Lucy*—and I love how it sounds. I love hearing him say my name. But unlike study hall, this time he's very, very serious. "I can't do it. It's just not sane to drive on a frozen lake. If it was warmer, I'd get out my phone and Google could explain it all to you."

"But we do it *all the time* here. Don't you remember where you are?" I'm desperate to have him understand how much it means to me that he gets in Brady's truck.

Chase laughs. "Minnesotans obviously don't understand science, and Nebraskans like me understand that fishing is for summer, not winter."

"CHASE!" I'm desperate.

"Lucy!" He thinks all this begging is funny—it's obvious. "Forget it. No way."

It's all I can do not to scream. My plans are ruined.

~~~~~~~~~~

Chase Baldwin moved to my little town of Malmo, Minnesota, in September, just after the school year started. He had to—his dad came to be the plant manager for Essex Filters, the place in town where everybody's dad works, including mine. Essex Filters is one of the largest national manufacturers of air filters for every kind of gasoline engine. Boring. There's another Essex Filter plant in Gothenburg, Nebraska, where Chase lived his entire life up until he moved to Malmo. Chase says Gothenburg wasn't that exciting, but compared to Malmo, it was Disneyland. Ha. I looked up Gothenburg, Nebraska. Malmo has 2,500 people in it. Gothenburg has 3,500, so it's not like he lived in the big city or anything. Chase also told me that it was seventy-five miles to the nearest Target from his house. It's only fifteen miles from here, so I win.

He says he hates it here except for me.

I don't understand how someone can miss a nothing place like Nebraska.

When he came in September, ninth grade had just started. We have a brand-new school, Malmo Consolidated, so we were all trying to figure out where our classrooms were. In that way, he fit right in, since we were all lost at the beginning. But our class is pretty small—eighty-seven—so once we found our classrooms and lockers, he stuck out like a palm tree in a snowbank. First of all, he wore cowboy boots on the first day he came. With loud boot heels and everything. Every time he walked down the hall, it sounded like he was walking into the Last Chance Saloon. Before I met him, I didn't think real people wore cowboy boots, just people in movies. And of course everybody stared— and I mean everybody, students and teachers—when he clicked down the hall. I don't think there are any cowboys in Minnesota. There aren't in Malmo, anyway. When he really wants to flip people out, he wears shirts with pearl buttons and a huge belt buckle. I know he has a cowboy hat, too, because I've seen it at his house. But he doesn't wear it in public. He says he doesn't want the stereotype to be reinforced any more than it has to be. Which leads me to my second point about him.

Chase is a really smart cowboy, which surprised everyone. People had a hard time looking past the shirts, the boots, and the belt buckle. Chase has already taken the SAT and the ACT, and he could go to college tomorrow, if he were done with high school. He told me this on Christmas break, when we were driving up to the Twin Cities with his mom to spend our Christmas money at the Mall of America. I saw his mom smile when he was telling me. But he says he doesn't care about being smart. He goes to school because he likes having friends like me. I think that's dumb. I'd do anything to be done with high school and be gone from Malmo. But he thinks it's important to be doing things with people who are his own age. He doesn't want to go to college until he's old enough. I think that's really weird.

The funny thing is, Chase doesn't act smart at school. He acts like a regular ninth-grader, somebody who talks about football and basketball—he loves Minnesota's pro teams, so the guys in my class liked him immediately for that—and he pretends to be someone who *doesn't* like math homework, even though he secretly does. He fits in with the mathletes, the jocks, or whatever group he wants, except for the arty theater kids. They're still suspicious of his boots. I'm the only person he's told about the SAT and the ACT, and he only told me because I caught him reading a book about quantum physics and its intersection with trigonometry. He looked so guilty. He was supposed to be reading a graphic novel for English class. He takes study hall very, very seriously.

And he likes that I'm smart, too. Everyone's always surprised about my brains—after all, the daughter of someone who works at Essex Filters couldn't possibly be a candidate for scholarships, could she?—but Chase likes that he can talk to me about almost anything, and I can mostly understand it. Or at least I can learn about it (and find it on Google). Sometimes we talk about silly stuff, too—are sea turtles ancient dinosaurs with shells? what if they're really mutant sea robots?—but it's all fun.

I love that we can be smart together. I love that his boot heels make such a cute noise when he walks down the hall. I love when he wears his huge belt buckle, because it's so goofy. I love his smile. I love that he doesn't make fun of me for not really understanding quantum physics. I love that he FaceTimes with me so we can watch *Harry Potter* movies together. And of course he has no idea I like him, which was fine for a while, because things stayed simple. But then I decided Valentine's Day was exactly the right time to tell him how I feel.

Which brings us here. To this frozen lake. On a freezing cold February night.

~~~~~~~~~~~~~

"Chase, you really need to get back in the truck now. Driving on the ice isn't a big deal. Honestly, it's not."

He looks very secure in his knowledge, standing there in the February darkness. "I'm not going anywhere. You have no idea what could happen."

"Um, yes, we do. People have been driving on ice in February in Minnesota since cars were invented." At least I hope that's true.

"How much does a pickup weigh?" He's actually asking me this.

"You're the smart one. You tell me." I'm getting mad now. "Why do we have to play twenty questions? Please just get back in!"

He decides to lecture me. "The average pickup weighs between two and three tons, and I'm guessing Brady's pickup is average, since it's pretty small." He points at Brady and the truck. "Add three people to four thousand pounds, and then expect that weight to be supported by twenty inches of ice? Like I said, it defies the laws of physics."

"But it doesn't, Chase! People do it all the time. And . . . you just have to believe me, okay? We have to go to the fish house."

"Why? What's so important in the fish house?"

"Just . . ." I don't want to ruin the surprise. "We just want you to have a nice Minnesota winter experience. Brady thought you might like it."

"Brady wants me to come?" This intrigues him, for some reason. "Do you ice fish a lot with your older brother? That's just weird. How come you haven't mentioned this to me?"

"We don't do it a lot. But our fish house is a good place to hang out." Our fish house is pretty crappy, actually, compared to a lot of other people's, but it's nice enough. Our neighbors have carpet and a satellite dish, plus beds with real mattresses. We have fold-out platforms, sleeping bags, ugly linoleum, and only a radio. And the generator is super loud, which we started up before we went to get Chase so I could plug in the red and pink heart lights that I strung around inside. Two huge pink-frosted cupcakes, a single rose, and a teddy bear are sitting on the table, looking adorable in the glow of the lights. It's all ready for Valentine's Day, *if* the valentine would get in the dang truck.

Chase won't give in. "So why do I have to go to your fish house today? Why not tomorrow, or why not after I've done some research about whether or not ice can hold a two-ton truck?"

"Because tonight is the night we go to the fish house. Because it's Tuesday. Because any night is a good night to go to the fish house." I'm out of ideas after that one.

Brady honks his horn, and I can tell he's not in this adventure for much longer. Good thing the lake's on the edge of town. He's going to ditch us in three seconds and we'll have to walk home.

"Seriously, Chase." I try one more time. "Just . . . trust me, okay? Trust me this one time."

"I trusted you when you told me to eat fried cheese curds, and that was a good decision. I trusted you when you taught me to snowshoe. This one I can't do." He crosses his arms.

I hear a whir.

"Chase!" It's Brady, with his window down. "Are you gonna get in this freaking truck, or do I have to pick you up and throw you in? I'll keep the stupid windows down. If we break through, you can swim out. All right? It's freaking freezing, and there's heat in the fish house. Let's go!"

A more-than-slightly-nervous grin flits across Chase's face. "For real you'll keep the windows down? It's below zero, you know. I can feel it in my frozen nose hairs."

"As a matter of fact, it's minus ten, but I'll keep the windows down. Now get the hell in here." *Bzzzzzzzp.* Window up for now. But Chase takes a step toward the truck.

"Come on. We won't sink, I promise. Brady promises."

"I'll go if I can sit in the middle next to Brady. And if I can lecture you tomorrow about how frozen lakes are not roads plus a couple other things. String theory, maybe. Or maybe the rate of decomposition in dead cats."

"Gross. No. But I'll let you lecture me about the ice."

"Fine." And Chase walks—carefully, delicately, watching his feet the whole time—back to the truck. Once he's in, I climb in after him.

Brady zips both windows down. "I promise you won't drown. But you might freeze to death before we get there."

Chase leans over me to put his arm out the window. "I'm ready to swim."

"Whatever." Brady snorts and then we're twenty feet out, forty, eighty, and Chase grabs onto me, as if I can keep him afloat if the ice breaks. It's a million degrees of cold in the truck, and I'm glad our fish house is only a half mile or so from the shore.

When we get there, Brady stops the truck and looks at his watch. "I'm giving you thirty minutes. That's it." He shifts the truck to P. "After that, I'm outta here."

"Thanks a lot, big brother." I know I can't do anything about Brady's declaration, but I reach over and smack the back of his head, just so he knows I'm mad. "Come on, Chase." I open the truck door and get out.

Chase looks between Brady and me, terrified. "He's staying here? In the truck? How come? And why do I have to walk on it again?"

"Dude, if it holds a truck, it will hold you. I can promise you that. And it's not like you're adding weight, you're just redistributing. If anything, that makes it better." I'm just freestyling now. "And it's warmer in the fish house. So let's go."

Crack. The ice makes a sound like a tree falling over.

Chase's face is a portrait of horror. "I'm not getting out of this truck."

"Seriously, it's all right. Sometimes the ice does that."

Chase looks at Brady. "Does it really? Or are we going to sink in ten seconds?"

Brady gestures to all the fish houses around us, which you can see only because there are lights in their windows. "This ice village has been here for weeks. It's Minnesota. This is what we do."

Chase looks slightly reassured, but only slightly. "I'm looking this up as soon as I can." The tone in his voice tells me how serious he is. He puts his feet on the ice, gets out, and stands very still. It's obvious he's waiting for it to collapse under him. "It's some sort of miracle that people don't die from this."

"Well, they don't." I grab his hand and pull him out of the way while I reach to shut the truck door. Sometimes people do die. But he doesn't have to know that.

When I open the door to the fish house, Chase bolts inside and seats himself in a lawn chair. Fast as he can, he whips off his glove and pulls out his phone, looking for information. Ten minutes go by. I'm losing time and money every minute Chase is looking at his phone.

"Want a cupcake?" It's all I can think of to say.

Chase lifts his head. "Cupcake?" For some reason, this word jolts him out of his physics coma, and he starts to look around. He notices the lights, the teddy bear and the rose, and the two giant cupcakes on the table. "What's all this stuff?"

"Do you know what day it is?"

"Tuesday." He looks at his phone again. "Tuesday, February 14." Pause. "Oh."

I make my voice light. "Happy Valentine's Day!"

"Seriously, Lucy?" His face tells me that I've just crossed a line somewhere, and it's not one he wanted to deal with.

"Well . . ." I have to save this somehow. "I like you. In, you know, that way. So I thought I'd bring you out here and tell you, since there's no one else to see me do it. Nobody else has to know." I hand him one of the giant cupcakes.

"Brady knows, doesn't he?" He takes a bite of the cupcake. "Did you make this?"

"Yes, and Brady doesn't exactly know. I didn't tell him why we were coming out here."

"Maybe he thought you just wanted to fish?" He takes another bite and gets frosting on his nose, the cupcake is so big. "And your mom probably wondered why you were baking cupcakes this huge. She probably guessed they weren't for Mr. Torkelson." He's our principal. Chase chews and swallows. "By the way, no ice is 100 percent safe to drive on, no matter what *Ice Road Truckers* says. The Minnesota Department of Natural Resources agrees with me."

"A whole state of people thank you for your diligence." I suppose it says a lot about Minnesotans that a whole state of people also disregard that statement.

He takes another bite of cupcake. "So I'm just going to say it: I don't like you like that. I just . . . well . . . I think Brady is more suited to being my valentine."

My mouth falls open, but I shut it fast. I had no idea. "Oh. Well. Um. That was blunt. Okay. I just . . . you know . . . we spend a lot of time together, and . . . you wear cowboy boots."

Chase looks at me over the top of the cupcake, which he's still shoveling into his mouth. "My uncle Dave is gay, and he wears cowboy boots." He glares, and I realize how stupid I must sound, even though I'm not the one from a hick state.

"I've never heard of a gay cowboy before, all right? Cut me some slack." I try and calm my face down with my icy hands. I'm blushing as red as the lights I've strung around.

"Can Brady come inside? Maybe he'd like the rose." He shoves the rest of the cupcake in his mouth, smiling around the wreckage. "I'll forgive you that cowboy boot comment if I can give him the teddy bear."

It clicks why Chase wanted to sit next to Brady in the truck. "Shut up, jerk!" And I can't help it—the tears escape, so I turn my back on him. If I'm lucky, a huge muskie will jump up through one of the holes, grab me, and pull me under. Then this can all be over.

"Oh, hey—don't do that. Please don't do that, Lucy. I'm sorry. I haven't told a lot of people about . . . this part of me. I don't mean to be rude. I'm sorry. The cupcake was delicious." I hear him get up; then I feel a hand on my shoulder.

I'm not going to turn around. "Have Brady take you home. Forget this ever happened, all right? Just forget it. I'll walk back." There's no wind. I've got enough clothes on to keep warm.

"Not until you tell me we can still be friends. And you have to turn around."

"Of course I'll be your friend. Who else would I talk nerdy with?" I mean about 85 percent of this statement.

Chase doesn't give up. "No, you have to turn around and say it to me. Otherwise it doesn't count."

I don't do it.

"Listen here, Lucy." He's trying to get me to laugh. "It's not a big deal. Nothing has changed except that you're embarrassed. I didn't want you to find out this way, but it's out now."

"Go find Brady. Take your rose and your teddy bear and go, okay?"

"Lucy, come on."

"You should have told me sooner. You didn't trust me?" It might be anger; it might be hurt. I don't know. The tears are still trickling.

"It's just . . . this is a small town. You have to be careful."

"It's the twenty-first century! Being gay is no big deal. Unless you keep it from people."

"Do you know that for sure?" His voice is icy, and his hands are gone from my shoulders. "Have you ever seen someone with FAGGOT cut into their chest with a screwdriver? I have. I'm really not interested in that."

I whirl around. "Did that happen to you?"

Now *he* won't look at *me*. "A kid a few towns over. But everybody knew about it. When the kid's mom called the sheriff, nobody would come to take her complaint."

I have no idea what to say. I truly didn't think that happened anymore.

"So, yeah, I keep it close, and yeah, I trust you, but no, I wasn't ready to tell you until you forced it with the cupcake." He smiles a little, though his eyes are still flicking from thing to thing, avoiding my face. "I haven't really been sure for very long. So it's all just . . . you know. New. Surprising."

I pick up his hand and hold it, which is the first time we've ever held hands. All of a sudden, making sure he's okay is way more important than any stupid crush. "I'm sorry about your friend."

"He wasn't my friend. Just a guy." Finally his eyes meet mine. "But, yeah. It wasn't good."

Silence. We hold hands. The generator growls on. He looks at the rose, the bear, and the cupcake. I look at him. I wish for a boyfriend like him someday. I wish for a decent boyfriend for him, too.

Finally I ask it. "Are you gonna tell anybody else?"

He looks away again. "We'll see. One person is enough for Valentine's Day."

"Do your folks know?"

"Yeah, they're cool."

"That's good, at least." I squeeze his hand and let it go. "So now what?" Though I don't really want to know the answer.

"Now we just . . . go on. Nothing's changed."

"Brady's going to wonder why you're carrying a teddy bear and a rose."

"We can pretend we're dating. At least for tonight." Chase gathers up his Valentine's Day loot. "It won't be the last time I have to act straight." The sadness on his face makes my heart hurt. "If we give Brady the other cupcake, maybe he'll keep this adventure to himself."

"It's okay if you come out. Nobody in Malmo will hurt you. I'll make sure of it."

His smile isn't very convincing. "We'll see." Then he opens the door and goes back into the frigid night. I check my phone. We have two minutes until Brady's deadline.

I unplug the heart lights and shut off the generator. The fish house is black and silent, but Brady's headlights illuminate the dark outside the window. I hope he and Chase are laughing and sharing that last cupcake.

There's nothing left to do but close the door and lock it.

Poetry Themes from Creative Writing Class

Joyce Sidman

Loneliness
> *Please notice me.*

Love
> *I'm crazy about you.*

Self-doubt
> *If you knew the truth, would you still love me?*

Deception
> *You're toying with me; I'm weak.*

Fear of inner violence
> *How dare you walk away from me?*

Dream about being a vampire
> *I am isolated, alone.*

Dream about death
> *No one told me it would be this hard.*

Detachment
> *Maybe someday I'll forget you.*

The power of friends
> *You broke my heart, but I don't care anymore.*

Gathering strength
> *You may ignore me, but I'll triumph.*

Making plans
> *I can break the cycle.*

The future awaits
> *I rise into the air; I fly.*

The Silver Box (An Excerpt)

Margi Preus

The following is taken from the forthcoming sequel to the novel
Enchantment Lake.

THE POLICE TAPE HAD BEEN REMOVED, and the huge summer
home was empty. Francie remembered how it had been all lit up
and looked like a cruise ship run aground when she'd attended
a party there in the summer. Now it was empty and forlorn,
leaves had collected on the many decks, and cobwebs clung to
walls and downspouts.

The once-immaculate sweep of yard now looked like a hay-
field, and Francie and her friend Raven had to practically wade
through it to get to the front steps of the house. At the far edge
of the lawn, the lake clung to the last of the daylight, emanating
a soft glow.

Francie shoved aside a layer of moldering leaves with her
foot as she stepped onto the deck.

"You're sure there's nobody here?" Raven whispered, following behind Francie.

"The person who owns it is in jail." Francie jiggled the door
handle. It was locked, and she moved along the deck to another
door.

"Won't all the doors be locked?" Raven asked.

"Yeah, probably."

Nonetheless, Francie checked the many doors while Raven
scanned the woods that ringed the property.

"You know there is a still-unsolved murder that happened
out here, right? You know that, right?" Raven said.

"I know, I know." Francie circled the house looking for any

doors she might have missed. "But this has nothing to do with that."

"Well, all the doors are locked," Raven said, after Francie tried the last of them. "I guess we have to give up."

"Nope," Francie said, producing a thin metal tool that she inserted into the lock and twisted until the door clicked open.

"Ooh, boy," Raven said. "Where'd you learn that trick? Don't tell me if it was in jail."

"I learned it from my brother."

"Theo? Where did he learn it?"

"I don't know, and I'm not sure I want to find out."

The place was stuffy, the air stale, with a faint scent of something sort of sweet and noxious, a strange odor Francie couldn't quite place. Rather than switching the lights on, the girls opted for flashlights and they roamed from room to room, the beams bouncing over furniture, lamps, artwork, momentarily illuminating the black eyes of a moose head on a wall and the beady eyes of a bear rug on the floor.

"This place has more eyes than a sack of potatoes," Raven said, shining her flashlight on Francie. "Are you sure you want to do this? You look kind of pale."

"I'm fine," Francie said, although a familiar cold tremor ran through her.

"Tell me what we're looking for again," Raven whispered.

"A small silver box," Francie choked out. She didn't think the place would affect her, but she had to admit that her nerves were jangled. "Um," she continued, trying to stay focused, "I remember one like it from my mother."

"You think it was your mother's?"

"I don't know," Francie said. "I only know the box disappeared at some point when I was little.

"How big is it?" Raven asked.

"Maybe about the size of a pound of butter," Francie answered. At least, that's how she remembered it. Was it? She really couldn't say for sure.

"And if we find it, we're going to do what?" Raven asked. "Take it? So in addition to breaking and entering, we are going to *steal* something?"

"We didn't break anything," Francie said. As for what they were going to do if they found the box . . . Francie hadn't quite thought that through. Maybe she just wanted to look at it. She didn't know. All she knew was that she had to find it. *Had to!*

"It's not in here, anyway," Francie said, moving to the next room. *Think!* she told herself. *You saw it, then things happened, and you got distracted. But you saw it.*

She stopped to picture the scene as she remembered it when she had seen it in this house. It had been so unexpected, yet there it was, exactly as she had pictured it in the years following its disappearance, ornately engraved and gleaming: the silver box. Maybe it was just a fanciful invention of her imagination. But she *had* seen it—a real thing—and it had been *here.* Hadn't it?

Even now, just thinking of it brought on a blur of memories: her childhood home, her father, a sunlit nursery, and then—an almost memory of her mother—a shred, a wisp, like a nearly remembered dream . . . she strove for it, but it eluded her, dissolving like mist. Oh, if there were only something she could remember!

There was so much not knowing in her life: Who was her mother? Why had she disappeared? *Why would no one tell her anything about her?*

Unless she understood these things, she could never understand herself, and she would always feel like she did right now: floundering, sinking, as if she were being pulled underwater. Or, like her character in the school play, buried alive.

"You are seriously creeping me out right now," Raven said. "You've been shining your flashlight on that table for about five minutes, and anyone can see there is nothing on it!"

Francie snapped out of her reverie and swept the beam over the room. "Let's just make sure we look everywhere," she said, letting her light come to rest once again on the same end table.

"Maybe the police took the box as evidence," Raven whispered.

"Why would they?" Francie whispered back. "And why are we whispering?"

"I don't know," Raven answered, "but it feels like we're not alone."

As soon as Raven said it, Francie felt it. The hairs on her arms and the back of her neck prickled.

Someone else was inside the house.

When they stopped to listen, they heard it: footsteps.

"Come on!" Francie whispered, moving toward the sound.

"Are you insane?" Raven whispered back. "We should be running away. It might be an ax murderer. It might be *the* murderer!" She clung to Francie's arm, trying to prevent her from going, but Francie plunged into the hall, dragging Raven along with her.

Peeking around the corner, Francie caught movement—a glimpse of a figure in a—seriously? a trench coat?—disappearing through an open door: a leg, a foot, one arm, a hand, and clutched in the hand, something that—had she imagined it or had there been just the faintest flash of silver?

As soon as the door clicked shut, Francie turned to Raven. "I think he's got it. We have to go after him." She charged down the hall toward the door.

"No!" Raven cried, running after her.

Francie already had her hand on the door handle when Raven reached her and yanked her away from the door.

"Think!" she said. "If you go out there, whoever it is will see you!"

"If I don't go out there, I won't see whoever it is." Francie tore away from Raven, flung open the door, and burst out onto the deck in time to see a fleeing figure headed for the beach. "That's him, getting into a boat!" she cried, and raced down the expanse of lawn while the mystery person started the motor and plunged away from the shore.

Francie watched helplessly as the boat headed across the lake. Then, before it receded into the gloom, the boat slowed. The trench-coated figure let go of the motor, reached down as if picking something off the bottom of the boat, stood, and, with an overhand motion, sent it soaring into the air. There was a faint splash, stillness (during which Francie realized she was holding her breath), and then the motor roared back to life and the boat disappeared into the darkness.

The color of Enchantment Lake could not be named, Francie thought, as she gazed at it from the bow of the canoe the next day. It wasn't blue or green or any color you would think water should be, but some new color, as yet unnamed, a kind of silver, each wavelet outlined in black. Along the shore it reflected the colors of the forest, only deeper, darker—the kind of place you dare not venture into, lest you never return.

"Are you looking?" Raven asked from the stern.

Francie turned her gaze downward as the canoe glided over lacy weeds, stretches of sand peppered with snail shells, and here and there the forlorn skeleton of a crayfish.

"Are you sure it's here?" Raven asked.

"You saw the guy throw it in the lake."

"Are you sure *that's* what he threw into the water?"

"Yes."

"How?"

"I *know*. I just know."

"You *think*," Raven said. "You just think. You could be imagining it."

"You heard the splash," Francie said.

"Yeah, but it could have been a rock. Or a bait box. Or a dead fish. It could have been anything!"

"It gleamed," Francie said. "Didn't you see it?"

"I didn't see any gleam."

"I did," Francie insisted. "I saw it flash inside the house, and I saw a glint when he threw it in the lake." Francie stared down into the water. She had to find it—*had to*. Not just to prove it to Raven, but everything depended on it—*everything*.

"Glint, gleam, if you say so," Raven said. "You know what? You are crazier than a loon." She squinted at the sun. "I really gotta go home now."

"Okay," Francie said. "I'll look more tomorrow."

But the next day rain pocked the surface of the lake, making it impossible to see anything underwater. And the day after that it was windy, the water the color of bruises, all chopped into foaming whitecaps. Big clouds, white as clean sheets, raced across the otherwise blue sky. Beautiful weather if you weren't hoping to find something on the bottom of a lake.

She stood by the picture window of her great-aunts' cabin and stared out at the water, first blue, then, as the sun passed under a cloud, turning jade green, then gray. It was a turbulence she felt inside herself, as if whitecaps churned within her. Wind roared in her head, and she could think of little else but wind, waves, and under the waves, somewhere, the silver box, rolling, turning, and tumbling.

Pressure

Swati Avasthi

Bharati Aunty

Too much in my hands. I balance the pitcher on my head. It takes a moment. I have been in this country too long. With my free hand, I push the doorbell and hear its two-note song. I glance at the windows to make sure no one has seen my Indian move. It has become habit to hide. I don't like the way Americans ask me about everything Indian. Their curiosity is so intense it's like watching lovers kiss. In my haste to remove the pitcher, I knock the side of it and nearly flood my hair with mango *lassi*.

Mango *lassi* is Rajesh's favorite, I realize. Thoughtless me, I'm twisting the knife. I want to dump the drink in the bushes, but the door swings open. Shobita. Her long, straight hair is tied in a ponytail, and she is wearing her white soccer jersey—a home game. Her sports bra makes her breasts look like one mass. I look away quickly. She turned fifteen two days ago, but she is larger than my B cup. No wonder my daughter, Ritu, insisted on a Miracle Bra. Shobita regards the mango *lassi*—a quick, mournful smile. She misses her brother.

"Bharati Aunty," she says. *Aunty*—an honorary title that, over the years of sleepovers and holidays that our families spent together, has become real.

She ushers me in, lifting the tray of *samosas* that is balanced on top of two casserole dishes. She leans over the *samosas*, smelling them, but does not take one.

It was only three months ago when I brought food on India's Independence Day. She and Rajesh were waiting for me in the yard as I drove up. Before I turned off the car, they dove in the back and uncovered the *samosas*. They each broke one open—a plume of steam and sudden scent of cooked potatoes. I miss her brother, too.

She waits while I slide off my *chappals* and leave them on the green mat beside other shoe couples. We walk into the kitchen, which is hopelessly out-of-date: no island, yellow walls, and brown compressed-wood cabinets. Depressed.

"Where's your mother?"

Kamala is nowhere to be seen. *Please, don't let that mean she is in bed again.* Two weeks in bed, eating nothing. Fasting, as if in protest against the turn her life took.

"On the phone. Don't worry so, Aunty. She started knitting again last night."

"Did she? That's something."

"Yeah. A sweater for when he is discharged. Yellow. She says it's the color of happiness."

I open the refrigerator door and push a margarine tub aside to make room for the *lassi*. "How's school? Ritu said you have Mr. Cole this year?"

Shobita toys with the end of her ponytail. "Uh, yeah. Geometry."

I hesitate. Why do I keep insinuating Rajesh into our conversation? Mr. Cole was Rajesh's favorite teacher and adviser for three years. I glance back at Shobita. She lets go of her hair and straightens up.

"How was your game? Did you win?" I finally come up with something that has nothing to do with Rajesh.

"Haven't played yet. I'm on my way out."

"So late?"

"State finals. Later draws a better crowd."

She kneels and roots around in a cabinet until she pulls out a kettle. She walks to the sink and opens the faucet. Water rains loudly into the kettle.

I pile my dishes in the fridge and start out of the room. "There's more in the car."

"I'll get it. One minute. You just sit down."

I turn a swivel chair to face her and sit, tucking a foot beneath me. She puts the kettle on to boil, faces me, and rests against the counter. A perfect mimic of her mother. She is growing up fast. Too fast. No cooking with her mother, spending time in the kitchen, rolling out dough together, like Ritu and I do. Instead, she had had to persuade Kamala out of bed when I couldn't make her even sit up. "I will not come out until you do," I had heard through the door. When they emerged, she was supporting her mother by her elbow as Kamala wobbled on atrophied legs. Watching Shobita now, I know that Kamala's strength has passed into her.

Shobita's head inclines, listening to her mother's tread coming. "I'll get the rest of the food."

In the doorway she steps aside, letting Kamala enter, and gives her arm an encouraging squeeze before disappearing. Kamala tucks the end of her sari into her petticoat. I look for signs. No red eyes, no puffy face or streaks down her cheeks.

"Good news?"

"Same, same. He will get better, though. I'm sure Rajesh will come home when he is ready."

When he is ready. An American phrase that sounds awkward from Kamala's mouth.

When Uma, another "aunty," had called to tell me that Rajesh had written a suicide note before swallowing half a bottle of pills, she asked, "What has he got to be depressed about? No one tries to kill themselves in India."

Of course not. India is perfect. If you ignore the poverty, disease, filth, crime . . . easy to romanticize the mother country, harder to live there, I don't say.

Uma continued, "I can't imagine what his parents are thinking."

They cannot believe this is happening to them. That they are failures, wondering what they did wrong. And of course, the one question none of us can escape: should we have stayed in India?

I knew all this, but I couldn't think of anything to say when I met Kamala in the blue and gray hospital emergency room. Silently, I held her hand. When the doctor came, I asked every question I could think of: "Will it hurt to have his stomach pumped?" and "Why does he need charcoal?" All the while thinking: *Should they have stayed in India? If they had, would they have picked up the signs? What do we miss in our American children that leaves them unprotected? Could I become Kamala, sitting out here, waiting while my own daughter gets a tube stuffed down her throat?* Kamala just swallowed and swallowed. I can still hear that gulping sound. It was the only sound she made all night.

The front door slams, and Shobita returns carrying the gallon-sized Ziploc of *puris*. Steam whitens the clear plastic. I should have made *chapatis*. They would keep better.

Shobita fusses with the teapot, lifting the top and plunking in cinnamon, cloves, and green cardamom pods. She gets down two mugs and opens the refrigerator door, disappearing from view.

"You made tea?" Kamala says, noticing for the first time what her daughter has been doing. "There is no milk."

A Land O'Lakes quart emerges from behind the door and waggles.

"Dad picked it up last night." Shobita backs out of the fridge, hooks her foot around the door, and pulls it closed. From outside, we hear a car door slam. She puts down the milk and smooths her hair. "Can you finish? I've got to go."

"Yeah, yeah. Go, go." Kamala waves both hands at the door. "Don't keep Mr. Cole waiting."

"Bye, Bharati Aunty."

"Bye."

Shobita hoists a purse on her shoulder and checks that she has house keys before she leaves.

"She's getting a ride?" I ask.

"With her teacher, Mr. Cole." A near-smile on her face. I've seen it before when it was full-blown, when Rajesh got into Yale or Shobita made National Honor Society. In India, "teacher's pet" is a point of pride. Ritu had to explain it was an insult here.

Kamala continues, "This way I don't have to worry about some teenager driving her. I know she's safe."

"State finals. You've never missed a game before."

Kamala shakes her head and swallows. I get up and pour a little milk in the white mugs. Put them in the microwave. Beep-ing as I punch in the time and start it. It whirs. I remove a few *samosas* and plate them while I remember how Shobita hadn't reached for one.

Kamala, I am worried about her. A fifteen-year-old should cry when her brother decides he wants to leave this world and she has to pry her mother from bed. If she is not crying to you or me, then to whom? She will break, and she does not see it coming. I don't say it. Already, Kamala feels like she has failed her son, her family. Rajesh has given her enough to worry about.

Milk out of the microwave. Sugar by the teaspoon. White wading pools. When the dark tea meets the milk, it stands—a separate pillar on the white. Then it blossoms into brown. We sit, stirring our chai. *Clink, clink.* The conversation of our cups.

Shobita

The score is 0–0. Opposing team's number eleven goes down mid-strike as her cleats lose traction in the mud. Our goalie, Caitlyn, kneels down and scoops up the shot on goal. The crowd cheers, even though it was an easy save. Soccer is big in our school.

Number eleven comes up, blackened, muck clinging to her blond hair. We're all having trouble finding traction, and the rain won't stop. I peel the jersey off my stomach and try to shake out the water.

Caitlyn punts it downfield, and with another pass, it's mine. When I see it coming, the world slows and silences. This is it, the moment I love most about soccer—the buildup before the goal. I can feel Emily, our center, moving upfield. I slip the ball under my foot, feint to the right until my shadow, number four, falls for it. I dart left up the sideline. Emily's just in front of the box. Her favorite shot.

I pass. Score. Everybody's on their feet. Three whistles—the end of the game. We're overcome by students rushing the field.

Emma, a sophomore, rushes up to me and hugs me, jumping all the while. "We won, we won. You did it!" She's on the junior varsity team—glory by association.

I look for Cole, hoping he walked out to the field after parking and didn't just drop me off and go. I'm hoping he saw me.

Before I climbed out of his car, he touched my hand and said, "You'll do great."

Coach Silverman is shouting. "Line up. Line up."

Emma's still got me in a death grip. Jump, jump, jump. Maybe she can make the varsity cheerleading team. I want to shove her off and go. Too rude. She releases me and runs off, hunting down her next victim.

I'm the last one to the line. I lift my hand, high-fiving the opposing team—a mumble of voices, but we all know the script: "Good game, good game, good game." I pass number eleven. She's red-eyed and the mud is still thick in her hair.

"Good game." She chokes it out.

I'm off, keeping up with my team. Nothing but air under us as we circle back to the locker room and run off the field, the crowd of students parting for our team. I can't stop smiling.

I pass number eleven again. She's leaning against a teammate's shoulder and sobbing. I hear her say, "I'm sorry. I slipped. I had the chance, and I blew it."

And I'm grounded, like a helium balloon that's been popped. I slow to a walk. *I cannot shake my failure. It sticks to me and drags me under,* Rajesh wrote in his note. People are rushing past me, hooting and slapping my back. I want to go back, find number eleven, remind her that it's only a game.

"Only winners say winning isn't important," Rajesh would say whenever I beat him at anything—chess, basketball, whatever our competition-of-the-month was. He would sulk. I would tease him or try to console him. Finally, I learned to leave him alone. It was that or let him win. Maybe I should have let him win more often.

It's a quarter of a mile back to the gym. By the time I get there, the river of people has thinned and disappeared.

As soon as I step into the hallway, the sound of the girls in the locker room eddies around me. I push open the door, and Caitlyn scurries past me. Her towel slips off, and I get a full frontal. She laughs and picks up her towel, wrapping it around herself as she runs on wet feet to the second bank of lockers. After a victory, we get dressed as fast as if there were a fire.

I'm the last one to the showers. So late that I don't even have to wait for one. I reach in and twist the faucet to hot.

"What kept you?" Emily comes up and pounds on my shoulder, a goofy smile on her face. She is wearing her purple bra and matching underwear. Must be going out with Kenny tonight.

"Sorry," I say.

Her eyebrows wrinkle in concern. I try to smile.

"We won, you know," she says.

All around me, the girls are celebrating, cheering peppered with hoots and squeals. I finally get the smile on my face, which is a good enough cover for Emily.

"Party. Kenny's house." She hands me my sample-size bottle of two-in-one shampoo and my towel. It's a best-friend thing: whoever reaches the lockers first gets the other's stuff, too. "Hurry up."

Fully clothed, I step into the shower stall, close the plastic half-door, and bolt it. My uniform can't get any wetter, and I like my privacy. Not like Caitlyn. I strip off my clothes and hang them over the door.

I've barely gotten the shampoo pooled into my hand when Emily calls over the shower stall door. "You coming, Sho?"

"Go without me. I'll catch up."

"You sure? No problem to wait." She means it, but I know Kenny will drive her, and he has to get home before the party starts.

"Yeah."

She shouts in the direction of the door, "Wait up." She shoves her feet into shoes, running out of the locker room with untied laces.

When I'm done, I turn off the shower. Silence. *Drip, drip.* Hard to believe the locker room was thronging with girls two minutes before. *Drip, drip.* I hate public showers.

Is Rajesh in a similar shower? I can't imagine what a mental hospital looks like. I haven't been to see him. "It would be too hard on you," my parents said. Haven't they ever heard of Alfred

Hitchcock's theory that imagination is worse than reality? Of course not. Alfred who?

I wrap my towel around me, grab my two-in-one, and walk to my locker. Bottle down on the bench. Combination lock: 34 right, 22 left, 10 right. I pull on the lock, remove its curved finger, and open the door. I stare at my clothes.

When Mom visits Rajesh, she'll tell him we won—one more thing to make him feel inadequate. He got a 2380 on his SATs, and my father said, "Where's the other 20?" Not perfect. Good enough for Yale, but not for my dad.

I googled suicide: 67,200,000 entries in 0.14 seconds.

I didn't tell Emily. We are called "The Pair" by everyone. One nickname for both of us, we're so close. She would want me to blame my parents, which I can't do, although I'm not ready to defend them. But I find myself practicing.

It's not their fault. They can't be expected to know us, either my brother or me. They don't know who Dr. Seuss is. They don't know that we sneak off and defile all their beliefs, stuffing burgers into our mouths with our friends. The largest ocean on earth separates India and America.

I dry off, rubbing my skin slowly—slowly, as if we lost.

It hits me . . . "Go without me," I had told Emily. And my mom isn't waiting for me.

Great. Now I have no way home. I yank my dress over my head, thrust my feet into my sandals, and burst through the door. The gym is empty. I glance around and see that I was wrong: Cole is sitting on the top of the bleachers, one leg crossed over the other.

"I didn't know if you had a ride home," he says.

Keys hang from his slender fingers. He keeps his nails manicured. Sometimes I watch his hands, dusty with chalk, while he writes up equations.

"I am stuck," I say. "Thanks."

I wish I had gelled my hair—something. I probably look like a drowned rat.

I watch him coming down—step, leg stretching over the metal seat, step.

"I'll take you home."

I want to ask him to take me to Kenny's, but it's twenty minutes from our mutual neighborhood, and he has already waited for me.

The rain slams against the tin roof, making it hard to hear. We walk through the gym to an open door. I can't see through the rain, which is coming down even harder now.

"I'll get the car," he says. Gentleman.

"Let's make a run for it."

I sprint to his car, the only one left in the parking lot. The rain immediately soaks my dress, and I splash through the inch of rain that has turned the parking lot into a lake. The car door is unlocked. I throw it open and sit. I hear papers rustling underneath me. Pressing my feet to the floor, I lift my hips and pull the damp papers out from under me. It's not usual paper, but thin carbon copies, each a different color, bound at the top by a perforated strip. I skim the front page.

Dissolution of Marriage
Susan Cole,
petitioner
v. Case No. DM-10211 9-8924
Justin Cole,
respondent

I glance up. The windshield is streaming, and through it, I can see his shape jogging toward me. I flip to the last page and see two signatures. Next to his, I see today's date.

I hear the latch release as he opens the door. The papers are none of my business. He'll think I was snooping. I throw them in the back and hear them rustle into a foot well. He darts into the driver's scat. His blue eyes are shining like when he presented the Pythagorean theorem. His breath comes in warm clouds, and I want to put my hand in front of them.

His marriage has ended; his family is falling apart. We have more in common than just geometry.

I never liked math before. Once when I was struggling with

algebra, Rajesh leaned over me, showing me. He said, "Just wait till you get Cole. You're gonna love him. He's so cool." Cool enough that we all call him Cole, like it's his first name.

"Did you watch the game?" I ask.

"You were great. Good assist."

I try to think of something to say . . . *Given right triangle ABC, if b=c, prove <C = 45°*. No, not as a student. Friends . . . common interests. I can think of nothing.

"How's your brother?"

He doesn't know about the pills. "It's a family matter," my mother whispered to me. Translation: *Don't tell anyone. They might discover we're not perfect.* No one else has asked about him. My throat constricts, and I swallow down the tightness.

"He's failing calculus and physics. How important is *that*?" I say.

"To him, very. His scholarship depends on his grades. Besides, he has never failed at anything. I imagine he has little experience in disappointment. A lot of pressure in college," he says. After my parents, college is nothing. "How are your parents taking it?"

I want to tell him, tell him everything, but I know I shouldn't. My family, my problems. "His grades? What they don't know won't hurt them, right?"

I don't want to return home, back to that mess. I want Cole to put his foot on the accelerator and watch the needle swing high and then hover. Can a car really go 120 miles per hour? Emily told me that sometimes when Kenny is driving, she climbs out of the sunroof and sits on the car. "It's like flying," she said.

Rajesh did everything right, and I've followed behind, measuring my footprints beside his. I can't walk that path anymore. I know where it leads.

~~~~~~~~~

"Hey, hey, what is it?"

He puts his hand on my shoulder. I want to stay right here, with the warmth of his hand in mine, inside this dry car. But I know I'll have to go home and make tea and comfort my mother and sit silent with my father and run our household, but in this instant, I want to fly away.

I take his hand—smooth, white fingernails—and look at him. His breath comes fast, his chest rising and falling, rising and falling. His gaze focuses on my mouth, my lips. He leans toward me. When he kisses me, the world blurs. Is this what it should feel like? If this is what I wanted, then why do I taste panic and trouble?

I let him kiss me.

He pulls away and stares at me as I slink back, away from him. He doesn't look like a math teacher to me anymore. Tears prick my eyes. No one holds up when it matters.

"Maybe," he says, "I should get you home."

We drive in silence. The rain streaming down the window has mutilated the shapes of houses and trees. As we accelerate, they blur into an abstract painting of fall colors—orange, red, yellow, brown. Out of the corner of my eye, I see him wipe his palm on his jeans.

When we get to my house, he stops and reaches for me as I unhook my seatbelt and turn away.

"I wish I had an umbrella to offer you," he says, and I look at him again

"It's okay. I couldn't get much wetter."

He wipes his palms on his jeans again. "Shobita, I'm sorry if . . . my job is very important to me."

"I know." Let him worry.

"I'll see you tomorrow?" he asks, all his certainty gone. Flop, gasp. Maybe he should stick with geometry, with theorems, rules, and proofs.

"Monday," I correct him.

"Right, Monday."

I push the door open and get drenched a second time on the walk up to my house. I fumble with the key to our front door.

Cole hasn't driven away. I know he's watching me. I wave my key at him, and his motor revs as his car finally moves on.

Why won't my hands work right? I wrap one hand around the other to steady the wobbling key and shove it in the lock.

Turn, click, and push. I close the door and rest my back against it, my soaked dress sticking to my skin. Dripping on the tile floors. *Drip, drip.* I leave my *chappals* on the green mat and walk to the bathroom, knowing I'm leaving pools of water with each step.

"Shobita?" My dad's voice.

I freeze. "Just me."

He must be in his study. Usually I hate when he doesn't come out, doesn't ask me about my game, but not now. I can slink off without seeing myself through his eyes.

I close the door, grab a towel off a hook, and wrap up my hair.

I swallow, trying to get the panic and trouble out of my mouth. It doesn't work.

I pull out my toothbrush and squeeze blue toothpaste on it. While I brush, the minty taste seeps into my gums, cleansing me. When I'm done, I decide it's time for a new toothbrush. I throw mine in the wastebasket and watch it float on top of an ocean of used tissues.

Bharati Aunty

While Shobita was at her game, Kamala and I visited Rajesh in the hospital. I had expected to wait for Kamala as I did before, sitting in a deep leather chair, staring at calming photographs on the wall. But when Kamala was called, she looked at me and said, "Will you come with me?"

We walked down the bleached hall and into a small, private room. Rajesh sat on his bed, one leg up, the other dangling. He was clean-shaven, and I wondered why they let him use a razor. He stood when he saw me and gestured as if inviting me into his home.

While we were there, Kamala sat tall and put her hand on Rajesh's. She listened and gave news, smiling. She showed him the yellow sweater she was knitting him and occupied him with questions about the color, the neckline, the pattern. He wanted a turtleneck, he said, but this time, one that didn't cut off the circulation to his brain. She laughed, and the sound bounced off the walls in his little room until Rajesh laughed, too.

When we returned to the car, she slumped in her seat and deflated. She closed her eyes on the way home, but I could tell she was not asleep; her hands kept working.

Now that we are back, I walk with her to the bedroom to get her settled. Her white sheets are rumpled from her earlier rest. She sits on her bed and reaches for the collection of shells on the night table. She chooses the large conch shell, plucks at the spines, and slides her fingers over the rough exterior toward the smoothness where the shell curves in on itself.

"Do you need anything? Water?" I ask.

"Do you think it was all right to laugh?" she asks. "You're a good mother."

"The perfect thing to do. You're a good mother, too."

She puts the shell down, next to the other petrified objects: identical clamshells split open for display, slender angel wings, a curled nautilus—former homes, now empty of life.

She closes her eyes and lies down. "I'll just rest for a minute."

I walk to the door and glance back at her. Her eyes are squeezed shut, and a tear pops out and slides past her temple. It falls, untouched, into the curve of her ear.

I close the door and lean my forehead against it. An argument starts in my head:

Nothing gave Rajesh the right to dismantle his family—not distance, not pressure of college. Nothing. Doesn't he know that there is a thread from him to Kamala, him to Shobita? Even one to me. Doesn't he know that it's never just his life alone? It's never just one person, just one story.

But then, doesn't he have the right to end his own pain? His life, his choice.

I chide myself in the wake of my American thought. *Too long in this country.*

I straighten up. I turn and drift down the hall, dragging my finger along the textured wall. It bumps and dips under my skin.

I will go to my house and sit with my daughter. She will ask me how the family is, and I will try to answer, but my words will fail to capture the emptiness of this house. Her brows will crinkle with worry at our helplessness.

When she was little, it was easy to fix her problems. If she had a worry, I would let her splash in a tub, and when she was dry, I would sit her on the counter. As a treat, I would bring my bottle of coconut oil, pour the clear liquid in my palm, and finger-comb it through her wet curls. And that would be enough.

Ritu does not use that oil anymore. She doesn't like the smell. "Too Indian," she says.

I try to erase thoughts that are too American, while she refuses anything too Indian, and I don't know how to close the gap.

I curve my finger under a framed Rajasthani tapestry and slow down, then stop. I step back, staring at the colors: orange, green, and white.

A thread is loose, looping out away from the pattern.

Behind me, the bathroom door opens so suddenly that I jump. I turn, and Shobita is standing inches from me. I am ready to laugh with her, but she does not return my smile. Instead, her face is blank, her eyes unfocused. She stares at me for a moment before she forces a company smile.

If I were in India, I would assume that she had only child problems—a lost soccer game. If it was serious, she would go to her mother or another aunty, but she has not come to either of us. Here, we must be vigilant for signs.

"Excuse me," she says, her voice formal, which is not like her. We are too close for that.

I reach for her, catch her around the neck, and pull her gently. The muscles in her face stiffen, erasing expression. She relents for a moment, indulging me, before she pushes away.

"I'll get you all wet. Too rude." She brushes at a spot of water already spreading on my cotton shirt. "I'm sorry."

"Clothes dry. And there's no Hindi word for 'sorry,' at least not one you'd use with family."

At the word "family," her lips tighten in pain. I watch her struggle to turn the grimace into a smile. I put my fingers into her wet hair and comb it, and the barrier crumbles. She falls against me, but I don't lose my balance. I don't step back.

Opposite Land

Pete Hautman

I HAVE BEEN TO HELL and it's not what you think. There are no blazing fires, no pitchfork-wielding devils, no seething rivers fouled with regret.

Well, maybe the regret part, but not for my sins. I mean, I'm only fifteen—I haven't had time to commit any of the really heinous ones. At least they didn't seem so heinous while I was committing them. I haven't robbed any banks or gotten pregnant. Yet.

No, the hell I have experienced not once but every year for most of my life is the Annual Christ Our Savior Lutheran Church Lutefisk Supper.

The event is, as my mother likes to say over and over again, *Not Optional.*

"I want everybody to see our beautiful family, Astrid," she says.

"We are not beautiful." I inform her. "We're the Dork Family. Look at my hair."

"Well, it is a little green. You shouldn't have tried to dye it," she says, not even bothering to disagree with me. "You'll look cute in that cloche hat of your grandmother's."

"Mom, it's not 1920."

"Suit yourself," she says with a firm smile. "In any case, you are going. And no makeup."

I'm not the only one whining. Jack doesn't want to go either. He's thirteen and therefore intolerable, but on church suppers we agree. Adam, who is nine, doesn't want to go because Jack doesn't, but he lets Jack and I do most of the complaining. Dora and Kate are too young to know any better. I think Kate actually *likes* lutefisk. She's only five and has no discrimination whatsoever.

I don't think Dad cares one way or another. He just does what Mom says.

~~~~~~~~

Dorkily, we troop into the church building and hang our coats in a coatroom filled with puffy down parkas and wool over-coats in colors like beige, mushroom, and taupe. My purple leather jacket looks all wrong, but at least it'll be easy to find. I lag behind as the rest of the Dork Family heads for the stairs leading to the basement dining hall, lest I be put in charge of kid control. My mom looks back.

"Astrid? Are you coming?"

"Yeah, I just . . . I have to use the restroom."

"We'll see you downstairs, then. In five minutes. We'll save you a seat." She stares at me until I nod, smiling brightly.

Five minutes I can stretch out to ten. I head down the hall past the church offices to the lounge area. Three vinyl sofas are lined up facing the floor-to-ceiling windows that look out over Hampton Lake. I walk past the sofas and stand with my nose inches from the cold glass.

They call it a lake, but it's really just a marsh. In the summer it supplies mosquitoes to the surrounding neighborhoods. Now, in mid-December, it's a frozen, white, trackless expanse studded with cattails along the edges. I imagine standing in the exact middle of it surrounded by white blank space, clean and alone. I stare through the glass, bracing myself for the hellish hour to come.

I am interrupted in my reverie by the sound of throat clear-ing right behind me. Startled, I whirl around. It's a boy, sitting up on one of the sofas. He must have been lying there, and I'd walked right past him.

"Hello," he says. "Sorry." He isn't talking normal—it's like he has an accent.

"I didn't see you there," I say. He has dark brown hair all the same length, just long enough to cover the tops of his ears, and light blue eyes.

"I was having a lying down." Definitely an accent, it reminds me of how my grandfather used to talk. He points out the window. "I am looking at this lake."

"It's more of a marsh," I say.

"I don't know this word."

"It's like a shallow lake. My name's Astrid."

"Astrid." He says my name the way it's actually supposed to be pronounced: *AH-streed*, with the "d" so soft it almost disappears. I don't usually say it that way because it makes people misspell it, but it's nice to hear somebody say it right.

He stands. He is taller than me by several inches, and he has broad shoulders. He is wearing a University of Minnesota hoodie.

"I am Andreas." His teeth are brilliant. "Very please I am to meet you, Astrid. I am visiting here."

"From where?"

"Oslo."

"Oslo, Minnesota?"

"Oslo is in Norway."

"Oh." Now I feel stupid. "Are you going to school here?" I gesture at his U of M hoodie.

"This, it is a gift from my aunt and uncle who I am visiting." He looks over his shoulder, then turns back to me. "I like this hat you are wearing on your head," he says.

"Oh!" I reach up and put one hand on the felt cloche. I'm saved from the embarrassment of explaining why I'm wearing my late grandmother's hat by a booming voice.

"Andreas! We thought we'd lost you!"

It's Mr. Gunderson, followed closely by Mrs. Gunderson.

"Sorry. I was looking at the, ah, marsh," Andreas says.

"That's a *lake*, son. Hampton Lake!" Mr. Gunderson pats him on the back, letting him know it's okay to be mistaken.

Andreas looks at me, confused.

I say, "That's what it's called, but it's really just a marsh." I never did like the Gundersons. Ever since their daughter got married and moved away they've become oppressively active in the church, always sponsoring this and that, letting the rest of us know how inadequate we are.

"Lake, marsh, river, pond—it's all water under the bridge." Mr. Gunderson claps Andreas on the shoulder; Andreas doesn't like it, but he keeps smiling.

"Under the bridge?" he says. "What is this?"

"It's just an expression," I say.

"Andreas here is our nephew; he came all the way from Norway for the holidays. You're John and Kathy's girl, right? Aster?"

"*Astrid.*" Andreas and I speak as one, and this time we say it the same way.

"Astrid. That's right. Well, we've got two big weeks planned for this young man—we want him to meet the whole family. Tomorrow we'll be heading up to St. Cloud for a couple days so Andreas can meet his second cousins, two twin boys, turning five this year! Then over to Lindstrom so he can see the teapot water tower, and then back to the Cities for my Sons of Norway meeting." He claps Andreas on the shoulder again. "You'll get a kick out of those fellas, Andreas. Some of them came over after the war, the big one, WW Two. They'll have some tales to tell, you betcha! Ha-ha."

Mrs. Gunderson, a nervous woman who reminds me of a stretched-out chicken, touches the sleeve of Mr. Gunderson's plaid sport coat.

"We should head down to the supper, dear. I think they're about to say Grace."

"Uff da! Right you are. Come along, Andy. You don't mind if I call you Andy, do you?" Mr. Gunderson grips his nephew's elbow. As they head for the stairs, he keeps talking. "Say, I bet you'd like to visit the Swedish Institute while you're here. They're almost Norwegian, right? Maybe you could pick up some souvenirs."

Andreas looks over his shoulder with the universal expression that means *Save me!* in any language.

I wish I could save the both of us.

I wait a couple more minutes, looking out at the clean white marsh, lake, pond, whatever. My mom is probably getting testy, so I will my feet to carry me down into the bowels of the church basement. The nose-wrenching smell of lutefisk hits me at the top of the stairs and increases in intensity as I descend into Hell.

~~~~~~~~~~~~~

I missed Grace, which is fine with me. Pastor Emmer can stretch a simple *Thank You, Lord* out to eternity. I stop at the bottom of the stairs and take in the scene—the long tables, recessed fluorescent ceiling lights, metal folding chairs, an artificial, tinsel-festooned Christmas tree in the corner, and various other Christmas decorations taped or otherwise fastened to the walls, plus a "He Is Risen!" banner left over from last Easter. It looks like a school cafeteria all dressed up for the holidays.

At the far end of the room the buffet line is forming, but most of the people are simply milling around, smiling and chatting.

There are three varieties of Lutherans present: old people, parents, and little kids. Maybe a hundred people and nobody my age. Clearly, my peers have been more successful in wriggling out of the event and are no doubt off doing something fun or, at least, less *not*-fun. The air is thick with the smell of people and food; I can hardly breathe.

I sense my mother's eyes on me. They are sitting near the front—Jack scowling, Adam playing with his plastic utensils, Dora and Kate fighting, my dad gazing off into his happy place—waiting for me to complete the Dork Family. I pretend I haven't seen them. I know I'll have to join them soon, but I hate the idea of Andreas seeing me in Full Dork tableau. I look and find him surrounded by a flock of white-haired women. A real Norwegian! It's like they're cooing over a newborn baby.

I try to cross the room to get to him, but too many people know me. Mrs. Halvorsen wants to tell me how grown-up I look. Everybody likes my stupid hat. Jimmy Kelso, who I babysit sometimes, wants to show me his scars from falling off his bike. Mr. Jansen, a thousand years old at least, mistakes me for his granddaughter. I've almost reached the fringes of Andreas's fan club when my mother's steely grip clamps onto my arm and her all-too-familiar voice stabs at my eardrums.

"Where have you *been*?"

"I told you, I had to go to the bathroom." I jerk my arm away from her. It's a safe move because my mom would never make a scene in public, especially in church, but I know I'll pay for it later.

She gives me a pinch-faced look. "Daddy and Adam are already in line. Jack is watching Dora and Kate. We saved a seat for you."

"Oh. Thanks." I attempt to edge away from her but she grabs my arm again.

"Why don't you get in line and get plates for Dora and Kate," she says, making it clear that it is not a question.

"Okay," I say. "In just a minute." I pull away and turn my back to her before she can respond, and continue making my way toward Andreas. I can barely see him through the haze of fluffy old lady hair. I wade into the scrum, inserting myself between two elderly matrons wearing nearly identical beige dresses. Andreas grabs my hand and pulls me all the way in.

"Astrid, this is my great-aunt Gerd!" I look around at the six biddies with no idea which one he means.

Thinking quickly, I say, "Andreas, I'm supposed to tell you to get in line for the buffet."

"Oh, yes!" one of the women says. "We wouldn't want you to miss the food!" The others nod in agreement, and I'm able to separate him from the pack.

"Thank you," Andreas says, looking much relieved. "They were standing very close. I could not get my breathing."

"Yeah, they looked like they were about to absorb you."

"Up-sorp?"

"Absorb. Like suck you up."

"I see." He is looking around, still with that trapped-animal expression. "There is a . . . odor. Smell. What is this smell?" He simultaneously smiles with his mouth and frowns with his eyebrows.

I laugh, and he sort of winces as if he's made some horrific social error.

"No, it's fine," I say. "That's the lutefisk."

"Lute . . ." He scrunches his eyebrows together hard. ". . . fisk? Fish?"

I nod.

"I have heard of this thing," he says.

"I thought it was like the Norwegian national dish."

He shakes his head. "We do not eat this thing that smells like this at home."

'What do you eat?"

"Pizza. Hamburger. You know—food."

"Me too," I say.

"But sometime *min mor*—my mother—serve us *farikal*." He senses my incomprehension. "A sort of mix-up with sheep's meat."

"Oh. Like lamb stew?"

"Yes!" He nods. "But I prefer something good. I like the french fry."

"Well, you're not going to find that at Christ Our Savior." I risk a glance toward the Dork Family table. My mother is laser-beaming me with her eyes. I look back at Andreas and see Mr. Gunderson approaching from behind him.

"Bogie at six o'clock," I say.

"What is—"

He's interrupted by Mr. Gunderson's hands landing heavily on his shoulders.

"Better get in line, son! You don't want to miss out!" He steers Andreas toward the buffet line, keeping his hands on his shoulders.

With a quick, apologetic glance at my mother, I follow them and slip into line just ahead of Andreas. Mr. Gunderson, distracted by a friend who wants to show him pictures of his grandchildren, releases his grip on Andreas and moves off.

"I thought he would not ever let go," Andreas says. "Like he, how did you say it? *Upsorp* me."

"Yeah, he can be kind of overwhelming." As we shuffle forward, I scan the room and spot a table near the back where nobody else is sitting yet.

"Maybe we can sit together?" I say.

"If my uncle does not abduction me first."

"So how come you came over here all by yourself?"

He shrugs. "I have some troubles at home."

I like the sound of that. "What did you do?"

"Things I am not supposed to."

"Murder? Rape? Terrorism?" I grin to let him know I'm kidding, but he doesn't laugh.

"None of these things."

"Oh, well, that's okay then."

Mrs. Johanson, the mountainous queen of the Christ Our Savior kitchens, has planted herself behind the steam table. She has a spatula in one hand and a ladle in the other. When she sees Andreas, her face lights up.

"*Velkommen Norske!*" she brays.

"Thank you very much," Andreas says.

"Just a small piece for me," I say, holding out my plate.

Still smiling at Andreas, Mrs. Johanson plunks a random slab of fish on my plate and ladles about a cup of white sauce over it. For Andreas, she searches the serving tray for the largest piece and places it delicately on his plate. It must weigh half a pound.

"A taste of home for our cousin from the old country!" she says proudly.

Andreas manages a sickly smile as she slathers on the sauce.

"Enjoy!" she says.

We move on to collect boiled potatoes, peas, and a square of Jell-O salad from the other servers. Once we're through the line, I lead Andreas to the back table, still unoccupied. I do not look in the direction of the Dork Family, though I can feel my mother's eyes on my back. We sit down across from each other and contemplate our meals.

After a moment, Andreas speaks.

"I do not think this I can eat."

"I do not think this I can eat either," I say. I might be able to manage a few bites of the potato, but it is perilously close to the gelatinous lump of lutefisk.

"What is this thing?" He pokes at the cube of Jell-O salad with his fork.

"That's Jell-O salad."

"What is?"

"It's lime Jell-O with shredded carrots and, um, I think celery. That's mayonnaise on the top."

He gives me a look so overflowing with desperation and horror that I almost laugh.

I can hear my mother's voice in my head: *At least try some!*

I venture a nibble of potato. It is, thankfully, tasteless. Andreas does the same, from the side farthest from his enormous slab of lutefisk.

"So what did you do, really?" I ask. "I mean, to get sent here."

"Some things." He is embarrassed. "It is nothing." He looks around. "I do not like people so much."

"Oh."

"I like you," he says quickly. "But this"—he gestures at our surroundings—"this I do not like. I have the bad attitude."

"I get that." *Bad attitude* I have in abundance, or so I have been informed.

Andreas pokes doubtfully at his lutefisk.

"You have to at least try it," I say.

"You are not."

"I've had it before." I fork off a small piece of the gelatinous fish flesh and hold it near my lips. "It's not so bad if you ignore the smell, texture, and appearance."

He follows suit. We hold forkfuls of lutefisk before our mouths, daring each other with our eyes to eat it.

"This, it is not like real fish," he says.

"No kidding. They cure it with lye, dry it, then soak it in water for like a week to get the lye out."

"Why is this?"

"I have no idea. Then they boil it. You mean you really never had this in Norway?"

He shakes his head.

"Are you ready?"

He compresses his lips, then nods slightly.

We put the lutefisk in our mouths.

It is like I remember: a lump of fishy, stringy, unevenly congealed gelatin. I move it to the back of my mouth and swallow. Andreas is chewing his with an expression that is somewhere between curiosity and revulsion. For a moment I am sure he's going to spit it out, but he manages to swallow. He puts his fork down. His eyes are watering.

"I do not like this lutefisk." He looks past me. "My uncle is waving for me to go to him."

"Ignore him. He'll make you eat more lutefisk. That's what they do."

Andreas stares bleakly at the gigantic slab of fish on his plate. "I do not think I can."

"Me neither." The air in the basement is thick and too warm and filled with muzzy chatter and the dull clicking of plastic utensils, and I am suffocating. I push my chair back. "I have to go."

"You are leaving me?"

"No. Come on. I have an idea."

He stands and, with an apologetic wave in his uncle's direction, follows me to the stairs.

"Where do we go?" he asks.

"We need our jackets," I say.

He follows me upstairs to the coatroom. I find my thin purple leather jacket, then laugh when I see Andreas put on a puffy, blaze orange parka.

"What is funny?" he asks.

"We're opposites."

"Opposites?"

"Purple and orange."

"Oh." He laughs. "I get it."

~~~~~~~~~~

It's farther than I thought. I wish I had something on my feet besides my Reeboks. We have to walk down the hill behind the church through two feet of crusty snow. A couple of times Andreas has to grab me when I almost fall, but we make it down to the shore and crunch through the rim of broken cattails, and then we're on the ice. The snow there isn't as deep—it's been blown away by the wind.

"The ice, it is safe?" Andreas asks.

"Probably," I say. "It's been frozen over for a month." I fold the curled brim of my grandmother's hat down so it covers the tops of my ears. Andreas doesn't have a hat. His down parka has a hood, but he leaves it down. The cold doesn't seem to bother him.

We weave around the low drifts, sliding our feet along the ice beneath. In one spot the snow has been completely blown away; the ice is black, and when we look straight down we can see our reflection.

"Are there lutefisks in here?" Andreas asks.

I laugh. "No fish. Just turtles and frogs. And leeches."

We reach the center and turn to look back at the church, at the big windows overlooking the frozen marsh, at our two sets of tracks cutting across the whiteness. Above us is a great blue bowl of sky, flecked with wisps of cloud. We are only a short distance from the church, but it feels like a different planet, a different reality, clean and crisp and silent, as if we've stepped through a portal into Opposite Land.

"This I like," Andreas says. He tips his head back and inhales through his nose, then blows it out, making a cloud of his own.

I imagine how we must look from the church—two dots, one purple, one orange. Is anyone watching? I can't remember the last time I was so far away from anybody. Except I'm not alone; I'm with Andreas. And my feet are cold, and frigid air slips up under my thin leather jacket.

"I'm cold," I say, as I start to shiver.

He puts his arm around me.

We stand there, one dot in the middle of the white, and we breathe.

Chant for a Winter Dawn

Joyce Sidman

Let the frosted trees turn into clouds.
Look at them, glowing in the winter dawn:
they long to be weightless.
Let them step from their roots
and fly.

    And the clouds:
    let them become trees.
    All night, they have hovered low
    among the branches, icily clinging.
    They crave the shape of something.
    At dawn, let them stand,
    strong and straight,
    holding up the sky.

And me?
Let my thoughts turn to poems.
As I wait, feet planted in snow,
breath clouds rising,
let beauty speak to me
in words I can understand.

Lone Star

Shannon Gibney

KOLLIE WAS OVER IT.

He had officially had enough of the mindless name-calling, the pushing disguised as playful jostling in the lunch line, and the theft of his school supplies. Last week during soccer practice, one of his schoolmates had even had the gall to spit on him while they were lined up on the sideline, waiting for the signal from their coach to begin the play. Anger grew deep in his belly as Kollie remembered the shock of the slick wetness oozing onto the back of his neck, the snicker behind him as he gasped in disbelief. One of the black ones had grinned at him then, and it seemed as if he was daring Kollie to hit him in retaliation. It took all of his self-control to resist what he knew would result in yet another trip to Principal Schmidt's office and a call home to his weary mother.

He swore under his breath as he walked into geometry and found his place beside Abraham. The two of them had lived three houses down from each other since the sixth grade, and their mothers had signed them up for the same Bible study group at the church. That, and the fact that they were both Liberian, was the most they had in common, however, and some days Kollie wondered if he even liked Abraham.

"Good morning, Comrade," Abraham said, far too brightly. "You are exactly seven minutes late."

Kollie took out his phone. "Six. I had to urinate." He threw his book on the table and then slouched down in his chair.

At the front of the room, Mrs. Walker turned around from the blackboard, startled by the loud noise. Kollie knew that she wouldn't do anything, though, because she was scared of him. She smiled at him nervously and waved. Kollie nodded at her absently, then pulled his ball cap down over his eyes, how he liked it. She faced the blackboard again and continued writing some theorem that was basically illegible to him. He didn't know why he even bothered with this class. Who would ever need to know anything about the circumference of circles, anyway? His daddy told him he was buying a basement club in Crystal for him, where he and his friends could spin the latest tracks for their friends and relatives and make plenty of cash. It would only be a little while longer until the deal was done, and then maybe he could focus on making his dream a reality and forget all this school nonsense.

"Sonja says she is finished with Clark now," said Abraham, his pencil diligently moving across the paper, taking down the notes on the lesson.

Kollie pretended not to care, but his palms began to get sweaty. "Really?" he asked, as evenly as possible. Sonja was the flyest girl in school. She dated both black and African guys, which was pretty rare for a black girl. Kollie had heard that her father was Kenyan. There was something about her—maybe the way she smelled like clean soap, or the way her medium-sized, perky breasts peeked out of her T-shirts, or maybe even her hearty laugh—but Kollie had a huge crush on her. He had been trying to get up the nerve to talk to her all year, but she always seemed to be surrounded by so many people.

"Yes," said Abraham. "You should get with her."

Kollie laughed. "Just like that?"

Abraham looked at him sideways. "Just like that, Comrade. Why not?"

Kollie thought about it for a moment. *Why not?* He grimaced. For starters, Clark, her now ex-boyfriend, had just beat the crap out of Hassan Mohammed, the biggest, baddest African dude in school. At third-period lunch, Clark had pushed Hassan to the ground in front of all their friends, yelling: *Why y'all jungle animals here, anyway? Minnesota's too cold for y'all. Can't run around here butt naked, like, Owwwwoooo!* (Accompanied by monkey-like gestures and noises.) Hassan tried to get back up, to fight back. But Clark knocked him down again. This time with a punch, followed by another punch.

Jake Evans, the white star of the football team, was clapping and laughing with his crew, like they were watching the Superbowl or something. And all the teachers and lunch monitors were just pretending that nothing was going on, like usual. But Hassan and his Somali crew had had enough, and lunged at Clark and his boys. After that, it was sheer pandemonium, with food, punches, and sweat flying everywhere. The principal had to call in the police department to get everything calmed down again, and Clark and Hassan were threatened with arrest. In the end, they were just issued warnings, but the incident was why the school was still on lockdown. No, Clark was one black dude a skinny Liberian guy did not want to mess with.

"Let me think about it," Kollie said, as casually as he could muster.

Abraham laughed. "Think all you want. Just don't be surprised if someone else gets her while you are doing all that thinking."

~~~~~~~~~~

Kollie was tired.

"We're now beginning our unit on the Great Migration north," said Mrs. Jackson, in his next class, American history. Mrs. Jackson was the only black teacher in the whole school, and as a result, her classes tended to be filled with black and African students. The white kids had plenty of other choices.

Beside him, Tetee groaned. "What the hell," he said to their entire table. "Again?"

Kollie laughed openly.

Mrs. Jackson whipped around and eyed him. "Is there a problem, Mr. Flomo? Something you want to share with the class?" Her tone was icy, her arms crossed.

Kollie sat up in his seat, a bit chagrined despite himself. Although he considered himself an American, he had spent his first nine years in Liberia and had therefore had it drilled into his very marrow that teachers were not to be disrespected—at least, outwardly. That reverence that was his de facto stance toward them was a liability in this new context, in which it was clear to all of them that American teachers were out to destroy them rather than raise them up. It was far easier to just ignore them, like they did Mrs. Walker, and pretend that they were not even there. But Mrs. Jackson had a hardness in her, like so many black women, and wouldn't allow that.

"No, Ma'am," he said softly.

"Good," Mrs. Jackson said. "Just let me know if you do have something to add. I value your considerable critical faculties, Mr. Flomo, when you choose to apply them appropriately."

Kollie blushed, hoping fervently that none of his boys saw. Mrs. Jackson was undoubtedly referring to his reading logs on *The Warmth of Other Suns*, which she had given very high marks.

Mrs. Jackson finally broke from his glance and addressed the entire class. "Now then, let's begin, people. I want to start with what might sound like an obvious question to guide our discussion: Why would anyone ever want to leave their home?"

Because they have to, Kollie said in his mind, before he could stop himself. *Because there is no food, no work, no school, and they have no choice. Or because war was imminent, and there are soldiers who would kill for a cassava leaf.* He and his family had been stranded in a refugee camp just outside of Accra for three years as the second civil war was finally ending, waiting for whatever papers the people in charge said were needed in order to come to the West. If he tried hard enough, he could still see a dusty orange road in his memory, the compound in the village in Lofa County where he was born and lived the first five years of his life. The goats who lay lazily in the road and would not get up, the mist that covered the tips of Mount Wuteve at dawn. But they were all a patchwork of faded images now; there was no narrative to hold them together and give them meaning.

"War," a white kid said from the front of the room.

"People leave their homes when they're being treated like second-class citizens," said a black girl from the front of the room.

"Because the white man is a crafty devil and drives them to it," said Henry, the black kid in the middle of the room. Henry was Clark's best friend and a point guard on the basketball team. His father was the assistant principal of the school, and some people said he got special treatment because of it.

An audible cackle passed through the room, as the black kids reacted to his comment.

"That's racist," said the same white kid at the front of the room. "And stupid."

"Is that right?" Henry said, and began to stand up. "You got anything else you wanna say, you ignorant—"

"Enough!" Mrs. Jackson exclaimed. She walked over to Henry. "Sit down."

Henry looked back up at the white kid in the front of the room, who was cowering in his seat. You could tell Henry was seriously contemplating what it would feel like to pummel his pale flesh.

"Sit. Down," Mrs. Jackson said again, this time getting up in his face.

Tetee looked from Kollie to Abraham, his eyebrows raised. Things at Brooklyn Center High School had never seemed calm, but lately it was like everything—all the old animosity between the white kids and the black kids, all the hostility between the black kids and the African kids—was rising to the surface. And it looked like there were only a few adults in the building, Mrs. Jackson being one of them, who actually wanted to deal with it.

Mrs. Jackson gestured back at Henry's chair, demanding that he take it, and he finally did, grudgingly. Then she slowly walked back to the front of the room.

"We talk about these things because we have to," she said, "not because we want to."

Kollie sucked his teeth. How many things a day did he and his friends *have* to do, anyway? Was this the best way to spend the precious few years of youth?

"You all think you hate each other precisely because we *don't* talk about this stuff." She sighed. "You don't realize it yet, but that is the real tragedy. Not a name somebody got called."

It was strange, almost like she had forgotten that they were there and was talking to herself rather than the class. The atmosphere in the room was still electric though, and everyone was awake and leaning forward in their seats, waiting for the next explosion.

Mrs. Jackson shook her head, as if waking herself up. "But

we will have these discussions in my class, and when we do, we will conduct them respectfully." She looked meaningfully at Henry, who was still defiant, and then at the white kid, who was still cringing. "Understood?"

They both nodded. Henry rolled his eyes.

"Good," she said, her voice returning to its normal, conversational tone. "Now then. Back to the topic of leaving home. During the Great Migration African Americans did so at a rate and number so high that it changed the entire face of the country. To them, the often violent system of racial separation throughout the South known as Jim Crow was something no one should suffer through if they had a choice, so they made the decision to leave for what they hoped would be better, more welcoming communities up north. Unfortunately, that wasn't always or even generally the case."

Kollie let her voice become background noise, as he worked out the beats to a new track he was working on. He closed his eyes and wondered what it would feel like to have his own music blasting through the speakers of his own club, while he and Sonja danced, their bodies pressed against one another.

~~~~~~~~~

"I heard you flunked chemistry. Again."

No matter how high he turned up his music, it was never enough to drown out his little sister, Angel.

She leaned into him, picked up one of his headphones, and whispered in his ear. "Mom said this was your last chance, and you messed it up. So that's it—you're going back to Liberia."

Kollie snickered and turned up the Kanye.

This was the threat that was always lobbied against Liberian and Somali boys in Minnesota by their parents: *Shape up, or we will send you home. And there, they don't love their children too much to teach them respect. There, you will learn the value of everything you just junk away here.* His mother, who worked nights as an LPN at Abbott Northwestern Hospital and was finishing up her coursework to be an RN at St. Mary's during the day, often told him the very same thing, late at night, when she stumbled in after her shift to find him playing Minefield on her iPad, throwing another suspension warning letter at his feet. But he knew she would never actually do it. He was her only son, and she had hid him, fed him, and taught him throughout the war and its aftermath. All her hopes were with him.

Angel put a hand on her hip and wagged her finger at him. "Hear me? You're gonna be on a plane to sad little Africa this summer."

Kollie sneered but decided not to give her the satisfaction of acknowledgment. She wasn't worth his time.

"Okay, whatever," she said, and turned around. "Don't know why I bother anyway."

Kollie didn't know why, either. He had no idea who she cavorted around with or what she did in school, and he didn't want to. He knew she was an academic superstar because she dangled it in his face every chance she got. The brilliant younger daughter who everyone liked, and the delinquent older son who just wouldn't try. That had been their identity and relationship to each other as long as he could remember. He didn't hate her; he just found her irrelevant.

Angel threw herself down on the couch and began to scribble something on a piece of paper. She was two years younger, in the ninth grade, but sometimes it really felt like two decades. Everything was just easier for her, and he didn't know why. Maybe it was because she was a girl. Or maybe because she had left Liberia before it had begun to mean something to her.

She shoved the paper in his face. DAD CANNOT SAVE YOU FROM EVERYTHING. ESPECIALLY YOURSELF, was scrawled across it.

He turned off his music, finally, and then slowly, deliberately, began to rip the paper into long shreds. The way that their father doted on him, and ignored her, had always been a sore spot with Angel.

Right hand on her hip again, she stuck out her tongue and then ran from the room.

~~~~~~~~~~~

The prayer room was also a problem.

It was a makeshift space, set up on the second floor beside the new atrium. Principal Schmidt had brought in movable walls to be placed around a small set of prayer rugs at the request of Somali students so that they could complete their *salat*, or five ritual prayers, during the school day. And the prayer room did have a steady stream of Somali students leaving and entering it throughout the day, proving its value. Unfortunately, it also blocked a small part of the beautiful new set of windows that had recently been constructed in the atrium—something that irritated some longtime Brooklyn Center High School parents, as well as some members of the school board. Some students and parents were also concerned that Muslim students were being given "special treatment," as "Christian students have not been given their own place of worship." (Principal Schmidt's response to this had been that no Christian students had requested specific prayer rooms, unlike Muslim students, but that if and when they did, he would seriously consider it.) This did not stop them and their (mostly white) children from grumbling about it from time to time, but they knew when it was best to back down, and in this case it was before parents of the Somali kids made contact with the ACLU.

The real tension was with the blacks, though. They had previously used the space now occupied by the prayer room as an informal lounge. Students would come between and after classes to gossip, share news, freestyle, and even rehearse dance moves. "It was *our* place. Our one space where we could just chill and be us in this whole raggedy school," the Black Student Union leadership had told Principal Schmidt. "So, of course, you had to take it away from us." Some of them would still loiter around the prayer room, presumably out of habit or to antagonize, trading the dozens, laughing loudly, or even talking about how the space was really theirs. The Somali students mostly tried to ignore them, although lately nerves had been frayed on both sides.

"I don't know why they think this is some MLK Day march,"

Kollie's friend Haji said, as he walked to the prayer room for his midday prayers. "What they need to do is clear out and get over it. Allah got no time for such lazy men-o. No wonder they can't graduate, and white man got no job for them." Kollie and Tetee cracked up and patted Haji on the back. Although he was Liberian, he was also Muslim and so had found a way to float between the Somalis and Liberians.

Haji saluted good-bye to his friends and then entered the prayer room. He smiled easily at the black guys in front of him and nodded to them. They did not respond, except to grimace. Kollie watched, his stomach beginning to churn, as they crossed their arms and blocked Haji's way. Their faces were covered in disgust, and when they pushed Haji, he couldn't say he was surprised. Kollie felt a scalding fury bubble up, and before he knew it, he was rushing toward them, ready to knock them down. It was Abraham, who came out of nowhere, who saved him. Abraham who caught the fist Kollie sent toward the jaw of the bigger black guy before it hit him, grabbed his shoulders, and held him back. *It's not worth it*, he said in his ear. *They're not worth our futures.* Kollie could not stop himself from lunging at them again, but this time, Haji lodged his small frame between them.

"Listen," he shouted. Then in a normal voice: "Listen to your brother, Kollie. Don't let this be the thing that ruins your life in America."

The black guys were pushing back on his friends, ready to fight him.

Kollie would still have grabbed for them, but Abraham, Tetee, and Haji were holding him back.

"Don't think this is over!" he yelled at the black dudes, as his friends pushed him down the hall.

"We're counting on it, jungle monkey," the bigger guy threw back at him. "Best watch your back."

And then he was around the corner, out of their sight line. "Get off me, man," Kollie told his friends and shrugged off their hands.

Tetee held up his palms. "Easy. Easy, Comrade."

Kollie scowled. Then he put his hands on his head and kicked the nearest wall. The yell he emitted at the same time could be heard all the way down the hall.

~~~~~~~~~~~~~

At dinner that night, Kollie picked at his fish and rice. His mother sat across from him at their modest kitchen table, almost inhaling the food she had cooked the weekend before. After working a double shift at the hospital, she had stopped at St. Mary's to complete her biochemistry exam. She was only three classes and a board exam away from achieving her RN degree. His mother eyed him wearily. "How was school today?"

Kollie sighed. He wished she knew how much he wanted to be the son she could be proud of, not the one she had to worry about constantly after making herself sick through too much work. He wished he could tell her something good. "Fine," he said softly.

The garish topaz clock his parents had purchased in the Dollar Store ticked in the silence between them, but did not fill it. Angel was at a yearbook meeting, and his father was working late (they all knew he was at his girlfriend's place, but "working late" was what they always said), so it was just the two of them.

His mother glanced at his barely touched dinner. "You want something else? Or are you just not hungry?"

When he had first come, all he had ever wanted to eat was soup and rice just like every other Liberian he knew, but in the past few years his palate had become decidedly more American, and he preferred a well-done hamburger and fries to a bowl of *torgubee* any night. But that wasn't why he wasn't eating now. He had actually lost his appetite. "I'm fine," he said.

If his mother didn't buy it, she didn't let on. She shrugged her shoulders and scooped up the last few bites on her plate. "A boy need to eat-o." Her blue hospital scrubs clung too tightly to her stomach, which was becoming thicker more and more rapidly it seemed to him. In Africa, fatness was seen as a sign of prosperity and even status, but here you were thought to be lazy or even a bad person if you were big. He knew she ate because she was sad and also because she was lonely. A devout Baptist, she allowed herself only this one vice.

"I ate at school," he said. Then he stood up and grabbed his plate. The dishes from the last few days were stacked in the kitchen sink, almost overflowing onto the counter. If he couldn't be the son she needed, then the least he could do was the dishes. He began to run the water, then grabbed the scrubber. His father would have laughed at him for doing women's work if he were here. But he was not here.

"Ah, I almost forgot!" his mother exclaimed suddenly. She sat up in her seat and raised her right index finger, punctuating the important words for emphasis. "Your teacher Mrs. Jackson called me this afternoon."

Kollie felt his arm stiffen. The dishwashing soap he was squirting onto the scrubber landed on the side of the sink instead. "She . . ." He swallowed. "She called you?"

"Yes," she said brightly. "The two of us had a nice, long conversation, all about you."

He tapped his toe on the tiles. This was not going the way that most talks about school did—she seemed genuinely excited about something. "Really?" he asked, cautiously.

"Yes, really," she said, laughing. "Don't look so surprised, Kollie. I always knew you were capable of reaching your potential. It was just a matter of you having the right instruction and the right environment."

Now he was absolutely perplexed. What on earth was she talking about?

She stood up, pushed in her chair, and brought her plate to him. "She said she wanted to tell me herself about a beautiful essay you wrote about Bigazi and the people who lived there before and during the wars. She said it was one of the best in the class and that she is going to ask you to read it at the Black History Month assembly later this month. She said that when you described the children in church, the planting and harvesting of groundnuts and cassava leaves, the beauty of the rivers, the quiet at dusk, and the aimless bullets that tore through compounds in the dead of night, it almost brought her to tears." She was standing so close to him now. She took his hand. "I know I don't know how hard it has really been for you here, to adjust to the new culture. They say that America is the land of opportunity, and I suppose that it is. If you want to better yourself, they will give you the opportunity to do so. But if you want to destroy yourself, they will give you that opportunity, too."

The energy she was emitting from her eyes was too strong for him. He looked at the floor.

"And I know as a black boy, they will convince you that it is in your best interest to destroy yourself." She sighed. "I don't know why the whole world over, the worst thing to be is a black boy, but that is how it is. Especially in this country."

He wanted to leave badly then. That feeling he had had earlier in the day, of a scream eating his gut from inside out, was bubbling in his belly again, and he didn't know how much longer he could control it.

She brought his chin up, so he had no choice but to meet her eyes. "I am just so glad you are now making the choice to better yourself," she said quietly. "Your father and I, the whole family, really, we have always had such high hopes for you. Angel is smart, and she works so hard . . . but she doesn't *feel* like you do. You feel everything, which is why it is hard for you, I know. But it is also why you are meant for great things. And it makes me happy that you have not forgotten home. You are our black diamond, Kollie. And you are just beginning to shine."

She was crying now. He swallowed the lump in his throat and wrapped his arms around his mother. How he wished he could tell her about everything at school, the teasing, the bullying, but he wanted her to be proud of him more. Let her have one thing in her life, for a moment at least, that made her happy.

"I love you, Ma," he said, as he rubbed her back.

~~~~~~~~~

Kollie threw the first punch.

Midway through the Black History Month celebration, while he was seated on the stage, waiting his turn at the mic to read the essay Mrs. Jackson had loved so much, he saw Clark push Sonja off the fourth row of the bleachers. She landed with an unceremonious thud and screamed, interrupting Principal Schmidt's long monotone speech on the courage Black Americans had exhibited throughout history.

"What the hell is *wrong* with you niggas?" Sonja's best friend, Aisha, yelled, leaping down two aisles of the bleachers to help her friend. Aisha was Tanzanian, although she had lived in America since grade school.

"Shut up, you stupid jungle animal," Henry told her.

Sonja was moaning on the gym floor, holding her right thigh in pain. Several teachers were looking on in confusion, fear barely masking their features.

Before he could consciously think about it, Kollie was off the stage, on the ground, and running toward Sonja. When he got to her, he saw that her face was stained with tears and that her left shoe had fallen off.

"I'm okay," she said to him as he leaned into her. "I'm okay." She was wearing a spotless white cropped shirt and tight blue jeans, and she smelled of flowers.

"Are you sure?" he asked.

"Yes." She nodded. "I just . . . need some help getting up, that's all."

It was the longest private exchange they had ever had.

He nodded and held out his hand. She smiled at him and was moving her hand to meet his when Clark shouted, "Leave her alone, you freak."

Kollie flinched and then grasped Sonja's hand.

"I said leave her alone! Or I will beat you and your skinny ass all the way back to—"

Kollie dropped Sonja's hand, stood up, and lunged at Clark with all his might. He remembered the spit on his neck, the names that were hurled at him daily, his stolen school supplies, the attempted attack on Haji, and so many more indignities he had suffered through daily from these animals, and he found that his fist was endowed with a kind of terrible force that stunned everyone around him. He began to pummel Clark, who staggered backward after the first few punches, then Henry, who jumped in to try to defend his friend, then three other members of their crew. When Hassan Mohammed and his crew saw what was going on, they jumped in and started hitting on pretty much any other black kid who had said or done anything to them—boy or girl—and pretty soon, the entire gym was in a state of chaos. They had to take Clark away on a stretcher after what Kollie did to him, and three other students were hospitalized. Kollie was suspended for the rest of the term, effective immediately. He didn't think he would ever forget the sad, slow shake of Sonja's head as she watched a police officer lead him away.

<hr>

As he stepped off the plane and onto the jetway, a burst of warm air hit him and stopped him. He blinked in confusion, remembering where he was, while at the same time trying to forget again.

Monrovia. Liberia. It was the middle of the rainy season, and everywhere it smelled of red clay, earthy and rich. The other passengers on his flight were queuing up, preparing for entry with their passports, but he found that he was stuck, could not get his legs to move. There, up above him at the top of the last building in the airport complex, waved the flag of what he supposed was his country now, as before. It was just like the American flag, with red and white stripes bound across it, left to right. Except that in the corner, there was only one star, almost engulfed in a square of blue. It seemed so singular to him as he stared at it in that long moment. Some would call it pronounced, prideful even, but he would not describe it that way. What he would say was that the sole star of the Liberian flag was so alone that it didn't even know it had come from fifty other stars on another flag. And that this was a measure of just how lost it really was.

The Ocean Where the Dreams Go
Trần Thị Minh Phước / Phuoc Thi Minh Tran

The Ocean

In my teenage years, I loved spending countless hours on the beach, letting my dreams go wild. The ocean was always so peaceful, beautiful, and relaxing. I was often mesmerized by the small, calm waves moving rhythmically in and out, in and out, lapping against the shore. The whirling winds that chased the busy hermit crabs as they burrowed in the deep sand made me laugh. The happy seagulls riding on the high tides moving up and down amused me. The big and round jellyfishes being washed to the shore reminded me of my auntie's delicious, crunchy, refreshing jellyfish salad, tossed with basil, mint, roasted peanuts, and her culinary secret ingredients.

It has been more than ten years since I left the refugee camp and resettled in Minnesota. Things happened and things changed. I finished school, worked as an educator, met my husband, and got married. Our children all have the middle name Duong, which means "blue," to remind us of the ocean. The same blue ocean on which we each spent hours and hours, days and days—hopeless, thirsty, and hungry—in a crowded boat. The same blue ocean we saw as we each flew on a plane to America, leaving our family, friends, and everything we knew behind. We saw the same blue water in Lake Superior when we traveled there the very first time.

The deep blue water, the happy seagulls, the fresh breeze, the rocky beach, and the singing waves keep my family coming back to visit Duluth every summer. My boys love to slap the water with sticks they find along the shore, and my girls feed the hungry seagulls and chase after them. My husband enjoys taking tons of photos, and I am captivated by the beauty of nature. As years have passed, Lake Superior has become my ocean, its slow waves reminding me of the ocean of my childhood.

When I was young, I was fond of the ocean, the beach, the morning breeze, the softly moving palm trees, and long walks across the wet sand. My favorite things to do at dawn were to chase the seagulls and to run as fast as I could back to the beach before the waves crashed into the shore.

Sometimes, far away on the horizon, I would spot a funnel stretching from the bottom of a cloud to the ocean. Rather than being scared of it, I was fascinated by the natural forces of Mother Nature's masterpiece. It looked like a powerful dragon fiercely flying high in the sky, swooping down occasionally to drink water from the ocean through the waterspouts along the coast before heading straight back to the dark sky.

The ocean was always my comfort zone. She was my dearest friend, gentle and charming. The beach was my dreaming place. I truly appreciated all the gifts that nature gave freely to us. I dreamed of visiting the sea kingdom one day and collecting all the jewels and rare corals. Most of all, I dreamed of getting a better education and becoming a marine biologist someday. I wanted to study all the animals, plants, and corals in the ocean and other deep-sea creatures as well.

Unfortunately, my dreams were interrupted after the Fall of Saigon on April 30, 1975. My school was closed. I stopped going to the beach, and I longed to return someday to let my dreams go wild again. I held on to my memories and happiness as long as I could.

An Unforgettable Journey to Freedom

It was early morning on August 19, 1978. The rain was falling hard, and the horrible winds were howling. My family had decided to escape from Vietnam by boat like other people who had risked their lives in search of freedom and a better life. I didn't know if my family still remembered that my eighteenth birthday was coming soon, just two weeks away. "It will be fine.

There are more important things for us to remember now," I told myself. Per the instructions, we were all divided into small groups and told we would meet later in an undisclosed location before catching the big fishing boat.

I will never forget that fateful day. We pretended to not know each other. Everyone was quiet, except my little brother. "Where are Daddy, Lan, and Cúc?" whispered Trúc.

"I don't know; be quiet please," I replied back, "but for sure they are with other groups, not far behind us." Trúc nodded his head repeatedly as he glanced back at my mother. He was afraid of getting lost.

The sun went down fast, and not much later total darkness surrounded us. Everyone was anxious and waited to be called by the boat captain. For some reason, we were divided again into groups of two before heading to the small river. I was paired with a little girl about thirteen years old named Hoa. "It will be okay," Mom softly assured me while squeezing my cold hands. "We'll all meet at the big boat."

We finally got into the small wooden sampan. It was still raining cats and dogs, and the thunder rumbled from the sky louder and louder. In the murky light and from such a distance, I couldn't see what was happening ahead on the water except for intermittent gunshots and loud voices. I was so scared. Suddenly Hoa started crying, but quickly she covered her mouth with both hands. "Thank God!" I mumbled.

The small rickety sampan finally brought us to the big boat. There were about thirty people already there, mostly men. Both Hoa and I looked around in the dark and couldn't find our families. More little sampans arrived, and still there were no signs of my loved ones. The waiting time was so terrifying. We heard more gunshots. The captain started counting people on the boat and then said anxiously to himself, "Where are the other fourteen people? Why is it taking them so long?"

Thirty minutes passed, and again there were gunshots. Suddenly the boat captain decided to depart and leave the other passengers behind. I was hoping that he would change his mind. I prayed and prayed. It looked like Hoa was going to say something to me, but I couldn't hear a word. I was crying hard knowing that the rest of my family was left behind with the other unfortunate passengers.

In the Stormy Ocean

After leaving, we struggled for days and nights in the stormy ocean. Again and again we were sucked down. Water rushed in, and our fragile boat was flooded. Just like a roller coaster, the high angry waves pushed us up higher and higher at mighty speeds before we were dragged down again into the deep dark ocean. We shouted for help, and we knew that we were not going to make it to the land of freedom. I held Hoa as hard as I could and knew definitely that only God could save our boat, give us some strength, and tame the angry ocean. We wanted to see our families and our friends, and we didn't want to be taken under by the deadly waves.

I didn't have the energy or the strength to think of my family, even though I was very worried about them. Most of my time was spent trying to survive the cruel ocean that once was my dearest friend. I felt betrayed and abandoned. She didn't help us. Instead our little boat was tossed up and down and around and around by her angry waves. The thundering sounds of torrential rains rushed toward our boat. We screamed as the raging waves dumped on us.

Eventually the rains subsided and stopped attacking us. I could see the ripples on the water surface when the breeze blew. Suddenly, I noticed oily bubbles emerging from the bottom of the sea. There were pots and pans, broken suitcases, a conical hat, and clothing floating everywhere. I realized that we had just passed a recently wrecked boat, and I prayed for those unfortunate families who had lost their lives in search of freedom.

I felt my pain, my agony, and my fear. I believed that God had protected and shielded us from the deadly high waves and the dark ocean. We were so blessed and very lucky. We had survived an unforgettable sea crossing.

In the Refugee Camp

After ten nights and nine days in the stormy ocean, the high waves had carried us to a long coast in the middle of nowhere. Luckily, we were rescued by some warmhearted fishermen. We were too weak to walk, suffering from starvation, dehydration, seasickness, and other illnesses. Later we learned that we had landed on the eastern shore of Malaysia in the South China Sea. After preliminary paperwork and interviews, we were transported to an island to join other survivors who had been the first to come in the mid-1970s. They called us "boat people" because we fled our country by boat.

I was really frightened on the first night in the refugee camp. I was so scared of the big, ugly black rats scurrying everywhere in the long house, along the fence, inside the instant noodle bag, or underneath the cupboard.

Three days after arriving at the camp, I celebrated my first birthday away from home, my first without my family, relatives, and friends. I was devastated and felt empty. I cried a lot on my birthday, which I had never done before.

I decided to go to the beach. Sitting there, I saw a small island in the far distance and thought to myself that on the other side of the sea, Mom, Dad, Lan, Cúc, and Trúc would be anxious to learn about my whereabouts. It was amusing to see thousands of hermit crabs crawling on the beach, then quickly disappear into sandy holes as soon as they detected my footsteps.

I found an empty fish can washed up on the shore. That sparked an idea in my head. I mixed the brown sand with seawater and the fish can turned out to be a great mold to make a nice round cake shape. I gathered some colorful broken seashells and decorated my eighteenth birthday cake. I added some green seaweed for a final touch. My eyes filled with tears as I thought of the family that I had left behind. I closed my eyes and prayed. I could hear the crashing of the waves, the cawing of seagulls, and the blowing of strong winds. I opened my eyes, and my special cake was gone. It had washed away into the ocean. Filled with sadness, I went back to the camp.

"Big Sis Mai, where are you going? I have been looking for you everywhere since morning!" Hoa shouted at the top of her lungs. Far away, I could see her running toward me as quick as lightning. "It's my birthday; I wanted . . ." Before I could continue my story, Hoa rushed to the rocky shore and ran back. She pressed a wet blue rock on my hand and said eagerly, "Make a wish and toss it into the ocean." I silently made a wish, and then, to her surprise, I slipped the special gift in my pocket."

Friendship

Four months after leaving Vietnam, I finally received news from my family. They were now home after being arrested and put in jail for two months. I had adjusted to the life in the camp and made new friends. I was volunteering at the hospital and working as an interpreter at the New Arrival Center.

At the refugee camp, there were many places where people could meet, talk, play, and watch the waves slamming their way to the shore before they were ripped back out to the ocean. However, I was the only one of the refugees who ever woke up early to go to the beach and contemplate nature. I had been watching the sunrise by myself for the past three months.

It was this morning routine that grounded me while at the camp. I was looking for the solitude and the serenity of nature that had brought me such joy in the past. One morning as I was approaching the sandy beach, I discovered that I wasn't the only visitor. I wasn't happy. I saw someone leaning against the big rocks and facing the ocean. Someone had stolen my favorite spot. I was angry because after my sea voyage it had taken me a while to regain the same comfort with the ocean.

Closer to the beach, I could clearly spot the thin and willowy girl with long black hair in white pants and a blue blouse. She was about thirteen years old. Her eyes were closed, and her tiny hands were in praying position. She must have been dreaming or praying because she seemed not to notice my presence.

She opened her eyes when she heard my footsteps dragging through the wet sand. I passed by her and slowed down. She made a small sigh. Something about her seemed vaguely familiar. Looking straight into her sad eyes, I recognized her. "Are you Tú? Do you remember me?" I asked. "I was your interpreter two days ago at the New Arrival Center, and my name is Mai," I told her. She nodded slightly without saying a word. She was crying. "Let's go chase the waves and see who will collect the most seashells today," I said. We both had a fun-filled day. I was much more fortunate than Tú. She was the only survivor from her family.

Their boat had sunk just a couple miles away from safety. She had washed up to the shore near the camp. God had blessed and protected her. I was so excited to introduce Tú to Hoa.

The Ocean Where the Dreams Go . . .

After that day, Tú, Hoa, and I became best friends. They were like my little sisters. I promised myself to never ask Tú about her lost family because I knew it was too painful and terrifying for her to remember that horrible day. Every time we met on the beach, we let our dreams go wild and talked about everything except the terrible sea journey. Sometimes we would dream of our future homes.

Tú dreamed of a garden where she would grow many of her family's favorite plants. Leading up to the house there would be a wide double border of multicolored tulips, which were her mom's favorite early spring flowers. There would be a tall bush of bamboo tree by the fountain for her daddy and a mango tree for her younger sister. For herself, she wished for a tapestry of fragrant forget-me-nots scattered around the house.

Hoa wished to build a tree house with the front facing the ocean and the back leaning against the mountain. There would be an orchard where one could find delicious tropical fruits, such as rambutan, starfruit, mangosteen, mango, dragon fruits, and many more. Then a bonsai garden with decorative bamboo benches to add to the elegance, beauty, and serenity of her dream home.

I longed for a cottage near the beach where my family and friends could gather to celebrate all occasions. I imagined children running wild on the beach harvesting seashells and chasing the seagulls. I would plunge into the clear, calm water of the ocean and enjoy snorkeling all day long.

After a little over a year, I left the refugee camp and resettled in Minnesota, the Land of 10,000 Lakes. Shortly after, Hoa re-united with her aunt's family in Canada. Only Tú was still waiting in the camp. I wrote to Tú often, almost every two weeks for a couple of years, but eventually we lost contact. I later learned that she had resettled in France. We had all promised each other that after we found our new homes, we would go to the beach every year in August to pray for the people who lost their lives in search of freedom and to celebrate our irreplaceable friendship. With this promise in mind, Duluth became my family's favorite place to visit in the summer.

Ocean Dreams

In the cloudless sky
As transparent as crystal,
Far away from the horizon,
Swallows are coming back.

In the quiet and peaceful night
As calm as a wonderful dream,
Far away from the storm,
Dolphins are swimming freely.

In the middle of the day
As restful as profound sleep,
On the beautiful beach, by the cottage,
I am there, swinging slowly on the hammock.

Closing my eyes,
Taking a deep breath,
Listening to the birds chirping,
I am there
To let my dreams go wild.

Adrift

Mary Casanova

The following is adapted from Ice-Out, *the sequel to the novel* Frozen.

IN KOOCHICHING COUNTY, ON THE FRINGE of northern Minnesota, nineteen-year-old Owen Jensen takes a train to see his girlfriend, Sadie Rose. It is late February 1922.

After a long train ride and a stop in St. Paul to find someone selling roses in the dead of winter, Owen reached Johnson Hall, an imposing two-story building on the Gustavus Adolphus campus. He tapped the brass door knocker, which produced a murmur of female voices within. With the bouquet of roses in one hand, he finger-combed his hair back from his eyes with the other, but the waves flopped down again.

Speaking face-to-face to Sadie Rose was the only way. Too much had happened since Dad died. Letters were inadequate to explain his jump-off-a-cliff decision to start his own Studebaker business. Add to that the letter he'd received just days ago from Sadie Rose, telling him she'd been asked to the Spring Ball. Not to worry. A thoughtful guy. Another music major, a clarinetist. A friend named Samuel, she'd written. Right, Owen thought. *Sam-the-damn-thoughtful.*

The door swung open, and a middle-aged woman with a tight collar, buttoned to her chin, smiled cautiously. "Yes, may I help you?" she asked, while behind her several college students clustered together, peering out at Owen. All dressed in layers of lace and silky fabrics, they at first reminded him of angels or a bouquet of faces, some pretty, others not as much. A sweet smell of perfumes and soaps wafted toward him, reminding him that his world of late had been filled with work and brothers and men. But he didn't want the company of just any female.

"Sadie Rose Ladovitch," he said. "I've come a long way to see her."

"It's after visiting hours," the woman replied.

"Oh, come on, Mrs. Ditzler, he's cute!" one of the college girls exclaimed.

"Let him in, please," said another.

At that, Mrs. Ditzler closed the door so that there was only a crack wide enough to reveal her taut face. "I'm sorry, she's not in."

"But you said it's after visiting hours. Where is she?"

"I'm not at liberty to say."

His heart dropped. "I took the train down from the border. I've come all this way, just to give her these flowers." He held out the flowers as proof. "And to see her just for a little bit."

"I'm sorry," Mrs. Ditzler said.

"Is she on a date?" he asked, bracing himself for the answer.

"Hey, I'm free tonight," one of the girls shouted, and an eruption of giggling followed.

"Girls," Mrs. Ditzler scolded, and then returned to the door. She must have taken pity on Owen, because she added, "If it helps, I'll tell you she's not on a date. Once a month, she takes the train to St. Paul for a meeting there. She'll be on the return train in the morning. She stays overnight with her family on Summit Avenue. It's a bit unusual, but she claims that these Wilderness Society meetings are educational in nature."

Wilderness Society.

Victor Guttenberg.

From the first summer he'd come to know her, she'd been interested in supporting Victor's cause to save Rainy Lake and the northern waterways from E. W. Ennis. Ennis, with his industrial ambition and unlimited money, allegedly had plans to turn the eighty-mile-long lake and watershed into a series of sixteen hydropower dams. Owen knew Sadie cared about protecting the islands and inlets from high levels of flooding. If Ennis got his way, the grand lake would turn into a giant bathtub—a reservoir—all with the purpose of keeping his mills and expanding empire thriving. But Owen had no idea she was staying overnight once a month to attend Victor's meetings.

He gripped the base of the bouquet as his hands dropped to his sides. "I know all about these meetings. I'm from Ranier."

"Washington State?"

"No, up north. Near International Falls. These meetings, they're about the wilderness there. Trying to protect Rainy Lake."

The woman nodded politely, but the door was now closing.

Owen pushed the toe of his boot in the door. "The meeting. Do you know where they meet?" He glanced at his watch. "If I catch the last train north to St. Paul, maybe . . ."

"Young man, I have no idea," Mrs. Ditzler answered, this time glancing down at his boot. "And please remove your foot from this door, or I'll have to phone the campus police."

"The Yangley Building!" one of the students called from behind. Then she wedged her rosy face just under Mrs. Ditzler's. "They meet in the basement there. And she said meetings sometimes go half the night."

"Thanks," Owen said, and grinned back at her. He removed his foot from the door. It closed with a resounding thud.

He spun away and ran down the sloping campus toward the river and back toward the depot. He swung himself aboard the train north just as it began to chug out of the station. Finding an open seat, he drew a deep breath and dropped his head into the bouquet of roses.

They still smelled sweet.

He couldn't wait to give them to her, but then he realized that she wouldn't be alone. She was at another meeting with Victor Guttenberg.

From the first time he made a dairy delivery by boat to Falcon Island, Owen had always gotten along with Victor. But as Sadie's interest in preserving wilderness grew, the more she enjoyed speaking with Victor about it. And the more she spoke with him, the more a slow fire of jealousy built in Owen. What if her interest in him had become something more? After all, Victor was a Harvard grad. He'd explored vast stretches of wilderness by canoe and had the muscles to prove it. He was articulate and an imaginative storyteller. What did Owen have to offer in comparison?

The train swayed and clattered alongside the Minnesota

River. Mile by mile, Owen clenched his jaw, willing the train to move faster. Everything in him felt desperate to see Sadie. It was as if he'd grown short of breath these past weeks.

He needed to see her just to fill his lungs again.

<hr/>

When the train at last crossed the Mississippi River and slowed to a stop in downtown St. Paul, Owen hopped out. Under the cavernous ceiling of Union Depot, Owen hurried along marble floors toward the building's entrance and out into the crisp night air. He checked his pocket watch; the hands read 9:32. The girl at the dormitory said the meetings went "half the night," but that was all a matter of perspective. He had to hustle.

From the window of a horse-drawn cab, Owen peered out. Patrons flowed into the Shubert Theater. In the distance, gold-gilded horses dotted the massive dome of the State Capitol. As he turned the corner, he spotted the St. Paul Cathedral topping another hill. Everything about the city was grand.

He hopped out at the Yangley Building, paid the driver, and stepped out onto the slushy street. The lights were out in the upper stories of the towering brick building. He wondered if he had the right place. From what he could see, there was nothing going on. He stepped up to the entrance doors of heavy wood and glass, but they were locked. A white-haired doorman limped toward the door from a bellman's counter inside, where a small lamp burned softly.

He cracked the heavy door and peered out.

"Young man," he said, "the offices are closed up tight for the night."

"I'm part of a meeting," Owen ventured in a whisper, hoping that if a password was needed, he could come up with whatever it might be. "The name Victor Guttenberg? Does that mean anything to you?"

"Ah, perhaps," the elderly man replied. "And you are?"

"Owen Jensen."

"Wait here," the man said, locking the doors before turning away.

Owen waited as the man disappeared into the shadows.

Growing impatient, he glanced up and down the street. With a clunk, the door unlocked again.

"Come in," the doorman said. "And forgive me for making you wait in the cold."

"I—" Owen began, but stopped short.

Several feet beyond the door stood Sadie Rose. He absorbed her in one glance. She cut a sleek silhouette, with a tailored jacket and skirt that flared just below her knees. Legs that curved at her calves and tapered to slim ankles in stylish heels. Her felt hat, with a tawny brown ribbon and a single pheasant feather, dipped slightly over her right eye.

"Owen?" she said. Her luxurious curls framed her face and dark eyes, which held surprise and something else. "What— what are you doing here? Is something wrong?"

He strode straight up to her, wrapped his arms around her waist, and lifted her off the ground, his lips meetings hers. "I just had to see you."

She stepped back and looked up at his face. "It's just so odd," she said quietly. "You took me by surprise. We're in the middle of an important meeting."

Her reaction stung. He had taken a risk in surprising her, but even with her plans to attend a dance with someone else, he'd expected she'd be happy. Not that she had to leap into his arms, but this? "Important," he repeated.

She nodded, her eyebrows drawn. "You know these meetings are quite secretive. I'm not sure how the others will feel about your knowing about them. I must have let it slip and mentioned this location, otherwise how—"

"The girls at your hall told me," he said.

"Oh."

Her face flushed. "I'm not great at keeping secrets, apparently."

"No, but I am. I won't tell another soul," he assured her, placing his hand briefly on his heart. Then he reached for her hand.

It was warm and soft. And the familiarity of her skin made him feel that everything could go back to normal. "Sadie, how about if you and me, we just head out and find someplace where we can talk, be alone."

She glanced back toward the elevator door and then turned to him. "Owen, I am terribly sorry to put you off, but I committed to this meeting. I'm part of it. They need me." She pulled her hand from his.

He was taken aback. "And you think I don't need you?" His words carried a tone of bitterness.

Her lips tightened, as if to hold back what she really wanted to say. Maybe there was already more between her and this Sam fella than she'd let on in her letter.

"My dad died," he blurted.

"Oh, no!" she said. "Owen, I'm sorry. So that's why you came straight here. When?" She tilted her head at him, then stepped closer and hugged him.

"Nearly two weeks ago," he said, breathing in the sweet scent of her. He rested the top of his chin on her head.

Again she pulled back. "Two weeks? But why didn't you tell me right away?"

"I tried, but I could never get through on the line. When I tried to write about it, I just couldn't."

She nodded. "What happened to him?"

"Heart attack. Died in his sleep."

"Oh, Owen. I'm so sorry, I truly am." She threw her arms around his waist. "How terrible for you," she murmured into his shoulder. "I know you weren't always close, but he was your father. You were lucky to have him beside you all those years."

For a few moments longer, Owen savored her touch. He kissed the top of her forehead lightly. "I've missed you, Sadie. I had to see you."

She nodded, then again glanced at the elevator, as if remembering her greater commitments. "Oh, I feel terrible, but I must get back. You can join us if you promise to be a bystander. It's all young lawyers, and they are risking their jobs to meet like this. That's why the basement . . . and candles."

Owen rested his eyes on her. She had no idea how absolutely beautiful she was. And from head to stylish toe, she was dressed as smartly as any young woman in the Twin Cities. Of course she'd captivated the attention of Sam, the clarinetist. And she no doubt was winning the admiration of these young attorneys as well as Victor Guttenberg.

He seethed with frustration. If Owen went down to their secretive meeting, there was no telling what he might say or do. How could he watch her in the soft glow of candlelight without wanting to have her to himself? How could he bear to know that she met with these men, taking notes or whatever she did, every single month? He had thought she was his, that she'd promised her love to him. But maybe he'd been wrong to assume such a thing. Here he stood, in a heavy wool jacket and wool cap. Downstairs, those attorneys were likely sporting the newest fashion in clothing and touting the latest political news and gossip. Even Victor, with his Harvard experience, probably left his wool shirt behind for something a bit dressier; he was always entertaining and unmatched at playing the violin. No, if Owen showed up at that meeting, he'd be a damn fish out of water.

Everything primal in him wanted to grab her hand, tell to get her coat and boots, and insist that she take the train north with him. Tell her that "wilderness" was endless, and it was never going to disappear. He was standing there, right in front of her, his heart outstretched in his hands. He wouldn't wait around forever. He held his emotions on a tight leash.

"No, you go to your meeting," he said, his voice gruffer than he'd intended. "Don't worry, I didn't make this trip just for you. I had other business anyway." A lie, but he didn't want her to think he'd made this whole trip for the sole purpose of seeing her. He suddenly felt pathetic. Some tragic figure in a play. "I'm heading back," he said.

"Owen, please," she began, hurt flashing in her eyes, and crossed her arms.

Before she could walk away from him, he spun away and strode out the entrance door. He needed to take charge of his own life.

Outside, Owen refused to look back. He set off like a man on his way up. Head high. A purposeful stride. He filled his lungs with air, damp and chill, and exhaled puffs of white as he followed the city streets back to Union Depot.

And that's when he remembered. He'd completely forgotten the bouquet of roses on his seat in the horse cab. After all the effort he'd gone through to find her fresh flowers, he'd blown that, too.

"Wouldn't have made any difference," he muttered, as he stepped inside the depot's vast emptiness. A policeman strolled the corridor, whistling as he twirled his nightstick. Owen found an empty bench. He didn't dare lie down, for fear of looking like a tramp or vagrant.

He let his mind drift.

Victor Guttenberg was only a few years older, yet he'd accomplished so much in a short time. His own island on Rainy Lake. An explorer. Heck, he'd paddled clear up to Hudson Bay with his Ojibwe friend, Billy Bright, and back; the first white man to make the journey. And now, Victor had gone from standing up locally against E. W. Ennis's plan to build hydropower dams, which would change the natural pathways of a long chain of lakes, to taking his fight to St. Paul and beyond.

What did Owen have to offer Sadie Rose in the shadow of someone such as Victor Guttenberg and his attorney friends? It was a long shot to think Victor could actually stop Ennis's industrial might—it was like Jack and the Beanstalk and the all-powerful Giant—but Owen admired Victor for trying.

In comparison, what was he doing with his life? Keeping a creamery going, a roof over the head of his mother and brothers. Starting a business in the lot behind the White Turtle. And in the process, losing his girlfriend.

He'd figured if he couldn't afford college, then he'd strike out on his own in business. The only way out was up. Despite his father's strong protests about Owen taking out a loan from Harvey Pengler, who ran the largest bootlegging ring on the border, Owen had gone ahead. He'd signed on the line, took the check to cover inventory for a dozen glistening automobiles—Studeys, as everyone called them—and now awaited their arrival on the "lot" behind Harvey Pengler's hotel.

But then Dad's heart suddenly gave out, leaving behind his lifeless body and a marginal business. Owen grieved, sure. Truth was, all those years of his father's drinking had—

disappointment by disappointment—hardened Owen's heart against him and encased it in ice. He grieved what *might* have been between them as much as he grieved his own fate now. He was the eldest, with five younger brothers and Mom frail with her own sorrow, and running the family creamery had fallen on him like a steamship anchor. How in the world was he going to run the creamery and his new business and hope to ever pay off his loan to Pengler?

In contrast to the echoing train terminal, a memory surfaced of a sunny afternoon on Falcon Island with Victor, Trinity (whose family owned a neighboring island), and Sadie. They swam off the island's eastern point, pulled themselves up onto the warm rock, and dried off in the sun, laughing as Victor told about barely surviving the last leg of his expedition home from polar bear country. He told of stuffing straw in his boots and pants, of breaking through ice as it formed ahead of them on rivers and lakes.

"November?" Owen had said, shaking his head. "That's winter up here. What were you thinking?"

Victor crossed his arms over his swim tank suit. With deeply tanned skin, Victor stared Owen down, as if he were a Greek god and truly offended. But a half second later, he broke into a broad grin and laughed out loud. "Clearly, Owen, I was not thinking!"

Trinity tilted her head back, her blonde hair glistening as it dried. "You have to be tough," she said, "if you're going to be wild."

"*Wild,*" Sadie said. "Up until meeting all of you, that word never existed in my vocabulary."

"That's why I'm your new best friend," Trinity said. Then she motioned to Owen and Victor as well. "We're your new best friends. Here to help, as needed. Isn't that right, Owen?" she teased.

Owen and Sadie shared a glance. By that point in the summer, they'd already become much more than friends.

Now on a bench at Union Depot, he let out a long sigh. He forced himself to sit tall, pulled his cap over his eyes, and waited for the next train north.

A haze hung in the air, a softening of winter's sharp edges, as the March sun warmed the forests around Rainy Lake. It warmed loggers as they felled virgin pine, stripped them of branches, and rolled them to the frozen shoreline, waiting for spring, when the logs would be floated down the lake and down the river to the paper mill.

One week after Owen returned, the sun warmed rooftops around Ranier and train cars loaded with lumber. Sun warmed the backs of mutts, ambling in search of scraps from tavern to restaurant, garbage can to dump pile. Sunshine warmed the backs of horses, pulling wagons and sleighs through town and out onto the endless lake, still frozen hard as granite. Sun warmed the tops of twelve shiny Studebakers, sitting in the cleared lot behind the White Turtle Restaurant and Hotel.

A large ring of keys clanked on his belt loop as Owen swept snow from the tops of his inventory. Even if he hadn't yet sold one, he was right to go with quality. He'd done his research. They'd been the strongest-selling automobiles nationwide for the past decade. The company had started building solid horse-drawn wagons and then horse-drawn automobiles. Then in 1904, they'd produced the first electric-operated Studey, which didn't catch on. But now they made gasoline-powered beauties. He folded his arms across his chest and admired his fleet, each one individually handcrafted, unlike Ford's mass-produced factory models. A Ford was cheaper, sure, but a Studebaker was built with genuine craftsmanship.

He hoped folks would be willing to pay a little more for quality.

He just had to get the word out. When the ads he'd purchased in the *International Falls Journal* started running soon, folks would begin to come by. Plus spring, technically, was around the corner. But who was he kidding? This far north, there wasn't spring. Winter gradually released its hold until one day you looked again and it was summer.

Snowbanks clung against the back of the White Turtle and four-foot icicles dangled from its roof, but Owen imagined blue open water, the sound of motorboats, and tourists hopping off passenger cars. Two months or so to go. When summer finally struck, who would resist taking one of these Studeys out for a spin? Who would resist driving with their sweetheart or parking by the pier when the sun set on Rainy Lake, the sky amber till 10:30 or 11:00 at night?

He sure wouldn't.

And there she was—her lovely face—framed again in his mind.

Owen removed his derby, ran his hand through his thick hair, as if to rid her from his head. She had other interests now. Between her life of music on campus and her meetings with young attorneys, they shared less and less in common. It was time to loosen his grip on her and let her live her life.

Easier said than done.

As he turned from the lot and headed toward the creamery, he glanced past the empty pier at the frozen bay. As he walked, the memory returned. It was last August, and they'd been fishing on Sand Bay.

She'd sat on the middle seat, her fishing line off one side of the boat. He sat in back, his line off the other side. They were fishing for walleye, jigging where the water ran deep, a hundred yards upstream of the lift bridge. A half dozen walleye already hung on the stringer. The sun was setting, a regular fireball. In its light, Sadie's face glowed. All around her, the water flickered with tongues of orange and red. While he was admiring her, her rod bent sharply toward the water. "I have a big one!" she shouted.

In the same instant he felt a solid tug on his own line. "Hey, me too!"

"Sadie," he coached, "if it's a northern pike, you gotta tire it out, give it some slack, then bring it in again. You gotta work it."

He gave a quick jerk of his line, hoping to set the hook, and when he did, Sadie's rod flew from her hands and out into the choppy water.

"He yanked it right out of my hands!" she said, standing in the boat. "I couldn't hang on to it!"

And then Owen reeled his line in, chuckling, until he produced her rod at the edge of the boat. "Looks like we caught each other."

She laughed out loud and then restrung her hook with a fresh silver minnow from the minnow bucket. But as soon as her line was back in the water, she burst suddenly into tears.

"What's wrong? Did you get hurt? The minnow? You know I'll bait your hook for you." He couldn't understand what had triggered this. Was it something he'd done?

She pressed her hand across her mouth, placed her fishing pole in its holder, turned toward him, her knees touching his, and buried her face in both hands.

"Sadie, sweet Sadie. A bad memory?" he asked. He knew she had memories and nightmares sometimes, because she'd told him. Memories of being out in a snowstorm, terrified, searching for her mother. Nightmares of things she'd seen at the boardinghouse. Things no child, she'd said, should ever see.

But always, she'd told him her secrets in whispers. And not once with tears.

"Sadie, Sadie," he whispered. "What's wrong?"

He dropped to his knees on the damp floor of the wooden boat. He wrapped his arms around her shoulders. He lightly kissed the top of her head. But she kept crying, her back heaving. He didn't know what to do, didn't know what to say, so he waited. When her breathing returned to normal and she sat up, wiping her eyes, he held her face in his hands and kissed her forehead, the tip of her nose, and then her mouth. Together they shut out the world, and the anchored boat cradled them, bobbing on the chop as the darkness enveloped them.

At last, Owen asked softly, "Can you tell me now?"

"In three days," she began, "I go back to school."

He nodded. "You have to. You're starting your junior year."

She drew in a breath and held it. When she exhaled, she said, "I don't want to lose you!"

To that, he'd laughed lightly. "I'm not going anywhere," he replied. "I'll be right here when you return."

Only now, as he approached the squat brick building of Jensen's Creamery, did Owen wonder. That night in the boat. Had Sadie seen a different future . . . and understood that things would change between them? Since that night, he'd always thought Sadie's outburst of tears had been sweet, an unnecessary worry about *his* finding someone else.

He never imagined she'd be the one to drift away.

We Were Boys Together

Kao Kalia Yang

OUR FAMILIES LIVED in the McDonough Housing Project. We were neighbors and friends. We were seven months apart, Tou and I.

In the summer mornings, before the wash of sunlight crossed the sky, we used to catch common swallows for breakfast. We needed no alarm clock to get up for our morning birding sessions. Somehow our bodies jerked awake in our different beds, beside our different sleeping siblings, and without brushing our teeth or washing our faces, we would meet up outside his townhouse.

I brought my father's old fishing lines. Tou borrowed the top of his father's old Weber grill. We found suitable sticks in the dark beneath the tall trees in the communal yards. We tied a long length of fishing line to the middle of the strongest stick we found. We used the stick to prop up the old Weber top. Tou had pieces of white bread from the cupboard. We placed the bread beneath the Weber top. We strung the line through the fine sieve of their kitchen window screen. Inside his kitchen, with the window open, we sat waiting for the birds to come. They always came with the first stretch of gray. Fearlessly, they entered our trap. We waited patiently. We never pulled the line until there were at least two birds crowded around the pieces of bread. We took turns jerking the line, watching the stick fall and the heavy Weber top close on the birds.

We were careful to be quiet even in our excitement. We didn't want to chance waking up Tou's parents or siblings. We certainly did not want to scare the little swallows with their puffy morning bodies. We talked in whispers.

"I'm going to open the lid. You are going to cup the birds as quickly as you can with your hands. Once you get them, put them in the old rice bag."

A good morning generated about seven swallows—enough for all our brothers and sisters to partake in a meal. Once neighbors started moving, front doors opening and people leaving for work, we knew it was time to stop. We suspected that the work of catching swallows for breakfast was illegal, and neither of us wanted our parents to go to jail. We cleaned up our operation, untied the fishing line from the stick, replaced the Weber top on its base, and threw the sticks on the ground. We gathered our bag of swallows and headed for my townhouse.

My mother and father worked the third shift as assemblers in a factory. They didn't get home until three in the morning. This meant they usually slept, if all went smoothly, until nine. When my siblings woke up, they would be excited to hear about our morning catch. Although Tou and I were only nine, we both knew how to cook. It is a responsibility of the oldest.

I got the rice going in the rice cooker as fast as I could. I filled one of my mother's thin metal pots from Thailand to the halfway point with water. From our freezer, I grabbed two stalks of lemongrass. I wet the stalks at the sink. I pounded them with the pestle. I put the stalks to boil in the water, watching as they turned the water green. As I prepared the fresh chili, green onion, cilantro, and sliced tomatoes, Tou was busy wringing the necks of the little swallows, dressing them with experienced hands over the trash bin. He used the tip of my father's big Hmong knife to make a slit beneath their bellies, took out the innards, and rinsed them clean. He chopped off the crooked heads and the dangling feet. Once I told him I was ready, he dropped the bodies of the birds into the water. I seasoned them with pinches of MSG, salt, and black pepper. We sniffed the air in the room—spicy and sweet from the tomatoes and herbs of our swallow stew.

When we were happy with the taste of the broth, we turned off the stove. We got out our big bowls, one for the rice and one for the birds in their broth. When the table was set, Tou went to get his siblings from his home and I went upstairs to wake up mine. It was then that I stopped to brush my teeth and comb my hair.

Around the table, all nine of us stood, with our metal Chinese leaf spoons in our hands. We ate spoonfuls of warm rice and drank deeply from the rich stock of the swallows. We gave our youngest siblings the drumsticks of the swallows. Tou and I sucked the juices from the necks, using our fingers to gather the thin layer of meat from the bone. We knew there would be none for the adults. Afterward, we cleaned the little bare bones of the birds from the table, washed the dishes, and told the younger ones to stay put at our house or they could go to Tou's, while we adventured some more.

There was a large grove of trees and a wetland to the west of the McDonough Housing Project. Tou and I often wandered through the trees, into the swamp, among the cattails to catch frogs, baby ducks, and other things. We liked to spend our afternoons there. Beneath the tall trees, we shared stories that we had heard from our mothers and fathers. We also talked about life, how hard it was to be the oldest boys in our family, how embarrassing it was that our parents did not speak English, how stupid it was that the police wanted to catch innocent people for everything in this country—from leaving your kids home alone because you have to go to work on the third shift to simple things like catching squirrels and swallows so you can make breakfast for your younger brothers and sisters. It was in that grove of tall trees that Tou shared a story that would change the way I saw Tou's father and my own forever.

Before this point, I had known Tou's father only as a quiet man with a broken smile. When he spoke, the few times I heard him, his words were blurry, hard to hear. I never asked why because Tou was my friend and he was Tou's father and I assumed he had been born that way, with no front teeth, twisted lips, and what appeared to be only part of a tongue.

Tou and I were on different branches of the same tall tree. He was lying back on a large limb, his hand cradling his head. I was seated, my feet dangling in the air, a hand on either side. The heavy canopy of the summer leaves hid us from the world.

We were in a haven of sweet-smelling green leaves. The sky was little more than blue patches that filled in the holes among the leaves. The wind rustled gently.

Tou said, "Did you realize that when our fathers were in the war they were our age? Just boys?"

I said, "Yeah, I guess they were."

He said, "Can you imagine us being soldiers, carrying guns, defending our families, killing people, seeing people die?"

I said, "I guess you just do what you need to do in times like that."

He said, "I asked my mom if my dad had been born with his mouth handicap yesterday. She told me his story."

I said, "What is his story?"

Tou said, "It was 1975. My father was my age now. He was carrying his little sister on his back. They had gone to the river to fetch water for the family. All was quiet. He was not expecting anything to happen. He had gotten the pail of water. It was in his hands. He was scrambling up the climb from the river when his little sister, who had been quiet on his back, began crying. He jostled her softly to quiet her. She was only a baby, you know. She continued to cry. All of a sudden he heard a voice call, 'We have to shoot. The baby is going to notify the villagers of our position!'

"The bullets started coming. My father fell down the incline. The pail of water went tumbling back to the river. He didn't care. He tried to maneuver the baby underneath his body, but she was tied up with the carrying cloth. He heard a bullet pass by his ear. He felt the baby's head drop on his shoulder. Hot liquid began seeping from her head. The bullets were going left and right. He scrambled toward the river's edge. He had no choice. He jumped into the cold currents. Bullets fell around him. He went underwater, but he couldn't stay there for long. He needed to breathe. He surfaced. A bullet hit him in the mouth, went through his lip, destroying his two front teeth. He could feel it lodged in his throat. My father thought he was going to die for sure. He heard more bullets, more yelling.

"When my father woke up, he was home, resting on a mat

beside the family fire ring. The house was full of people. His mouth was swollen. He couldn't ask what all the people were doing there, but two of the villagers shifted, and my father saw that his baby sister was dead, lying on a makeshift platform beside their east wall.

"When my mother met my father, she thought that he had been born with the broken lip, the missing teeth. She married him because she had lost her family in the jungle and needed another family to take care of her. She never asked and he never said. It wasn't until right before my grandma died in Thailand that she told my mother about what happened to my father. My mother tried asking my father about it once, but he just shook his head and then said it was hard enough getting the necessary words out into the world; there was no need to spend the time and energy bringing up old wounds. She told me the story but asked me never to ask him about it."

I couldn't see Tou's face as he was telling me the story. He was looking at the leaves and the pockets of sky overhead.

I said, "That's a sad story, Tou."

He said, "It is."

He asked, "Does your father come from sad stories, too?"

I said, "I don't know."

My father and I talked often about the war and life in Laos, but never about the actual killing or the sadness of it. I know that he had a prized buffalo before the war. I know that he lived in a village surrounded by flowering trees that bloomed and covered the mountains in scented white. I know that he grew up by a river, catching small fish and cooking them for himself and the village children. I know that he had been to school and that he had been a good student before the war entered their village and his education stopped. I know that he met my mother in the refugee camps of Thailand. I know that I was born there. I know only the things that my father has chosen to tell me, mostly the things he believes I need to know in order to make good decisions regarding our lives in America.

I guess my father, like me, doesn't like to talk about the hard things. For example, I tell my father about my grades and scores on math tests. I talk to him about how the younger children are behaving on the school bus and with their friends. I interpret the things we see on the news, tell him what the weather forecast looks like for the next day. But I don't talk to my father about the boys and girls who point to my short pants, at my bare ankles, and laugh, or the teacher who is always frustrated because I can't say her name right. "Roberta." The "r" always comes out as an "l" in my throat—despite how much I try, so I have stopped calling her by name. I don't talk to my dad about the money I need for the field trip to the zoo. I know he doesn't have any money. Even if he wanted to, he wouldn't be able to give it to me. My father and I know the sadness in our lives, but we don't choose to be sad together.

In the evenings, Tou and I gathered with our brothers and sisters and other neighborhood kids and played touch football on the green area beside the playground. The playground was always full of broken bottles, too dangerous for any kid to really play on. So we took to the green grass. We chose team captains by doing our version of rock-paper-scissors. We didn't know all the rules about football, but we used our shoes to divide the green grass into lines and understood that we had to defend our final lines. It was sweaty, fast-paced fun. It was always the sound of some mother's voice calling her children inside that told us the day was done. In the fallen dusk, Tou and I parted ways, waving in the air and saying, "Remember we have to bird tomorrow."

Those five years that our families lived in the project were the best years of my youth, my boyhood. I was twelve when we moved out of the project and into a government-subsidized house in a normal neighborhood. I was happy for the move. I knew I would not get to play with Tou anymore, but the move was more exciting than our childhood fun. We parted happily.

Tou and I next saw each other on a hot July day during the annual Independence Day Soccer Tournament at McMurray Fields near Como Zoo. Our voices were changing and our conversation was halting, but it was a meeting of old friends. When we saw each other at the annual Hmong New Year Celebration in downtown Saint Paul, we shook hands and acted grown-up. One year, he had a girlfriend. Another year, I did. Our lives continued with our families, each of us caught up in our own young adulthood.

I was twenty when I heard of Tou again. I was a sophomore at the University of Minnesota–Duluth. My roommate was also Hmong. I had no idea that he was even related to Tou. I hadn't talked of Tou in years. But one day after class, he told me that his second cousin had killed himself. I was curious. I asked how. He told me that he had hung himself from a tree. I asked why. My roommate said that he didn't know but that he was going to drive down to the Twin Cities for the funeral. I asked if I could come along—I didn't have a car on campus, but I wanted to come home that weekend. He said, of course.

We were on a sleepy stretch of the drive down. It was snowing lightly, but the wind was calm. My roommate sat far back from the steering wheel, his right hand on the wheel, the left tapping lightly at the window. He said, "The guy was cool. He was still single, like us. He worked the second shift at a factory. He took care of his mom and dad. I think his mom will be okay, but his dad—I am worried about him. Man hardly talks. He has a handicapped mouth. Tou talked for him all the time at family events and meetings. Tou really took care of the old man, was his voice, you know."

When I realized that it was Tou, my childhood friend, the tears came quickly. I just kept seeing us in that tree, him lying down on that limb, looking up at the sky, telling me the story of his father's broken mouth.

When I had hold of my voice, I asked if it was a traditional three-day, three-nights funeral. My roommate nodded.

I asked, "Can I go to the funeral with you? Tou was my friend back in the McDonough Housing days. I'd like to see his family again."

We went directly to the Hmong funeral home in Maplewood. The parking lot was only halfway full. I was used to seeing the lot overfull. I had a big family. We always showed up in a big way at family events like this. I guess Tou was young, and he hadn't lived long, and there weren't many people who knew him, people who wanted to see him off.

Inside the funeral home, there were men and women in all colors of clothing. Not everyone could afford black. At the entry to the viewing room, there was a picture of Tou, a much more mature Tou than the kid I remember, wearing traditional Hmong clothes. The picture had been taken at one of the booths at the New Year Celebration. There was a mural of a traditional Hmong house in the back. Tou was smiling. He was carrying a woven bamboo basket on his back, a prop. By the picture, there was a wreath of white roses, a banner of yellow, Hmong words written carefully across it in black marker: *Ib Tug Tub Zoo*, A Good Son.

There were many empty seats to choose from. By the casket up front, Tou's mother sat with a piece of tattered paper napkin in her hands. Around her, a few elderly women stationed themselves, touching her shoulders occasionally, a sign of comfort. I looked for Tou's father everywhere that night, but I did not see him. On my way out, one of his younger brothers caught me and thanked me for coming. I said it was nothing. I said that when I knew it was Tou, I had to come.

He said, "Tou's going to be happy you came."

I nodded.

I wanted to ask why Tou killed himself, but it was not the right place and it was not the right time. I said I would return to the funeral in the morning.

I did not go back the next morning.

At home, I told my parents and my siblings what happened to Tou. My brothers and sisters had suggestions for what might have caused Tou's suicide. The burden of caring for his family must have been heavy. Maybe he had gotten with the wrong crowd; he was always so eager to break rules as a kid. Perhaps he was mentally unstable—seeing as how his father hardly talked and all. I just shook my head at all the reasons why Tou may have killed himself. My mother told them to quiet down. She looked to my father who filled the silence with a familiar lament, "His parents had traveled so far to bring him to this country, overcome so much. How sad for them, that all of the hardship was for nothing."

That night, I thought long and hard about Tou before sleep came to me. I didn't think about why he had died or how he had died. I thought about how we were boys together. I thought about the early mornings we spent catching swallows. I remembered the taste of that delicious stock. I thought about our talks in the tree grove and hunts in the wetlands beside the McDonough Housing Project. I missed my friend.

~~~~~~~~~~

It has been sixteen years since Tou's death. Last night, he visited me in a dream.

I was a grown man visiting a relative in the McDonough Housing Project with my wife. As we entered one of the familiar townhouses, a boy rushed up to me and grabbed my hand. I looked down. He was about nine. He was a mixture of myself and Tou. I allowed him to drag me toward a door. He opened it. The room was full of people. I saw Tou's father standing in the middle of the crowd, an old man now, as old as my own father. His hair was white, thin. He wore a sweater that hung over his slender frame. He looked lost. His wrinkles fell heavy around his tired face. Beside him, there was a young man. The young man scared me. He was gaunt. He was pale. His black hair was spiked up. His face appeared to be bruised. His eyes were like holes in his face. He stood close to Tou's father, his hand on the old man's shoulder. He turned his head and looked directly at me. I took a step backward. The boy was gone. My hand was free, but I could not move my feet. I watched as the scary young man grew tall before my eyes. His features changed; they became Tou's. Tou became my age, thirty-six, his brown eyes looking down at me. The fear was gone. I found myself rushing toward Tou, reaching to hug him, looking up at him.

I woke up crying for the time when we were boys together, talking of the past, walking toward the future, unafraid of what it held.

Why Does Dr. Seuss Rhyme All the Time?
Questions for the Authors

THESE QUESTIONS WERE ADDRESSED to the authors in this book and were submitted by fourth-graders from Urban Academy Charter School and ninth-graders from Ms. Cocchiarella's Achieve Class at Como Park Senior High, both in Saint Paul, Minnesota.

What are your dreams like? Do you dream about fantastic creatures and interesting people?

ANIKA FAJARDO: I dream about really boring activities like shopping for shoes and getting parking tickets. I also have a recurring dream that I can fly (the trick is to get running really fast and take big leaps). But the most creative part of bedtime is just before I fall asleep. It's that moment when I'm cozy in the blankets and it's dark and quiet. Maybe I can hear someone else getting ready for bed, and the cat has settled down at the foot of the bed. That's when I have ideas for stories and characters and themes. I don't always remember these ideas in the morning, but the act of thinking them up helps my writing.

LYNNE JONELL: My dreams are sometimes boring and sometimes interesting. My favorite dreams are when I get to fly and when I discover that I can breathe on my own underwater, like a fish. I don't recall dreaming about any fantastical creatures, but I did once have the most boring dream in the world that ended up turning into my first novel for kids, *Emmy and the Incredible Shrinking Rat!* So you never know . . .

WILL ALEXANDER: I wish I knew! But I never remember my dreams. Never. Sometimes I can almost remember remembering . . . but even that slips away from me before I even open my eyes. I'm a little bit jealous of people who can recall the fantastical things that they did while dreaming.

How often do you write each day?

ANIKA FAJARDO: I think about writing at least a dozen times each day. I actually write much less frequently than that. I'm usually at my desk for a couple hours two or three times a week while my daughter is at school.

LYNNE JONELL: I try to write every day, but I don't always do it. I do find that I need to vary the places where I write, though. Some days it's outside (summer only!), some days it's at a coffee shop or the library, and sometimes I even write at home in my office. There is something about going to a new place that gets the creative juices flowing.

WILL ALEXANDER: I tend to write all morning long and then deal with other sorts of business in the afternoon. Occasionally I'll try to write at night, very late at night, because it feels mysterious and strange to be awake and telling stories when everyone else is asleep. But that rarely works. The things I write at night make very little sense to me when I read them later.

How long does it take to come up with a new plot?

SWATI AVASTHI: I find plots everywhere. Let's say I'm taking the bus. Suddenly, I start thinking, "What if?" What if someone I wronged got on the bus and sat right next to me? What if they had been planning it? Plotting for me is perhaps similar to paranoia. The hard part is making the plot work! My story in *Sky Blue Water* took me two years to write. Writing it wasn't about knowing what was going to happen; writing it was about making what happened mean something, something about who we are as people.

MARCIE RENDON: I seldom have trouble imagining stories. It is harder for me to find time to write them all down. Many are still in my head waiting for the opportunity to come out through the keyboard.

MARGI PREUS: You can come up with a plot in five minutes, but as soon as you create some characters, they all seem to get their own ideas of how things should go, and then it's anybody's guess how long it will take to sort things out.

What are the steps to becoming a writer? What courses should I take in college?

SWATI AVASTHI: The best step to become a writer is to feed your curiosity. Feed it by writing a story to see what will happen. Feed it by reading everything you can get your hands on. Feed it by allowing yourself time to dream and imagine. There is no proper path to becoming a writer; everyone gets to it differently. So follow your curiosity and it will lead you where you need to be. That's why I think you should explore your interests in college. I imagine that many of your interests will be about stories and language.

MARCIE RENDON: I did not learn how to write in college. I love to read. I am a compulsive reader and do think that that is what really taught me how to write for a reading audience.

MARGI PREUS: Read, write, repeat. Find out who the good teachers are at your college and take courses from them—no matter what they teach. Learn as much as you can about as many things as you can. Creative writing courses are okay, but you still have to know something else so you have something to write about.

Where do you draw inspiration for your characters? From real life? From other books? From movies?

SWATI AVASTHI: I develop my characters based on the problem they are facing. Who would be in a situation like the one I'm thinking of? Why would it matter to that person in particular? What are the circumstances of that person's history? From there I think I borrow bits and pieces of characters from myself and people I know. My antagonists are almost always based on someone I dislike. It's fun to get revenge on my enemies writer-style—by putting them in a story.

MARCIE RENDON: The characters in my stories appear in my mind and more or less take over once I find the time to sit down and write.

MARGI PREUS: Not movies. If you write characters inspired by film or television characters, your writing runs the risk of reading like a movie or television treatment (most likely one that's already been done). If you want to create interesting and complex characters, write from real life. Start by writing character sketches of people you know, and go from there.

Do you think one of your books will ever become a movie?

WILL ALEXANDER: It's certainly possible. I find the prospect more worrying than exciting, though, because I would have absolutely no control over the moviemaking process. Some of my favorite books, like *The Dark Is Rising* by Susan Cooper and *A Wizard of Earthsea* by Ursula K. Le Guin, have been adapted into vile and terrible films. The authors couldn't do anything to stop them or fix them. I would hate for that to happen. Then again, some film adaptations are amazing. I wouldn't mind if one of my books inspired one of those.

Why does Dr. Seuss rhyme all the time? Is it important for poems to rhyme?

JOYCE SIDMAN: Not all poems rhyme. Nonrhyming poems, or free verse poems, concentrate more on meaning and on surprising the reader with unexpected combinations of words and images. Rhyming poems appeal to our love of patterns and rhythm. They are more like a song or a dance—they make your whole body come alive!

Do you write children's books to escape the harsh realities of being an adult?

JULIE SCHUMACHER: No. I think being ten or twelve or fourteen has its own harsh realities. Sometimes being an adult is much less complicated—and generally adulthood comes with more freedom. I write kids' books because I'm interested in the age groups I write about. Adults seem more stable to me and therefore (at times) a bit less intriguing. The emotions of younger characters can be a lot stronger.

PETE HAUTMAN: Good question! I write for both younger and older readers, and it would be more true to say that I write adult fiction to escape the harsh realities of being a teen. It can be painful for me to remember what being a teen was like—the powerlessness, the restrictions, the uncertainty, and most of all the expectations that get piled on by adults, by our peers, and by ourselves. Being an adult is in many ways easier.

KURTIS SCALETTA: No way. I write children's books to remind myself of the harsh realities of being a child. And because books then were my biggest solace, I want to provide that same comfort to other kids.

What do you do to relieve writer's block?

JOHN COY: For starters, you don't have to believe in it. How would your principal react if your teacher called in and said she had teaching block or your librarian said she had library block? They have a job to do so they do it. It's the same with writing. I believe writer's block is perfection wearing a clever disguise. If you don't expect to be perfect, you can sit down and get words on a page and then make them better and better and better. It's that easy and that difficult.

JULIE SCHUMACHER: I go for walks. I read whatever I can get my hands on and write notes in the margins. And I try to keep writing, completing a certain number of words or pages per day. I try to remind myself that words on the page, no matter how limp and uninteresting they may seem at first, are always better than no words on the page. Once I put the words down, I can try to improve them, one draft at a time.

KURTIS SCALETTA: It helps to do something else—either

change practice, like writing in longhand instead of keying on a computer, or start a new project.

PETE HAUTMAN: I write something that has nothing to do with whatever I'm stuck on—even if it's just a grocery list or a poem about salamanders. Anything to get my fingers moving. Later, I might be able to go back to what I was stuck on and see a way to make it work.

Is writing hard? Or is it fun?

JOHN COY: Yes and yes. Writing is hard and it's fun. Like lots of things, it's satisfying after working hard to look back and see where you were and what you have accomplished.

JULIE SCHUMACHER: Definitely both. Sometimes it's great fun; at other times it's very frustrating. It's like most of life: to do it well, you need to struggle with it, through happy and sad, thick and thin.

PETE HAUTMAN: Both! If it comes easily, it's boring—like climbing a small hill instead of a mountain. "Fun" and "hard" are not mutually exclusive. There is nothing more satisfying to me than struggling hard with a scene or a chapter and having it come together.

KURTIS SCALETTA: I think it's hard, but not as hard as "real" jobs like cleaning toilets or teaching. And it's fun, but not as fun as going to a carnival or playing baseball.

What have you had to do to help get your book promoted and out in the world?

JULIE SCHUMACHER: Like any other writer, I try to stick up for what I've written, to nudge it onto the center of the stage as if it were a shy little thing. I'll talk to students at schools, or do Skype book club visits, or "real" book club visits, or readings, or e-interviews, or whatever (within reason) it takes.

KURTIS SCALETTA: You know, that's the hardest part for me—

self-promotion and extroversion don't come easily. I've visited schools, done events at libraries and bookstores, and gone to conferences for librarians and teachers and creative writers. Looking back I'd say it's also the biggest reward, because of the people I've met and friends I've made. But it's still not easy.

Prompts for Classroom Discussions and Creative Writing Activities

Stephanie Watson and Sarah Warren

THESE PROMPTS WERE INSPIRED by the creative writing programs at the Mid-Continent Oceanographic Institute in Saint Paul, Minnesota.

Understanding Your Audience

In "The Creature under the Bush," Jane and Bill go to great lengths to convince Karl the kobold that he should move out of Jane's house and back into the woods. To do this, they first had to consider what would make Karl want to leave. Then they had to carefully develop a plan. Next, they had to convince Jane's parents to let them ride the city bus.

Discussion

1. What aspects of the kobold's personality did Jane and Bill use against him?
2. How did the author, Lynne Jonell, reveal the kobold's personality and characteristics throughout the story?
3. What facts about Jane's parents did Jane and Bill use to convince their parents to let them take the bus to the park?
4. Can you think of an example in your life where you've had to convince someone to change his or her opinion?
5. Can you think of a career that might involve changing people's opinions?

Writing Prompt

What is one thing you feel passionate about? In one sentence, explain your opinion. For example: "Hot Cheetos are good for you" or "Teddy is the best quarterback in the NFL" or "I should be allowed to wear sneakers to church." Now, think of someone who doesn't share your opinion. Why do they disagree with you? What would it take to make them believe otherwise? Write a short essay to try to change that person's mind.

Step by Step

In "We Were Boys Together," the narrator describes how he and his friend, Tou, would make soup for their siblings each morning. The author, Kao Kalia Yang, uses very specific language to describe the vegetables and the order in which they go in the pot.

Discussion

1. What are some of the adjectives Kao Kalia Yang uses to describe the various items that went into the soup?
2. Describe what you had for breakfast or lunch today. What words can you add to give a better description of your meal?
3. Besides a cookbook or recipe, can you think of other places where step-by-step instructions appear?
4. List some common words or phrases that might appear in a recipe or set of instructions. Why is each step important? What might happen if you left something out?

Writing Prompt

Think of a task you know how to do very well, like pumping up a bike tire or cooking an egg. Now think of a particular person for whom you will write step-by-step instructions of how to do this task. Be sure to introduce the topic and give a preview of what you're about to explain. Use specific, detailed language. As you write, keep your audience's age and skill level in mind. Use transitions as you move from step to step.

A Place in Time

Authors often make very specific word choices to give you a strong visual picture of a place you probably have never been. Look at these two examples:

It was the middle of the rainy season, and everywhere it smelled of red clay, earthy and rich. ("Lone Star," by Shannon Gibney)

The lake and the strip of gravelly sand in front of it (the beach was a giant cat box, my mother said) were full of people. It was a weekday, but the sky was as blue as a balloon, and the walkways and the water and the sand were full of bikers and swimmers and strollers and ice cream vendors and volleyball players and people lying around getting cancer because of the sun. There were leftover streamers on the slide and on the swing set from the Fourth of July. ("Strange Island," by Julie Schumacher)

Discussion
1. Mary Casanova's "Adrift" takes place in two distinct locations. Can you remember where they were?
2. What are the differences between the two settings?
3. Why do you think the author chose to set her story in these locations?
4. How does this contrast between the two settings help you understand who the two main characters are and what they think about the world?
5. The story was told mainly from Owen's perspective. How would the story have been different if it were told from Sadie's point of view?

Writing Prompt
Close your eyes and think of a place that's very familiar to you. How does it smell? What does it sound like? What do you see around you? Who else is there? Do you know anything about the history of the location? Make a list of these details. Now write a paragraph to describe this place to someone from another country or another planet.

Around the World
In "The Ocean Where the Dreams Go," the narrator migrates from Vietnam to Malaysia and then to Minnesota. Migration is when a person or a family moves from one place and settles in a new location. Often people who migrate move a long distance,

to a whole different country or continent. But migration within a country is also possible.

Discussion
1. Why did Mai and her family have to move?
2. What were some of the challenges of her trip?
3. Have you ever moved to a new place? What were the challenges? What was exciting?
4. What do you miss about your former home?
5. Why did the author choose to begin the story in Duluth and then go back in time to her childhood in Vietnam?

Writing Prompts
1. Pick a place where you have always wanted to live—Chicago? Paris? Shanghai? Hollywood?—and pretend you just moved there. Write a letter to a friend or to your parents describing your new home. Include as many details as possible. Is the weather nice? What does your home look like? What do you do for fun? If you've never actually been to this place, you can either make up details or visit the library to research facts.
2. Imagine there was a disaster or conflict in your neighborhood and you had to leave your home by the end of the day. What are the three most important things you would take with you? Write these down and describe why they are important to you.

Telling a Tall Tale
In "Max Swings for the Fences," Max tells a lie when introducing himself to classmates at his new school. Over the course of the story, author Anne Ursu gives Max several opportunities to come clean, but each time he digs himself into a deeper hole.

Discussion
1. Why did Max lie?
2. Did Molly do the right thing?

3. What do you think will happen next for Max?
4. When you were reading the story, did you become anxious for Max? Do you think the author wants us to feel sorry for Max? Or feel mad at him for lying?
5. Have you ever told someone something about yourself that wasn't true? Why did you do it? What was the outcome?

Writing Prompts
1. Imagine you are introducing yourself to a new classroom. Write a paragraph describing yourself as truthfully as you can, including at least three details about your life. Physical characteristics like your hair color or height don't count.
2. What three things do you *wish* you could say about yourself? (Again, don't choose physical details.) Write a paragraph describing this made-up version of you.

First Impressions (Crafting the Personal Essay)
Sometimes your first impression of someone isn't true to who they really are. In Kirstin Cronn-Mills's "My Icy Valentine," Lucy makes several assumptions about Chase, the new boy in school, that are not accurate. In "Opposite Land," by Pete Hautman, Andreas's uncle assumes that all Norwegian people eat lutefisk, which turns out to be untrue. A better way to learn about someone is to ask them questions and invite them to share their own personal feelings and opinions. These questions are similar to questions that you might be asked in a job interview or on a college application. To make sure you are always making a great first impression, it's helpful to practice writing about yourself.

Discussion
1. Can you think of an instance where somebody decided what kind of person you were before they really got to know you? What did that feel like?
2. Can you think of a time when you made an assumption about someone else that turned out to be untrue?

Writing Prompts
1. What are you most grateful for?
2. What was the last thing that made you feel really happy?
3. Is there a story behind your name?
4. What are you good at?
5. What are you afraid of?
6. Who inspires you?
7. How have you helped others?

Bodies of Water

Minnesota is called the Land of 10,000 Lakes, so it's no surprise nearly every author in this collection chose to write about water in some way. In these stories, we see water as a place of recreation and reflection but also as a source of fear and destruction.

Discussion
1. What place or places have the most meaning for you?
2. Where do you go to find peace and quiet?
3. What have you learned about climate change? What might happen to our bodies of water in the future?
4. How might your life be different in the future?

Writing Prompts
1. Imagine that all the lakes are actually islands and the rest of the state is water. How would your life be different? Where would your home be? Where would your school be? Write a short story that describes a day in the life of a character who lives in this setting.
2. Write a short essay about a place that feels peaceful to you. Remember to use descriptive terms and to give the reader background on why it feels that way to you.
3. Contrast the different ways two authors in this book use water to express emotion, develop the plot, and create conflict.

Home Sweet Home
Discussion
1. What makes a place feel like home?
2. Can you think of a situation where someone made you feel at home in a new environment?
3. Have you ever had to adjust to customs in a new place? What was that like?

Writing Prompts
1. Describe your perfect home.
2. Describe how your family celebrates a special occasion.
3. Instead of birthday cakes and candles, come up with ideas for a new way to celebrate a birthday. Describe this new tradition in detail.
4. Describe a birthday party to someone from a different planet.
5. Sometimes the rules are different in different places. Describe how the rules are different in your home compared to a friend's home.

Looking at Language

Alliteration
Alliteration is when the same letter or sound is used at the beginning of several closely connected words in a sentence, paragraph, story, or poem. Repetition is a literary technique that involves repeating a word, a phrase, or a full sentence to make an idea or image clearer.

Poet Joyce Sidman uses both alliteration and repetition in her poem "The Blue between Us." There are thirteen different words that start with the letter B in the poem. The word "blue" appears twelve times.

Discussion
1. Why do you think she chose to repeat the word "blue" so many times?
2. What effect does it have on the poem?
3. Can you think of a song that uses alliteration or repetition?

Writing Prompts

1. Choose a color and use it five or more times in a poem.
2. Pick a letter of the alphabet and write a poem with at least six words that begin with that letter.

Metaphor

A metaphor compares one thing to another without using the words *like* or *as*. In her story "Fishing," Anika Fajardo uses a metaphor when she writes, "Eddie's plane ticket is a rock that we keep stubbing our toes on."

Discussion

1. What do you think she means by that?
2. How does this sentence help you understand how Little Eddie felt about Big Eddie?

Writing Prompts

Fill in the blanks in the following sentences.

_____ is a rock that I keep stubbing my toe on.
Create your own metaphors to fill in these blanks:
My best friend is a _____.
My future is a _____.
My mind is a _____.
The river is a _____.

Simile

Similes are a shortcut to describe a person, a place, a thing, or even an emotion. They are different from metaphors in that they use "like" or "as" to connect seemingly different things.

Read this paragraph from "The War between the Water and the Road" by William Alexander:

The park had two swing sets on the playground at street level, before the slope plummeted down to the pond. One was smaller and set up for younger kids. The smaller swings looked like armored underwear, impossible to fall out of. A more advanced swing set jutted up near the smaller one like a pirate ship bearing down on a weaker vessel.

Writing Prompts
Use similes to fill in the blanks:

_____'s handwriting looks like a _____.

Riding the bus is like a _____.

My dog is like a _____.

The car was like a _____.

The sky was like a _____.

Fashion Show
When stories are set in the past, authors often do research so they can accurately describe the clothing, automobiles, and buildings of the time. Read this paragraph from Mary Casanova's story "Adrift":

She cut a sleek silhouette, with a tailored jacket and skirt that flared just below her knees. Legs that curved at her calves and tapered to slim ankles in stylish heels. Her felt hat, with a tawny brown ribbon and a single pheasant feather, dipped slightly over her right eye.

Discussion
1. Which items of clothing from this passage seem out of place today?
2. Did the author do a good job of describing the girl? Can you picture her in your mind?
3. Why is it important to add details to a work of fiction?

Writing Prompts
1. Describe the outfit you're wearing today to someone from the future. Since we don't know whether kids in the future will wear jeans and T-shirts or space suits, be as detailed as possible. Describe the colors, the materials, and the textures.
2. Find five items of clothing (shoes, pants, dresses, tops, T-shirts) or jewelry from a magazine or newspaper. Write

descriptions for the items to help sell them. Look at other clothing catalogs and websites for reference. What descriptors are used? How are the materials described? What words are used to help entice someone to buy them?

~~~~~~~~~~~

Most of the authors included in Sky Blue Water, *including Stephanie Watson and Sarah Warren, who developed the discussion and writing ideas in this section of the book, are available for classroom visits and writing workshops. Visit their websites to learn more.*

Common Core English Language Arts Standards

Discussion themes and writing prompts have been designed to align with the following Common Core English Language Arts Standards related to both reading and writing. We encourage you to modify these prompts to suit your own classroom environment.

CCSS.ELA-LITERACY.W.5.2
Write informative/explanatory texts to examine a topic and convey ideas and information clearly.

CCSS.ELA-LITERACY.RL.5.3
Compare and contrast two or more characters, settings, or events in a story or drama, drawing on specific details in the text (e.g., how characters interact).

CCSS.ELA-LITERACY.RL.5.6
Describe how a narrator's or speaker's point of view influences how events are described.

CCSS.ELA-LITERACY.W.5.1.A
Introduce a topic or text clearly, state an opinion, and create an organizational structure in which ideas are logically grouped to support the writer's purpose.

CCSS.ELA-LITERACY.W.5.3
Write narratives to develop real or imagined experiences or events using effective technique, descriptive details, and clear event sequences.

CCSS.ELA-LITERACY.W.5.9
Draw evidence from literary or informational texts to support analysis, reflection, and research.

CCSS.ELA-LITERACY.RL.7.3
Analyze how particular elements of a story or drama interact (e.g., how setting shapes the characters or plot).

CCSS.ELA-LITERACY.RL.7.4
Determine the meaning of words and phrases as they are used in a text, including figurative and connotative meanings; analyze the impact of rhymes and other repetitions of sounds (e.g., alliteration) on a specific verse or stanza of a poem or section of a story or drama.

CCSS.ELA-LITERACY.W.7.2.D
Use precise language and domain-specific vocabulary to inform about or explain the topic.

CCSS.ELA-LITERACY.W.9-10.9
Draw evidence from literary or informational texts to support analysis, reflection, and research.

CCSS.ELA-LITERACY.RL.9-10.5
Analyze how an author's choices concerning how to structure a text, order events within it (e.g., parallel plots), and manipulate time (e.g., pacing, flashbacks) create such effects as mystery, tension, or surprise.

Contributors

William Alexander won the National Book Award for his first novel, *Goblin Secrets,* and the Earphones Award for his narration of the audiobook. His other novels include *Ghoulish Song, Ambassador,* and *Nomad.* He studied theater and folklore at Oberlin College, English at the University of Vermont, and creative writing at Clarion. He teaches at the Vermont College of Fine Arts. "The War between the Water and the Road" was written in Powderhorn Park in South Minneapolis.

Swati Avasthi is the author of two novels: *Split,* which received the International Reading Association Award and Cybils Award, and *Chasing Shadows,* which received starred reviews from *School Library Journal, Publishers Weekly,* and *Kirkus.* She teaches in Hamline University's creative writing program and lives with her two dogs, two kids, and one husband.

Kelly Barnhill is the author of several novels and short stories for adults and children. Her first novel, *The Mostly True Story of Jack,* received four starred reviews, and her second, *Iron Hearted Violet,* received a Parents' Choice Gold Award. Her most recent novel, *The Witch's Boy,* was a Chicago Public Libraries Best of the Best, a *Publishers Weekly* Best of 2014, and a finalist for the Minnesota Book Award. She has received grants and awards from the Minnesota State Arts Board, the Jerome Foundation, and the Loft.

Mary Casanova is the author of more than thirty books, from picture books to middle-grade and young adult novels. Her books land on many state reading lists and have earned countless awards, including the ALA Notable, *Booklist* Editor's Choice, and two Minnesota Book Awards. She frequently visits schools and libraries to meet her many readers. She lives with her husband and dogs in Ranier, Minnesota, near the Canadian border. For more information, visit her website at http://www.marycasanova .com.

John Coy is the author of picture books, young adult novels, and the 4 for 4 middle-grade series. His newest books are *Their Great Gift: Courage, Sacrifice, and Hope in a New Land* (with photographer Wing Young Huie) and *Gap Life*, a young adult novel. He lives near the Mississippi River in Minneapolis and visits schools around the world.

Kirstin Cronn-Mills is an adopted Minnesotan who has no earthly idea why people would drive on frozen lakes, no matter how thick the ice is. She has published three young adult novels and a few short stories and poems. She teaches, writes, and lives in North Mankato, Minnesota.

Anika Fajardo was born in Colombia and raised in Minnesota. She is the author of a forthcoming children's book on Hercules and a contributor to *Love and Profanity: A Collection of True, Tortured, Wild, Hilarious, Concise, and Intense Tales of Teenage Life*. A former teacher and librarian, she lives and writes in Minneapolis.

Shannon Gibney is a writer, educator, and activist in Minneapolis. She is the author of a young adult novel, *See No Color*. She is on the English faculty at Minneapolis Community and Technical College, where she teaches critical and creative writing, journalism, and African diasporic topics. She is a McKnight Writing Fellow and a former Bush Artist Fellow.

Pete Hautman is the author of more than twenty novels for adults and teens, including the 2004 National Book Award winner *Godless*, Los Angeles Book Prize winner *The Big Crunch*, and three *New York Times* Notable Books: *Drawing Dead*, *The Mortal Nuts*, and *Rash*. His young adult novels range from science fiction to mystery to contemporary drama to romantic comedy. He divides his time between Golden Valley, Minnesota, and Stockholm, Wisconsin.

Lynne Jonell is the author of seven picture books, four chapter books, and five novels for children. She has illustrated two of her books. Her novel *Emmy and the Incredible Shrinking Rat* won the Minnesota Book Award, and her novel *The Secret of Zoom* was bought by President Obama for his daughters. Her books have been published in nine languages and have received starred reviews in *Horn Book, Kirkus, School Library Journal, Publishers Weekly,*

Booklist, and *Sesame Street Parents.* Her newest novel and adventure/fantasy is *The Sign of the Cat.* She teaches writing at the Loft Literary Center and lives in Plymouth, Minnesota.

Kevin Kling is a writer, storyteller, and playwright from Minneapolis. He has written four books, including two books for children, *Big Little Brother* and *Big Little Mother.* His two story collections are *The Dog Says How* and *Holiday Inn,* and his plays include *Mississippi Panorama, Perfectly Persephone,* and adaptations of Kevin Henkes's *Lilly's Purple Plastic Purse,* Richard Scarry's *Busytown,* and Bernard Wabers's *Lyle, Lyle Crocodile.* He performs in many storytelling festivals.

Collette A. Morgan believes that sharing stories changes lives. In 1992, she and Tom Braun opened Wild Rumpus Books in Minneapolis. She has served on the board of directors of the American Booksellers Association (ABA), the Upper Midwest Booksellers Association, and the ABA's Booksellers Advisory Council, and has contributed to the joint ABA/Children's Book Council advisory committee.

Jay D. Peterson spent twelve years as the store manager of Magers and Quinn Booksellers in Uptown Minneapolis; he helped establish the new and used book retailer as one of the nation's top independent bookstores. In 2012, he was featured in *Read This! Handpicked Favorites from America's Indie Bookstores.* He is now project coordinator of In the Stacks, a program of Coffee House Press, and assistant director of corporate and foundation relations at Augsburg College. He has been a panelist, speaker, and moderator for the Minnesota Library Association, American Booksellers Association, Normandale Writing Festival, and the Twin Cities Book Festival. He enjoys volunteering as a classroom tutor at Como Park Senior High in Saint Paul.

Margi Preus is the author of several books for young readers, including *Shadow on the Mountain, West of the Moon,* and the *New York Times* best-selling Newbery Honor book *Heart of a Samurai.* Her mystery *Enchantment Lake* (Minnesota, 2015) is set in northern Minnesota, where she likes to ski, hike, paddle a canoe, or sit quietly with a book in her lap.

Marcie Rendon, enrolled member of the White Earth Nation, is a widely published playwright, poet, and freelance writer. She has written two nonfiction children's books, *Pow Wow Summer* and *Farmer's Market / Families Working Together*. She is a community arts activist, which means that she tries her hardest to support other artists, writers, and creators in pursuing their art. She is the creative mind behind Raving Native Productions, which produced *Bring the Children Home . . .* at the Minnesota Fringe Festival in 2015.

Kurtis Scaletta is the author of the middle-grade novels *Mudville, Mamba Point, The Tanglewood Terror,* and *The Winter of the Robots.* He also wrote the Topps League series. He won Reader's Choice at the 2012 Minnesota Book Awards for *The Tanglewood Terror.* He lives in Minneapolis.

Julie Schumacher is the author of *Black Box, The Unbearable Book Club for Unsinkable Girls,* and six other book-length works of fiction for teens and adult readers, including the academic satire *Dear Committee Members.* She is a professor of creative writing and English at the University of Minnesota.

Joyce Sidman is the author of the Newbery Honor book *Dark Emperor and Other Poems of the Night* and two Caldecott Honor books, *Song of the Water Boatman and Other Pond Poems* and *Red Sings from Treetops* (a Minnesota Book Award winner). Her book *What the Heart Knows: Chants, Charms, and Blessings* was a finalist for the *Los Angeles Times* Book Prize. In 2013, she received the National Council of Teachers of English Award for Excellence in Children's Poetry. When not writing or teaching poetry to Minnesota schoolchildren, she wanders the woods near her Wayzata home.

Trần Thị Minh Phước / Phuoc Thi Minh Tran spent ten months in a refugee camp in Malaysia before coming to America. In 1984, after a fifty-hour Greyhound bus trip from California, she reached Minnesota, where she found life's most precious treasures: education and a safe environment. She became Minnesota's first Vietnamese librarian and has been an active storyteller for more than twenty years. Her first book *Vietnamese Children's Favorite Stories,* winner of *Creative Magazine* 2015 Book of the Year Award and a Moonbeam Children's Book Awards 2015 Gold Medal, has inspired others to preserve their cultures through folktales and legends.

Anne Ursu is a lifelong Minnesotan (even though she's occasionally had to live elsewhere) and Minnesota Twins fan. Her books for young readers include *Breadcrumbs*, which was hailed as one of the best books of 2011 by *Publishers Weekly*, Amazon.com, and *School Library Journal*, and *The Real Boy*, which was on the National Book Award Longlist in 2013. She teaches at Hamline University's Low Residency MFA in Writing for Children, and she was the recipient of the 2013 McKnight Award in Children's Literature.

Sarah Warren is a teacher, artist educator, and author. She received a Legacy Award from the YWCA for supporting its mission, Eliminating Racism/Empowering Women. She was honored as a Cultural Caregiver by the Minnesota Women's Consortium. Her picture book biography *Dolores Huerta: A Hero to Migrant Workers* was selected for the 2013 Amelia Bloomer Top Ten Book List and received a Jane Addams Peace Association Children's Book Award honor. You can experience a Spanish translation of her book when you visit http://www.sarahwbooks.com.

Stephanie Watson is the author of the middle-grade novels *Elvis and Olive* and *Elvis and Olive: Super Detectives*, both Junior Library Guild selections. Her picture books include *The Wee Hours* (illustrated by Mary Grand-Pré), *Behold! A Baby* (illustrated by Joy Ang), and *Best Friends in the Universe* (illustrated by LeUyen Pham). She teaches writing workshops at schools, libraries, and the Loft Literary Center in Minneapolis. Learn more at http://www.stephanie-watson.com.

Kao Kalia Yang is the author of the award-winning *The Latehomecomer: A Hmong Family Memoir* and *The Song Poet*.